Sam North is the author of eight novels, including *The Automatic Man*, which won the Somerset Maugham Award, and *The Unnumbered*, which was long-listed for the Man Booker Prize.

Sam is also a screenwriter, and has worked as talent agent and script developer. He currently lectures in creative writing at the University of Exeter and lives in Devon.

Doc Martin

Practice Makes Perfect

Sam North

EBURY
PRESS

1 3 5 7 9 10 8 6 4 2

First published in 2013 by Ebury Press, an imprint of Ebury Publishing
A Random House Group Company

The Random House Group Limited Reg. No. 954009

Addresses for companies within the Random House Group can be found at:
www.randomhouse.co.uk

A CIP catalogue record for this book is available from the British Library

The Random House Group Limited supports the Forest Stewardship Council®
(FSC®), the leading international forest-certification organisation. Our books
carrying the FSC label are printed on FSC®-certified paper. FSC is the only forest-
certification scheme supported by the leading environmental organisations,
including Greenpeace. Our paper procurement policy can be found at:
www.randomhouse.co.uk/environment

MIX
Paper from
responsible sources
FSC
www.fsc.org   FSC® C016897

Printed and bound by CPI Group (UK) Ltd, Croydon, CR0 4YY

ISBN 9780091953485

To buy books by your favourite authors and register for offers visit
www.randomhouse.co.uk

Author's note

To adapt from whichever medium means writing on top of another writer's work; and it's been a particular pleasure to deconstruct the brilliant writing – especially the dialogue – of Doc Martin's creator, Dominic Minghella.

1

Dr Martin Ellingham squeezed into his seat: facing the direction of travel, with a table. It was a blessing, at the moment, that no one had taken the seat opposite, so he could stretch out his legs. He'd put his overnight bag next to him, which might discourage anyone from sitting there, in which case he was all set for the most comfortable journey possible for a man of his height and breadth.

But the carriage became more crowded and, a minute before departure, an elderly woman peered meaningfully at his bag. He was obliged to lift it onto the luggage shelf and accept her as a neighbour. Back in his seat, and with her unpacking a thermos and a sandwich box, he could feel that he was spilling over; the right hand side of his frame encroached on her territory and it would only be a matter of time before he jogged her arm while she was sipping a hot liquid, or . . .

'Would you prefer the window seat?' he asked. Surely the woman must see that if he was next to the aisle he could lean outwards, hold open the pages of the newspaper, and he could . . .

The woman blinked in surprise at being spoken to. 'Oh, how kind of you, but no, you have it. I'm perfectly all right.'

It was irritating. Why didn't she understand? He noticed her slight *delirium tremens*. Without thinking, strings of diagnostic computations unfolded before him: Parkinson's, excessive sensitivity to caffeine, alcoholism, shock, anxiety, cold . . .

With a mysterious lack of noise the train began to roll silently out of Paddington station. Only as it began to pick up speed did one '*clack*' add to another and it became the sound that he recognised from his childhood: a train journey to the West Country.

What did he remember best, about Cornwall? The light – yes, how the sunlight carried its colours differently. Perhaps, in Cornwall, the rain washed the air more clean than anywhere else, and so the light passed through fluently and elegantly. He remembered how the headlands boldly and obstinately stuck out against the sea, while the coves were shy, tucked away, often with small villages and beaches hidden among their folds. He remembered what almost seemed like conversations, during his childhood holidays, between himself and the sea. 'Now I will carry you,' the sea would say. 'Now I will bring you back.' And once it had said to him, 'See how I can pull you under.'

Portwenn, the little village closest to where he'd stayed every year with his aunt, was powerfully in his mind. The coincidence was an incidental factor in all this, for he didn't believe in fate, or in anything else. Nonetheless, it was

curious that it was the very same village. He remembered
the harbour walls, one from either side of the cove, solid
enough to break the rough weather in order to protect the
half-dozen fishing boats hauled up on the sand. Because
Portwenn didn't have a harbour, as such; just a beach.

From his childhood he remembered also the continual
hiding and revealing of things by that master magician, the
sea. The crab he'd found once, drifting in the tidal inlet –
he'd thought it was dead and he'd poked it with a stick to
find out, and still it had seemed dead. He'd lowered his hand
into the shallow rivulet of water and picked it up by one of
its legs, but then it had moved hurriedly and powerfully in
his grip, and, in fright, he'd dropped it . . .

Portwenn: year after year of childhood happiness, but
then suddenly, when he was eleven, the visits had stopped.
To this day he didn't know why. Something had happened
between his father and his aunt. The wrong words had been
spoken, maybe? Making this journey again now, with a job
on offer in exactly the same village, it was difficult to
imagine he wouldn't find out.

The first half hour of the journey had passed. It was too
hot. He thought of taking off his jacket, but he didn't want
to disturb the elderly woman sitting next to him. Sometimes
it seemed to Dr Martin Ellingham that the rest of humanity
was a long way off, far below, and he had to be careful not
to step on them, but none the less when things went wrong
he had to pick them up and move them around to where
they were supposed to be.

Thank heavens he could put his legs forward. It was the one thing that made the journey bearable.

And yet, here they were at Reading, and a woman came along the crowded train corridor, smiled and glanced at them all, and took the seat opposite. Martin had to draw back his legs, fold them into an impossibly tight space either under the table or right back underneath his own seat. He could lean forwards a few inches, but not to either side. His legs were either tilted to the right, to the left, or back. It was impossible to think of going all the way to St Austell like this. He'd break, somewhere. Or the table would break, or he'd simply explode.

Sometime in the past, he thought, somewhere on earth, the designer of this train carriage had sat at his drawing board, or at his computer, and he'd looked at the data for average human height and weight, and he'd looked at his budget for materials, and he'd slid the button down the scale just as far as he possibly bloody could; he'd sat there in his spacious office, with huge windows, and empty sofas, enormous armchairs, and he'd deliberately shoe-horned every economy-class passenger, for ever more, into . . .

He stopped himself from going any further down this track. It would only lead to feelings of bitterness. He could lean forwards a few inches. He could twist sideways to left or right, a bit. Maybe unfold his legs another inch . . . He hit something – the woman sitting opposite. He'd kicked her ankle. In the same instant he caught her eye.

*

Louisa Glasson, school teacher, pulled back her feet a touch, and glanced at the man opposite. A large, repressed-looking type, wearing an expensive dark suit, a green-and-red striped necktie and a blindingly white shirt. A man of middle years.

She returned her gaze to the landscape passing outside the window: small English villages passed by in a flash. They brought to mind her own small English village, the one she'd made her home, the one she cared about the most – Portwenn, in Cornwall. Somehow it didn't seem as English as these did; Cornwall was a different country. They even had a language of their own and a history that was more attached to the sea, and to France, than to the land. She loved the school where she taught: a white-painted converted chapel on the side of the hill.

The man opposite still looked at her, but she needn't look back. He'd soon tire of it, probably, if she didn't respond.

Louisa was used to this kind of attention from men. She had a face that was often looked at because it was a picture, and in a lovely frame. The jet black hair, if it was left down as it was now, fell on either side of her face in graceful curves. The peach colour of her cardigan warmed the light reflected onto her face. She had a steady brow, and an easy smile that seemed powerfully alive both in her eyes and in her mouth, which pleased onlookers. Anyone would seek out her face again. The whole village of Portwenn looked at her; it was one of the reliable pleasures for residents. The men, the women and the children of Portwenn had become altogether a better and a more glamorous population since she'd been among them. Her class rooms were crammed with children aged five to eleven years, and they shone if they were given her attention.

The drawback to being looked at was . . . people like this stupid man on the train. Every time she glanced back from the window, there he was, staring. He should know better, she thought. Where was his charm, for God's sake? Did he think he could sit and ogle her, as if she were a jar in a sweet shop?

And then it was a bit astonishing. He must be simple in the head, she thought, because he was actually leaning forward, and his stare was almost as if it were *her* fault. She didn't exist as a person but as an object, a face and a body for him to consider, judge, score out of ten? If that was the case, then she intensely disliked him for it, enough to meet his eye boldly, full time, and lean forward herself, and say, 'The view's out there, actually,' while she jerked her thumb towards the window. Her voice had the soft, blurred edges of the West-Country girl.

He blinked at that, she was pleased to see. And it worked. He looked embarrassed, as if he were about to say something, but then he surrendered and sat back in his seat.

Louisa's feeling of triumph was premature; five minutes later he was up to the same thing: just catching her eye and holding it. Staring at her, uncomfortably hard.

'Creep,' she said, directly to his face, even as she picked up her bag and coat. 'Boy, you have got a problem.' She got up and moved two carriages further down. She settled in – bag, coat, book – and congratulated herself. She'd never have to deal with him again; she'd escaped.

At St Austell station it was tricky to find a taxi; they'd all gone. Louisa had to kick her heels for five minutes until one came. 'To the Castle Hotel,' she said, as she slid into the back seat. 'And can you hurry, please? Seeing as I'm a touch late.'

'What's on, then?' the driver called back to her. 'Summat important?' He changed from second up to third.

'Yes,' she said. 'It's a new doctor for Portwenn, maybe.'

'Ah. This to be the job interview, is it? I've had a couple so far.'

'Yes. The job interview. There's only one candidate, but we can turn him down if we think he's awful.'

She made up the token woman, and the token Portwenn resident, on the panel that had been set up to approve the village's new doctor. It had been her ambition – although she'd never have said it – to have a woman doctor in Portwenn. She herself was a young female professional, and she'd wanted another one like her around the place. Besides, there were enough men already: her head teacher was a man, the surfers were mostly men, likewise the farmers, the fishermen. Men were just so, well . . . *there* all the time. With their hands on everything.

But she had been disappointed. They'd proposed some hot shot from London. She just hoped and prayed that when she clapped eyes on him, she'd know for sure it was going to work out. It was important for the village to have someone as good as Dr Sim had been. Someone who could listen properly. Who treated the whole person.

The hotel was a magnificent building, the size of a small stately home set down on a bluff of land that was like the prow of a ship heading out to sea; and her taxi swooped down the drive to the entrance like a galloping charger. She paid the driver and hurried into the lobby, hoping for everyone else also to have been just a bit late. She followed the signs pointing her towards 'Cornwall Primary Care Trust'.

She heard them before she saw them. A male voice, saying, 'And this is Hilary Richards, our District Nurse . . .'

She turned into the room and saw a group of men in suits, plus Hilary Richards the District Nurse. There was Bob Mathias, the General Practice Adviser, Chris Parsons, the CEO of the CPCT, and . . . she hurried onwards, ready to apologise.

'And this', Chris Parsons put out his arm to sweep her into the group as she arrived, 'is Louisa Glasson, our lay-member.'

The first thing she saw was the dark suit, the green-and-red necktie, and the blinding white shirt . . . it was *him*, the man on the train. She met his eye, and he looked blank or, at least, he wore a slight frown. She didn't bother to shake the hand he offered. 'Sorry I'm late,' she said, instead, turning to the others and moving away. 'I had to wait a bit, for a taxi.' She realised – of course, he'd have taken one of those taxis, ahead of her.

This was an emergency: it was no longer a case of her having wished for a woman doctor; the important thing now was *not* to have this man, never to allow him near Portwenn. Her heart leapt. And yet, how could she say to the others, when it came to it, that she didn't want him because he'd looked her up and down on the train? She couldn't say that.

During his interview, the list of his qualifications swamped her; she could quite see why everyone else thought he was good news. He'd floated down from some powerhouse medical career – a surgeon? There must have been a reason for his leaving all that behind. Could it have been sexual harassment? She looked at him closely: immaculately dressed in a suit and tie, a boyish complexion which added to the impression of youth, in a middle-aged man. A frowning, serious expression – superbly, powerfully confident. Almost belligerent. This could be a disaster. How could she tell everyone what had happened? She found herself talking out loud, almost by accident, her mind leaping ahead. 'And what is your attitude to female patients?' she asked. Her tone of voice rang in the air.

'Exactly the same as it is to male patients,' he replied. 'The responsibilities of the job are such that one's personal gaze, as it were, becomes completely other, different, and—'

'D'you think,' interrupted Louisa, 'that female patients, when faced with a male doctor, require a certain degree of respect?' She hadn't wanted to sound as shrill as that.

'More than a certain degree,' he replied. 'I think that patients of all types, whether man, woman or child, should be accorded the respect that comes at the same time as the duty is bestowed on one for the other. After all, one person, the patient, is putting their health, sometimes their life, in the hands of the other, who is a professionally trained individual. What we want from our doctors is breadth and depth of knowledge, and accurate, complete diagnosis.'

Still he had this child-like, frowning stare. And it seemed like he was in charge of the interview, instead of the other way round. Louisa found it infuriating. Towards the end, he even asked, 'So, any further questions?' And it was Chris Parsons, the CEO of the Trust, who gave the creepiest answer, 'Apart from, what have we done to deserve so eminent an applicant?'

Their smug laughter was the last straw – they were missing the point, she thought, something *was* wrong, that he'd give up a big career so early and come down here.

She thought of all the women of Portwenn, and she imagined his rude stare turning on them, one by one, when he wasn't in an interview situation, when he'd got the job . . . and his hands on everything. She saw that he was getting ready to stand; he thought he was in the clear. She'd been trying to work out a way of warning them, but she couldn't just announce to everyone, 'Hey, this was the man who stared at me on the train.' If she did, she'd turn herself into *that* type of woman, who stands up on her hind legs and complains about men.

He was on his feet – she had to do something. 'Can I just ask,' she blurted out – and she was pleased to see him sit back down. She could sense everyone's shock at her clumsy interruption. 'How would you describe your interpersonal skills?' she asked.

'I've been a surgeon for twelve years,' he answered carefully. 'I managed a team of senior registrars at St John's. I think that speaks for itself.'

'The classic image of the surgeon', she said, 'is of someone who deals with cases rather than individuals. Bodies, rather than people.' She was getting her confidence up now.

'My work is with the patients,' he said. 'That's nothing but dealing with bodies.' He frowned at her when he realised what he'd said. He tried to mend it by adding one word. 'People.'

'If you want to be a GP in our village,' she said, 'then social skills and a good bedside manner are essential.'

It was Chris Parsons, chair of the panel, who interrupted now. 'Louisa, I think Dr Ellingham is more than qualified . . .'

She interrupted, 'To alienate people, maybe.' She looked down the length of the panel. She was hoping that Hilary Richards would agree with her, but she had to find the courage to speak up on her own. 'I'm sorry but nothing I've seen so far convinces me that he's a proper replacement for Dr Sim.'

The interview came to an uncomfortable end, but the argument carried on during their discussion afterwards, while Doctor Ellingham waited outside. Louisa was the only one who disagreed; not even Hilary would back her up. She couldn't make them understand. And she knew, more than ever, that if she told them what had happened on the train, she'd be the one who'd be accused of bad behaviour. She couldn't stay in the room. She walked out; and what she heard as she left told her something else. Chris Parsons was asking Dr Ellingham to come in just as she walked past, and she heard him use the name 'Mart'.

Mart for Martin. So – Chris Parsons knew him, *personally*? It was jobs for the boys.

Louisa was furious, now; and she didn't even think what she was doing; she turned back and walked up to 'Mart' and drew a breath to warn him . . .

And she will remember forever that first touch, as he took her chin, and adjusted it sideways so the light fell onto her face more fully and he looked even more closely, right into her eye. It was a shock; she was taken aback.

'Vision a little blurred on that side?' he asked.

She had to agree. 'Yes . . .'

'Redness. Fixed, semi-dilated pupil, cloudy cornea. Bit of pain?'

'Sometimes,' she said. 'What—'

'Acute glaucoma.'

Louisa felt a sudden, cold drench of embarrassment. Never had she been so closely looked at – no, looked *through*. 'You're kidding.'

'You should see an eye specialist. Today.'

When they'd been opposite each other on the train he hadn't been looking at her as a woman, but as a patient. As a person. She had not been leered at, after all – she had been diagnosed. And during this whole interview, when she herself had been so rude, he'd not said one word. Not even in his tone of voice had there been an inch of reproach for her mistake.

'An eye specialist?'

'Yes,' he said. 'Today, if possible.'

'All right, I will,' she said, quietly.

The gaze between them broke. She could do nothing but carry on.

Before she left the room, she turned back, thinking to give him a small signal of an apology, maybe, but he was already being ushered by Chris Parsons back into the interview room. As the double doors closed behind them, she caught, as the last word of all, the name of her village – 'Here's to Dr Martin Ellingham, our new man in Portwenn.'

Portwenn was a dyed-in-the-wool fishing village, and it was given an extra, old-world charm because of the lack of a quayside harbour, offering instead a gently sloping beach protected by those sea walls, so the tide had to travel fast, hundreds of yards, to lift afloat the six fishing boats, which leaned slantways on the sand, patiently waiting at the ends of their leashes, as if keen to be put to work, to pull up lobster and crab, pilchard, cast drift nets for the herring and mackerel, year round.

Superimposed on top of this ancient fishing village – more obvious because it was summer – was a tourist spot. The fish market where the day's catch was sold had more of the flavour of a tourist operation, now, with its crab sandwiches and ice-creams. There were tourist signs hanging in the narrow alleyways. The pub cried out for tourists with its coloured chalk boards.

Dr Martin Ellingham stood and faced the harbour, waves repeating themselves on the shore just yards in front of him, and he didn't like the sound of his new title – a GP. A rural GP. In Portwenn, of all places, on the north coast of Cornwall.

It was just as he remembered it: the fishing vessels waiting at the ends of their ropes within the protective embrace of the sea walls on each side. He tried to summon some memories of the village from his childhood. It was a confused jumble: hiding away to read endless fly-blown paperbacks; an ice-cream melting and falling off its stick; his aunt leaning over him; the orange shrimping net stuck to the end of a piece of bamboo. His aunt making a fish hook for him out of a bent pin. The yellow plastic Labrador, bigger than he was, outside the chemist's, with a slot in the top of its head. He'd been given a one-penny coin, and he'd refused to go and put it in. He wondered if his aunt had really wanted to have them to stay for those holidays, or if it had been a bore for her. He remembered her impatience, and the rude, hurtful things she often said, but then the frequent kindnesses . . . So then, why had she suddenly *stopped* inviting him down here?

Most of all, what he remembered about his aunt was that things had to be *done*, as soon as she appeared. On his own, as a boy, he could read books or wait for hours next to his fish hook. As soon as his aunt appeared a pressure was immediately applied – he should be *doing* something useful, achieving something, even if it was a 'fun' thing, like running to the top of a sand dune. He wondered if it would be the same, now. They hadn't seen each other for years.

He turned back to face the village. It appeared smaller, of course. That was a function of his having grown taller, himself – all the way up to six foot three. In the tiny, steep alleyways that made up Portwenn's streets, he had the feeling he could step right over the small cottages, as if it were a toy town. Without question he was a giant; it felt like Lilliput, to him. He would stoop down to look in at an upstairs window, and reach in to take a pulse, or administer aspirin.

Somewhere, among these streets clinging to the steep Cornish hillside, there would be his first patient. The village was like a clockwork machine, finely tuned, and every person in the village was themselves like a small machine, running almost silently, with just the sound of gentle breathing, and a heartbeat. And without a thought as to why, or how come, this was his thing: the ins-and-outs of the human machine, how it worked. It just happened to be here, unfortunately, that he was doing it.

'A GP, in Portwenn,' he muttered under his breath.

He breathed in a further lungful of sea air, damp, clean, salty. Not at all what he was used to. Never again would he walk the corridors of a major hospital. No more of the surgeon's gown, no more of the surgeon's knife.

He looked down at his side to see a scruffy, long-haired dog sitting and staring out to sea. It was of a dark brown colour, almost black, and with all that fur over its eyes it was probably unable to see properly and had mistaken him for its owner. He took a step sideways, and then another. A dog's mouth was a seething nest of germs. Its fur was a repository for parasites. Any dog should be permanently attached to its owner by a short, unbreakable chain and padlock. Which didn't seem to be the case here.

He checked his watch. The small delivery lorry would be unloading from the big one at the top of the hill, and it would be driving down through the narrow streets. It was time for him to make his way up the western slope of the valley, and meet them at the surgery – his new home. And yet it was without the slightest sense of the importance of the occasion – it being merely the next step to be taken – that he started to make his way. This harbour, this pavement, the houses, the shops – he would come to know them, every inch, and the people who inhabited them, but he attached no romantic notions to this moment. He himself would become part of the machinery of Portwenn, and it was his function to make the surgery run smoothly. He was Portwenn's doctor. His reputation as a general practitioner started here and now. Behind him, like a different skin he'd once worn, he left his reputation as a surgeon in London, and he'd prefer not to look back on what now seemed like a distant past.

The dog, which was in fact perfectly clean and not in the

least infested with parasites, remained behind, still looking out to sea.

Not long after Martin had left the beach, the tide came up and lapped at the tyres of a Volkswagen Beetle that had been left parked there. A chalk board was handily placed against the wall of the fish market, which was meant to advise car-owners of the next high tide, but it hadn't been filled in. It was never filled in.

The tide crept up another few inches, until the wheels were submerged. Shouts were heard from the open windows of the pub, 'Volkswagen Beetle anyone?' It was a surfer's vehicle, from the boards attached to the roof. Someone shouted, 'It's Ross's!'

There came the sound of running feet, and exclamations. One or two gathered to watch and one man even waded out to look in through the driver's window to see if the keys were in the ignition. They weren't; and the door was locked. Very gently and beautifully, the Volkswagen Beetle lifted off the ground and started to float out to sea. It was a picturesque sight.

From the gift shop, meanwhile, Ross came running. He'd been so distracted by a customer that he'd forgotten about the tide. He raced down to the harbour in time to see there was nothing he could do; the Volkswagen was very slowly taking on water, sinking. A cheer and a round of applause greeted his arrival. He put his hands on his hips and watched. It was unfair. He'd been with a customer. If it hadn't have been for that customer . . . but then, he worked in a gift shop. Of course he'd be taken up with a customer. But it was a steep price to pay, to watch his beloved Beetle swim with the fishes.

The village of Portwenn was crowded into this sheltered cove on north Cornwall's storm-blasted, sun-kissed shore. The houses gathered more densely on the eastward slope of the steep-sided valley: here a hundred children aged six to eleven sat in rows in the converted chapel, which served as the school, and people queued for fish and chips, the hotels sent visitors out to the shops and pubs, and a thousand tiny cottages overlooked each other's roofs. The houses were attached, at their footings, to alleyways barely wide enough to allow a couple holding hands to pass by, alleyways so twisted that they always appeared to be in a hurry, with one corner coming so quickly after another.

On the westward slope of the village, however, just one small road traversed the cliff before coming to a halt, and turning into the coastal path that would continue across the cliff-top pastures.

Halfway up this slope, rubbing shoulders with one or two larger houses, the Doctor's surgery stoically kept off the weather. It was square, stone-built, with two bedrooms upstairs. The long-haired sheepdog, the same one that had come to sit next to Martin as he stood looking out to sea, now lay staring at the door.

And Martin came out of his new surgery with a particular

irritation: the estate agent's sign still declared 'Under Offer', which offended him. He'd made the offer; the offer had been accepted; here he was, moving in. It struck him as not particularly welcoming. He grabbed hold of it with both hands and tried to pull it out but it wouldn't budge. He wagged it back and forth, but it appeared to have been set in concrete. He gave it a sustained, heavy pull, but it wouldn't come out. It became a bigger irritation: Martin vs Sign. It was something else that must be added to a long list of chores: phone the estate agent's and ask them to remove the sign.

A further irritation was the way in which the removal men handled a box carefully labelled 'Fragile' as if it contained nothing but foam balls.

A third irritation crowded out the other two – someone called him by the wrong name, called him 'Doc Martin'. A young woman who clearly thought a lot of herself just baldly asked him, 'Are you Doc Martin?'

'No, I'm Doctor Ellingham,' he corrected her. It would have been expected that she'd apologise, and call him by his proper name, but the idea of good manners seemed to have escaped her.

Instead she said, 'I'm Elaine.'

Was he meant to know who she was? 'That must be nice for you,' he said. Funnily enough, he could hear in his own voice an echo of his aunt's; it was the sort of answer she would have given.

'Practice receptionist,' announced the girl.

Had he hired a receptionist? No. Had he spoken to anyone, placed an advertisement – no. 'I'm not hiring yet,' he said.

'I've come from Delabole.' She sounded annoyed with him, whereas it should have been the other way round: he had the right to be annoyed with *her*. And where, or what, on earth was Delabole? It sounded like a mental institution. 'I see. Is that far?' he asked.

'Delabole?' she repeated as if he were a child. 'There's no point in going and then coming back later. I might as well start now. Do you see?' And with that she walked into *his* doctor's surgery. The idea had obviously occurred to her that she was the GP, and he was the practice receptionist. He followed her in to try and correct the situation.

The phone was ringing even as he entered, but she seemed to have no trouble ignoring it. 'Feeling all right?' he asked her.

'Fine,' she answered in a sulky voice.

'No ringing in the ears, then?' He tapped the side of his head, and crossed the room to answer the phone himself. If she thought she was going to be the practice receptionist and she couldn't even think to answer the phone . . . He picked up the receiver. 'Martin Ellingham.'

And now there was a further irritation, because the voice on other end said, 'Can I speak to Elaine, please?' Once again Martin felt like her assistant. 'It's for you,' he said to Elaine.

'I'm not here,' said Elaine.

'Right.' Martin uncovered the receiver. 'Elaine's not here,' he said.

'Wait,' said Elaine. 'Hold on. Is it Greg?'

Martin wanted to put an end to this. He said into the phone, 'Greg, here's Elaine for you,' and handed her the phone.

Martin was obliged to listen as Elaine bullied Greg. 'Look, no,' she was saying. 'You're needy. I'm twenty-six, d'you see?' And then Martin found himself frozen out by Elaine's aggrieved stare. 'D'you mind?' she said. He supposed he would have to go into the next room.

To enter his consulting room was like stepping back in time. The sort of doctor who'd worked here would have worn a watch chain and mixed his own medicines in glass bottles in the pantry. There was no proper examination light; the couch had seen better days. The room smelled of TCP and plastic. He wanted to scoop up the whole lot and throw it out.

Under his hand the tap squeaked, as if it hadn't been used in a long while. The pipe kicked and a glug of brown water came out. To anyone else it might have seemed a ghostly place; it would have been easy to wonder at all the diagnoses that had been given in here, the way people's lives had changed, with bad news and good news dispensed. After all, to be a GP was not exactly to play God, but it was to be close up to where fate played its hand. But Martin was only concerned with the next task that stood in the way of his effective practice of medicine.

There was something ghastly in the fridge – as soon as he opened the door, a new smell invaded the room.

Elaine was there, again. 'Any milk?' she asked.

'One spore or two?'

'You what?'

'It has turned to penicillin,' said Martin. 'It's in the bin.'

'God, hello,' said Elaine. 'I need coffee.'

By hook or by crook Martin would bring this place up to scratch. 'Elaine, since you're here, a few things to organise.'

'Like what?'

'New exam couch.' He was pleased to see she had grabbed pen and paper, and was starting a list. Perhaps she'd be all right. 'Examination light,' he added. 'A functioning Sphygmomanometer.'

'Sphyg – what's that then?'

'It's for measuring blood pressure.'

'Oh all right. And I've got a couple of things too.' She tore off the sheet of paper from the pad and handed it to him.

Martin took the list and read down it. 'Milk. Biscuits.'

'While you're getting that other stuff you were talking about. Only I ought to stay next to the phone.'

'*Hello!* magazine,' read Martin.

'If it's there. Or *Heat* magazine if *Hello* is sold out.'

Martin was confused. This was a woman whom he didn't know – and he suddenly appeared to be running shopping errands for her. He had been handed a doctor's surgery out of the 1950s, which smelled like the inside of Florence Nightingale's medicine bag. Rotten foodstuffs in the fridge, apparently from the same era. The sign saying 'Under Offer', which refused, like Arthur's sword, to be pulled from the ground.

It was like the village of Portwenn had grabbed hold of his necktie and was tightening it, with both hands.

That night, the school teacher Louisa Glasson, and the new doctor, Martin Ellingham, with just the width of Portwenn's harbour between them, lay awake in their beds, thinking. Louisa stared up at her bedroom ceiling using only one eye, because an eye-patch covered the other one. She was thinking about the eye-drops she must put in, three times a day. She could reimagine the gaze of Dr Martin Ellingham, while she'd been on the train. A stern, persistent look . . . And she'd made a fool of herself; literally it made her squirm when she remembered what she'd said to him – 'The view's out there,' she'd said, and she'd jerked her thumb at the train window. How vain that made her sound! And then she'd said, 'Creep!' and 'You've got a problem . . .'

She put a hand over her stomach to try and settle her nerves. He would forgive her, she hoped. Having made such a fool of herself, it seemed like a top priority to mend the situation and allow him to think well of her. Maybe they could meet and laugh about it. Did he have a sense of humour? It hadn't seemed like it, during his interview.

She enjoyed the good opinion of most people, but with him, it felt like she had something to lose, for some reason.

She rose quickly, and went to her window. From a sharp

angle, she could look across the moonlit village and see the doctor's surgery, where it stood on the bluff looking out to sea. There were no lights on. He would be asleep in there, all alone.

It wasn't true – for, upstairs in his new surgery building, Martin also lay awake, remembering his first patient, earlier that day.

It hadn't helped that the man had rung the bell just after a whole spate of prank calls at the surgery door. A gaggle of girls had taken to loitering outside, making jokes at his expense. And so he'd tugged open the door, not disposed to be courteous, to find this old colonel type standing there, pulling back his shoulders and saying, 'Gilbert, Spencer, Lieutenant Colonel. Retired.'

And his reply had been facetious, 'Martin Ellingham, Doctor. Practising. I'm not open for another week.'

The old Colonel had been forced to insist, 'Look, it is urgent.'

And of course Martin had let him in.

'A bit of a problem . . . in the chest department, bit of excess weight,' the Colonel had said.

How could excess weight possibly be classed as urgent? Martin had felt his habitual irritation with people who didn't understand the meaning of the word 'urgent'. 'Fewer carbohydrates,' he'd said shortly, 'more protein, get some exercise . . .'

'Breasts,' the man had then said, sort of coughing out the word.

Martin had breezily replied that it was normal to have a bit of adipose tissue.

The Lieutenant Colonel, in his frustration, had done an extraordinary thing: he'd torn open his shirt and stared at Martin with a glare in his eye. And he'd been quite right to, because he was right, after all – there was a proper pair of womanly breasts bursting out from under the hairy chest of a retired Lieutenant Colonel in a Cornish seaside village.

Martin had expected nothing but coughs and colds and sore throats, and old folk who just wanted to talk. But here it was – his very first patient offered him a fascinating, rare case of gynaecomastia.

He puzzled over the case now, as he lay awake. Oestrogen in the water supply was a possibility. But that would mean a lot of men would be showing the same symptoms, and it would have become obvious before now. This man, Spencer, had held out until the last minute before coming to see him; that much was clear. His embarrassment had stopped him from coming before. And his shame had turned to anger when Martin had suggested the village's menfolk might need to start wearing bras. The Colonel had drawn himself up, buttoned his shirt and walked off, promising to visit the doctor in Wadebridge instead.

Martin swept back his duvet and sat up. He had to pace around. Gynaecomastia. He felt the usual pull of the logic: how the symptoms demanded the identification of their cause. Diagnosis requiring its running mate, prognosis, and the answering prescription. Somehow, that old Colonel had too much oestrogen in his bloodstream. Almost certainly it was down to something he was eating or drinking.

No matter that the Lieutenant Colonel had declared himself to be no longer Martin's patient. That was merely inconvenient.

Martin stopped pacing back and forth, and pulled back the curtains of his bedroom to look out over the village, which lay sleeping quietly in its cove. Hundreds of houses – and, in each one, a water supply. Why weren't there more cases?

Thus Louisa and Martin each stood in the darkness of their own rooms, and although there was too much distance between them to allow them to realise, they looked in each other's direction across the darkened village of Portwenn.

'Little Marty!'

It was *her* voice: it took him back to washing his hands before meals, to reading whatever books he could get his hands on, being instructed to collect eggs every morning from the hen house, walking down the cliff paths carrying picnics, lying flat out on the sand, being told he must learn to swim, being told he must mind the tiller in the dinghy. It was a voice that had issued a thousand instructions, many disapproving comments, as well as countless phrases of encouragement like, 'Jolly well done' and 'Good man'. He remembered particularly how galling it was for him, to know he was meant to find it exciting to hear himself described as a 'good man' or 'young man'.

'Aunt Joan,' he said.

The woman who came over the yard towards him hadn't changed; she was the woman of his childhood. The headscarf, the determined set of the jaw, the belligerent look, the rolling action of her walk. And of course she was in the middle of doing a task, a chore. There was always a list of chores at Haven Farm.

'You'll stay for chicken,' she said, and Martin felt the same old response rush to claim him: he must help with the chicken, peel the potatoes, or something – he must contribute to the general forward progression of life, at all times. 'Love to,' he said. He wasn't surprised there was no embrace, no wondering at how long it had been, no exclamations at how he'd grown. No, with Aunt Joan, it was straight into the present, what was happening now.

He followed her out of the yard and into a large, open chicken-run. The chickens scattered from under her feet; she seemed to be deliberately moving them around, looking for something. 'I always hoped you wouldn't look like your father. Oh well.'

Martin felt the familiar lurch of disappointment. He hated letting down Aunt Joan. And now he was doing so, just by looking like his father, her brother.

Aunt Joan swooped, and caught a chicken by its neck. She wrapped her hand around its legs and handed it to him. 'You as stubborn as him, too?'

'Um . . .' He took the chicken from her. It waved its wings; the weight of it thumped in his hand.

Aunt Joan answered her own question. 'Of course you are. We're all stubborn. Family thing. Have you heard from him?'

'Uhhh . . . no, I haven't.'

'God forgive me for cursing my own brother, but the man's a silly arse.' She nodded at the chicken dangling from his hand. 'That one will do for us. Will you do the honours?'

Martin knew that in the ceaseless queue of tasks that made up Aunt Joan's life, he was now being asked to wring the chicken's neck, while at the same time carry on with the usual burble of conversation. But he really did not wish to do so. He wouldn't . . .

As expected, Aunt Joan had no time for sensitive feelings. 'Oh come on,' she said, and took it off him. With a few sharp movements she wrung its neck herself. The chicken gave a ghostly flap of its wings, already dead.

But it was when they went indoors and she drew a knife from the block, that Martin couldn't stand it. The sight of the blade, in close proximity to the chicken's neck, and that chicken containing a volume of blood, a certain, crucial volume of blood that was about to be let out by the sliver of steel, the blade – that was enough.

Martin forgot what they were talking about; all ideas of proper behaviour fled. He could only get out. His feet, his legs, moved by themselves. Even as he left the room, Aunt Joan was still talking and he might even have been replying, he didn't know. His only concern was to remove himself from the danger of fainting, of giving way. To keep strong, he had to leave.

'For goodness' sake, Marty, whatever's the matter?' She still held the knife.

'Surgery to set up,' said Martin. 'Have to arrange a plumber, lot to do.' He left the house and was climbing back in his car when Aunt Joan caught up with him. He turned the key and the engine started immediately.

'The Large boys, for plumbing,' she was saying, always practical. 'They're in the book . . .'

Martin reversed the car, spun round, and drove off. He removed himself from the exact point where the knife would slice through skin.

When he was back in the perilously narrow lane he told himself to breathe, to calm down. The hedges flew past on either side. He would crash. He lifted his foot from the accelerator and allowed the car's speed to drop. He breathed more slowly; to hyperventilate caused more anxiety, creating a vicious circle. He attached the speed of his breathing to the slowing of the vehicle.

In the end he stopped completely and parked in a gateway. His aunt would think he was mad. Looking down on the village of Portwenn, he thought, 'Gynaecomastia.'

The main through-routes looked like arteries, the little alleyways like veins threading through the village . . .

No. He was calm, now.

Somewhere down there lived the retired Lieutenant Colonel. He couldn't stop puzzling over that case. He should get in touch with the surgery in Wadebridge, and admit his mistake, and perhaps together they could find a reason why a retired soldier in a Cornish seaside village should start to grow breasts . . .

Somewhere below, in that sleepy village, was the answer.

In fact, it turned out there were four sections to the puzzle, and Martin had to collect all of them before the picture became clear. And during the process he thought the puzzle had been made, before it became un-made, before it became made again. All the while, during the next few days, Martin blundered through the social geography of Portwenn; it would become an anecdote, in the end: how Doc Martin had reeled out of the pub, having become a patient himself, with a bleeding nose.

The first part of the puzzle was handed to him outside the gift shop. A vivacious looking woman, with a spring in her step and carrying herself in a jaunty way, came out into the street and hailed him. 'You must be Doctor Ellingham – welcome to Portwenn!'

'Hmm.' Martin knew perfectly well that Portwenn didn't welcome him, but no matter. The surgery was flooded, he'd had to run away from his aunt, he'd lost his first patient, the 'Under Offer' sign refused to come down, and a mangy, germ-infested, flea-ridden dog seemed to have decided that *he* was its new owner.

'You must come and see us one afternoon,' said the woman, breezily. 'At The Applegarth.'

If he were in a different mood – or if the village had been in a different mood with him – he would have liked this woman, who swung her arms merrily and had a quizzical, quick smile and a warm expression. 'Thank you,' he said, grudgingly. Somehow, he could never alter his mood to suit any given occasion. He was always in the mood he was in, and that was that.

'Actually, I need to come and see you, too.'

'I'm not quite set up yet,' replied Martin.

'Course. Just a repeat prescription. I'll come when you're ready.'

'Very good.' He could feel that she'd cocked a beady eye on him, as she walked alongside. He was rather hoping she'd go away, but it was not to be.

'Shall I tell you something? You're exactly what this community needs.'

Martin wasn't sure why she was bothering to flatter him. 'I think there might be one, or possibly two, people who would disagree with that.' His first patient, he thought. His practice receptionist. His plumber. His aunt. The school teacher, Louisa Glasson. It felt like quite a few people would drop-kick him out of Portwenn, if they were given the chance.

'Nonsense,' she said. And then she grabbed his wrist to look at his watch. 'Is that the time? My husband will shoot me. I suppose it would be against the Hippocratic Oath or something to dash off a prescription right now?'

'Can't do that, sorry,' he said.

'I shouldn't have asked. Apologies.'

'No problem.'

31

'It was just some of my cream, you know. Ladies of a certain age.'

'HRT cream?'

'Yes.'

'Any problems with it?'

'Far from it. Happy as a sand girl.'

There it was – HRT cream. The clue had arrived; it was the first piece in the puzzle, if only he had realised. But she gave her name as Mrs Susan Brading, not Mrs Spencer, so he didn't make the connection until later, when he was back at the surgery, dealing with the fall-out from the flood.

The plumbers were there – Large and Son, recommended by his Aunt Joan. Bert Large *was* large enough, at least in girth. His son, Al, was equally as lean.

Martin had walked in to find that everything was a bit better – at least there wasn't water spraying out of broken joints. He'd asked Elaine to fetch out Susan Brading's notes, and Elaine had come in waving them as if it were a triumph, to find a patient's medical records.

And what he'd read there had made him sit up and take notice. Bert Large's voice, prattling on, and Elaine's voice, prattling on, had both faded into the background. They answered his questions, and the second piece of the puzzle snapped into place.

It took only a search or two on the computer, and he was out of the surgery, and on his way to mending the situation.

It didn't concern him that Gilbert Spencer wasn't his patient anymore; Martin had the answer to the puzzle and it was his duty to deliver it. If Lt Colonel Gilbert Spencer wouldn't talk to him, then he'd ring the GP in Wadebridge.

He had the address and the post code from the file – The Applegarth was the name of their home. It was two-thirds of the way up the slope, overlooking the sea, a medium sized bungalow. As soon as he climbed from the car, Martin could hear the sound of the electric lawn mower. The square of grass at the front was already cut short, and was already striped with dead straight lines of dark green and pale green, yet here was Lt Colonel Gilbert Spencer, walking up and down, determinedly mowing it again. Martin caught his eye, but found himself waiting, while Gilbert carried on. Plainly he wasn't going to get the chance to catch his eye again.

Martin stepped onto the lawn, and called out to him. 'Lieutenant Colonel!'

The mowing continued. Gilbert had eyes only for his stripes.

Martin stepped closer. 'Gilbert.'

But Gilbert didn't want to know. 'You're not my doctor,' he said. 'I'm seeing the doctor in Wadebridge in the morning.' He smartly turned the mower and began to cut a new line. His chin was firm and he kept his eye on the alignment of the wheel and the cut grass.

Martin had no choice: he followed the orange lead of the mower to where it was plugged into the outside socket and unplugged it. The whizz of the engine stopped and a balmy silence descended. 'Gilbert, we're going to talk.' Martin was confident: he simply must deliver the answer and he

33

wouldn't leave until he'd done so. 'Perhaps I should talk to your wife instead,' he said into the silence.

Gilbert stood as stiff as a post, staring at the mower, which had stopped working. 'She's out,' he said.

'I saw her in village earlier and she said she was coming straight home,' said Martin.

'Can't help that,' said Gilbert, still looking at the mower and nudging it with his foot, as if it might start of its own accord. He gave the electric cable a hopeful tug. 'She's not here,' he added.

Martin felt his habitual frustration with people. He, Martin, could see quite clearly how Gilbert ought to behave, and what he ought to do, what he should think, and it was intensely annoying that he insisted on doing or saying something different. 'Well,' he said, 'if you still want to go to Wadebridge and inflict your pompous ex-military routine on some poor sod there, go ahead. I'll drive you over there myself.'

Even as he was delivering this reasonably sarcastic criticism of the Lieutenant Colonel, a motor car breezed up to the house and Susan Brading climbed out, smiling. She was sunny, optimistic, and the world brightened when she appeared.

At last, thought Martin, all the pieces of the puzzle were in the same spot; everything was about to fit together. He was impatient for everyone *else* to see how the puzzle had been made.

'Get out.' Gilbert Spencer took a step towards him.

'All three of us need to talk,' said Martin, 'and . . .'

'Please.' Gilbert's tone of voice was urgent, pleading. Suddenly, with that one word, 'Please . . .', Gilbert turned from a stubborn Lieutenant Colonel into a hurt, embarrassed child.

Martin realised that Gilbert hadn't told his wife about his problem. 'You have told her?' he began, doubting it was possible.

'Been wearing a vest,' muttered Gilbert.

'Doctor Ellingham!' Susan Brading sounded delighted. From the car she came across the lawn, full tilt, to soothe her husband, 'You must be starving, poor poppet.' And then she addressed Martin, 'Doctor Ellingham, will you stay for a bite?'

This was it, thought Martin, as they went indoors. At last. The whole thing was going to be cleared up. Susan Brading would reduce her fantastic over-use of HRT cream, and Gilbert's breasts would promptly disappear. It was a strange case, he thought. There was the strongest of intimacies between this couple, obviously, and yet these were private, medical areas, where nothing was said even between husband and wife, and the upshot was that a retired Lieutenant Colonel . . .

From his position in the living room, he couldn't help but hear the married couple talking in the kitchen. 'You're late again,' Gilbert was complaining.

'Silly, I told you, I was shopping,' replied Susan.

'Again. Did you get the moss killer?'

'Oh darling I'm such a fool, no I didn't,' Susan replied gaily. With her optimism and her cut-glass accent, she sounded like a 1920s flapper. She seemed like good fun.

And then she came in, so at last he could get on with what needed to be said. 'Susan,' he began, 'I was updating your patient notes. It looks like your use of the oestrogen cream is excessive.'

'Perhaps I use a squidgeon more than it says on the pack,' said Susan, wryly. 'It makes me feel ever so chipper.'

'There can be side-effects,' said Martin, impatient to move everyone to where they were meant to be. How much easier it would be, if he were a footballer. He could just kick the ball into the goal. It was this negotiating of ridiculous human frailties that was so time-consuming.

Gilbert looked forlorn, embarrassed. 'Looks like rain,' he said, 'I'd better go and attend to the . . .'

Martin stopped him. 'Sit down,' he said, abruptly. Miraculously, Gilbert did so. 'The thing is,' said Martin to Susan Brading, 'your husband came to see me with a complaint.'

'What?' She turned to her husband. 'Are you all right? What is it?'

'Nothing really,' muttered Gilbert.

'It's not nothing, is it?' said Martin, remembering the moment when the Lieutenant Colonel had pulled open his shirt. 'I think we need to discuss it.'

'I'd rather not. It'll be fine.'

'Then I think I should say.' Martin looked hard at the

forlorn Gilbert. 'He has gynaecomastia. It's a condition where a man develops chest tissue.'

'Breasts,' announced Gilbert and his eyebrows lifted, then dropped again. Plainly this discussion was going to happen, so he might as well get the nasty word out of the way.

Susan put her hand to her mouth. 'Haa . . . the vest in bed?' Her husband nodded. 'Why didn't you tell me?'

'Not as attractive as I used to be,' said Gilbert wearily. 'Aware of that.'

'Poppet.' Susan's voice was tender.

Martin's voice was utterly factual and straightforward. 'I think Gilbert's complaint might be related to the oestrogen cream. Oestrogen is a female hormone. Used to excess it's possible that during sex it's been transferred to Gilbert and . . .' he placed his hands on his chest.

'Gilbert, I'm so sorry.' Susan Brading was contrite. 'So, so sorry.' Her marriages always needed various forms of kindliness to survive, she thought.

'Not your fault,' said Gilbert.

Martin was in a hurry to leave. He wasn't used to being the bad fairy. As a surgeon, he had tried, as far as was possible, not to see his patients while they were awake and talking, and certainly never outside of a hospital, and never before diagnosis; now he was in someone's home while their secret lives were being revealed to him. He would like to disappear as soon as possible.

As he left the house, he heard Susan Brading's last call of, 'Thank you, doctor,' and, as he climbed into his car and drove down through the winding streets of Portwenn, he felt a surging good mood break over him, which had nothing to do with her charm, but was instead created by his own satisfaction at having completed the puzzle. The car's width filled the narrow street, its wing mirrors practically touching the sides of the houses as he descended, and he began to understand that if he stayed here, he would have a different map of the village, different from the map that most people would use, from shop to shop, or from the house of one friend to another's. His map would be marked with diagnoses he'd completed, and the very first one had just been put into place. He would never be able to drive past that cottage again without thinking, 'Gynaecomastia'.

If he stayed here long enough ever to drive up here again, of course.

His downhill route took him past the school, and he drove blindly past. It didn't occur to him to think about Louisa, except perhaps for the one part of her body that he'd been involved with – her acute glaucoma. It would never cross his mind to consider romance or love as a subject that was appropriate for him to deal in – he had observed the sexual instinct in others, of course, but it wasn't a path that had ever appeared for him to be able to take. And it was a path that led his patients inevitably to a variety of more or less uncomfortable diseases. That was all.

Martin sailed past the school, unseeing. He drove on down to the bottom of the hill, glancing sideways to see where the tide was. It was out – the boats lay stranded on their sides. He carried on up to the surgery and parked. Even the car seemed swifter, more willing today. He climbed out, and quite quickly managed to shrug off the feelings of revulsion at the sight of the ghastly dog that seemed foolishly to have adopted him as its owner. He even felt quite affectionate towards the immovable estate agent's sign. He walked smartly in. On seeing Elaine he had the unfamiliar sensation that she might be a useful and smart young woman. 'Good afternoon,' he said.

The expression on Elaine's face dropped to a surprised gawp. She plonked all her weight on one leg. 'What's wrong with you?' she asked.

'Nothing. The day has improved.' Martin swung through his surgery, thinking of how restful a place it was going to be, how modern. It was going to be a place where people were mended.

'Patient waiting,' said Elaine.

This patient would be the undoing of Martin's sense of satisfaction; he would cause a fight in a pub, and leave Martin with a bleeding nose; he'd be responsible for Martin's embarrassment on local radio; he'd be the reason for an almighty row between Lieutenant Colonel Gilbert and his wife. The first thing this patient did, though, was to throw into the air all the pieces of the puzzle that Martin had just fitted together so successfully.

He was a young man – handsome, making the most of the surfer look – and Martin happened to know he was the same young man whose car had floated off the beach on the high tide, the very first day that Martin had arrived.

Ross.

They shook hands manfully – but the first thing Ross said was distinctly not masculine. He blurted out, 'I've got breasts.'

Martin's frustrations returned at once: the practice receptionist, Elaine, was an idiot again; the surgery itself should be relegated to museum status; the wretched dog should be put down; the estate agent's sign was a harbinger of doom. The village of Portwenn was a scab on North Cornwall's coast. He'd thought he'd squared away this problem, already; he'd solved it, surely? It had been the first piece of cleverness that he'd performed in Portwenn – and now the strands of logic were broken up by this extra piece of information. Another case.

It would open the floodgates – he was sure, now, there would be others.

Ross's expression mirrored his own dismay. 'Oh my God,' said Ross. 'It's serious, isn't it?'

'No, sorry, it's nothing to do with you. It's just that I thought I'd worked it out, but you have just inconveniently proved me wrong, that's all.'

'I've been drinking the water,' said Ross.

'So has the rest of the village,' replied Martin.

'There must be something wrong with the water. No one's admitting it, but—'

'Hold on, let's just think about this,' said Martin.

All evening, all night, Martin was preoccupied. If it was something in the water, he'd have expected more complaints, and earlier on. It could be from a food source.

The first thing he must do, of course, was to call Gilbert, and Susan Brading, and advise them what had happened. An obvious next step would be to convene a meeting between Gilbert and Ross, so they could begin to discover what it was that both of them ate or drank? Where did the lives of the young man and the older man intersect?

On the Saturday morning, the morning of his fourth day in Portwenn, he called Susan Brading's number and left a message asking her to call him back.

He put his nose out of doors. The village looked different: the harbour area, just below him, was thronged with stalls and laced across with bunting. The lifeboat had been brought out of its shed and stood, a gleaming orange, on display. The tide was in, and many more boats than usual bobbed cheerfully within the embrace of the harbour walls. Of course, it was Lifeboat Day. Everyone would be down there.

He ignored the persistent dog – *why* did this dog hang around his door all the time? – and headed down into the village. Lieutenant Colonel Gilbert Spencer would undoubtedly be a supporter of Lifeboat Day.

Any form of organised frivolity passed Martin by; he alone was dressed in a suit and tie while everyone else wore colourful holiday clothing, to suit the occasion.

In fact, the first person Martin saw was not Gilbert but his wife, Susan Brading, who looked shiningly happy and alive, talking to someone in front of a stall. Martin was aware that he was about to spoil her good humour, just like his good mood had been taken away the previous day. 'Susan, I was looking for you,' he began.

'We were looking for you, too!' Susan gave him a carefree smile and grabbed his arm. 'Caroline here is our local radio star.' She turned to him. 'Caroline's in charge of the prize-giving.'

Susan Brading was dancing from foot to foot, and was already on her way. Martin was left with Caroline, who seemed to be solid on the ground.

'Kind of assumed you'd give the prizes for the children's art competition,' said Caroline, sensibly. 'It's usually the doctor's thankless task. Gig-racing, this year.'

Martin didn't know what gig-racing was, and he could see that Susan Brading was slipping from his grasp. 'I just need to talk to you!' he called as she moved off through the crowd.

'If I don't get inside and toss a few salads, the Committee will hound me out of Portwenn!' Susan called back.

The radio person, Caroline, was right there in front of him, like a boulder. Martin wasn't quite sure what he'd agreed to, if anything, but she smiled at him and said, 'Brilliant.'

He moved off. No doubt he'd catch hold of Susan Brading later, and meanwhile he could keep an eye out for Lieutenant Colonel Gilbert Spencer.

Martin really did hate any form of organised good fun. There was something relentlessly condescending in the tone of voice coming from the tannoy. The stalls were unforgivably twee. Every smile was painted on. Only the children seemed unpretentious and happy. And perhaps this gang of girl teenagers, the same gang who trotted through the village like a gang of bullocks dressed in what looked like underwear, calling out insults at him.

It seemed to Martin that everyone's voice was suddenly false. The sugary welcomes from the stall holders to their friends, hoping to attract purchases. The young woman who was drunk already, calling to her mates in a voice laden with fake *bonhomie*. Even the lifeboat looked fake, polished to within an inch of its life. He felt a relentless cynicism. He didn't belong here.

And here was a gang of child pirates, dressed to the nines, with some poor unfortunate adult who was obviously required to dress in the same way . . .

It was Louisa. The eye-patch, of course.

She caught his eye and smiled.

Just to emphasise his confusion, he found himself clumsily flailing among the musicians' stands, as they prepared to play.

'This way,' said Louisa. Suddenly she was right next to him.

They walked along the harbour side. Martin didn't in fact notice this, but because Louisa was next to him, dressed in a pirate costume, with the children naturally happy around her, Lifeboat Day seemed now a graceful and happy thing. The village of Portwenn was accustomed to how Louisa brought optimism to the place, and in her presence the occasion adjusted itself into a worthwhile celebration, full of charm, and what was more, one that would raise money for an important institution, Portwenn's lifeboat.

Martin was blind to this – he disliked the village, and was only looking out for Gilbert.

She looked up at him with her one eye and said, 'Your diagnosis was right. They've got me on drops.'

'Beta-blockers,' said Martin. 'Should clear up within a week or so. If not, go back and see your doctor.'

'I would,' said Louisa, 'but . . . I got off to a bad start with him.'

Martin was bluff, professional. 'I'm sure your doctor's professional enough to . . .' and then he realised. 'I'm your doctor,' he said.

Louisa nodded. 'I live in Portwenn,' she said. 'So I'm afraid you will have to be my doctor.' She glanced sideways at him. She remembered first coming to the village herself, and how she was expected to fill a certain role immediately, and how she'd had to feel her way carefully, and not make friends nor make enemies, just concentrate on that role – school teacher. She imagined it might be similar for him: the foot he'd have to put forward first would be the professional one. 'How are you finding us?' she asked.

'Irritating,' said Martin.

Louisa's heart quickened gleefully at his answer because

it was so politically incorrect. She was about to formulate a reply when he added, 'Apart from the local teacher. I've heard good things about her.'

Louisa loved that switch. It was so flattering; it mended everything at a stroke. When she would look back, over the coming years, this was the moment she'd identify as the one when it became possible that she could fall in love with Martin.

She drew a breath to reply, to say that the local teacher, when she'd first arrived, had found it hard to begin with, but she saw that his attention was elsewhere, over her head.

'Got to go,' said Martin and in two long strides he'd disappeared through the crowd. She was left standing on her own, dressed as a pirate, looking at him with her one good eye.

Martin had spotted Gilbert Spencer, just as he'd thought he might. Martin's height allowed him to keep an eye on the retired soldier; he followed him into the crowd. 'Gilbert,' he called. 'I need a quick word with you about your gynaeco-mastia.' It didn't enter his head that, with the inhabitants of Portwenn thronged around them, this might constitute a breach in patient confidentiality. Martin assumed that his patients took the same professional, objective interest in their conditions as he did.

'Please . . .' said Gilbert.

'It seems it's not the cream after all.'

This was a disaster. His wife's confidentiality breached as

well. 'For God's sake, man, not here.'

'Fine.' Martin steered Gilbert into the tiny fish market, which was empty because all the fishmongers had taken stalls outside.

'What makes you think it's not the cream?' asked Gilbert as they walked into the sudden gloom. It was difficult for his eyes to adjust.

'There's an unrelated case,' said Martin. 'Another chap developing breasts.'

'Who?' asked Gilbert. Their voices started to echo in the empty fish market. There was another noise as well, a sort of mechanical back and forth.

'I can't say.'

'Local fellow?'

Martin nodded. 'Young lad. Surfer . . .' Even as he said the words, Martin's eyes adjusted to the dark interior and his eye was inevitably, casually drawn to where the noise and movement was coming from; and he became aware he was looking at the very same surfer who had come to see him in his surgery, whose name was on his lips. Ross. Standing there. Or rather, tilting back and forth. And, rising up from the work surface in front of Ross was a naked female thigh. And the noise, that mechanical rocking, was attached to the action of Ross's hips.

'My God,' said Gilbert.

Ross froze, shocked. From the work surface a head bobbed up. A woman's head. Susan Brading. Gilbert's pretty, lively wife.

Stupidly, Martin said, 'Uh . . . probably not what it seems . . .'

Ross and Susan jumped apart. Both the lovers were hurriedly pulling at their clothing, staring at Martin and at Gilbert in disbelief.

Ross glared at Martin. 'What are you *doing*?' he cried angrily, buttoning his trousers.

Martin was still gawping, taking in the astonishing thought of *Ross* and *Susan Brading* in the fish market, in the middle of the morning, with hundreds of people walking past just yards away. 'Nothing,' he began, 'I . . . umm.' He was speechless.

Susan Brading's heartfelt voice rang out, 'Gilbert?'

The Lieutenant Colonel said mournfully to Martin, 'Probably was the cream, after all, then,' and he stoically walked out, stiff-legged, head down, ashamed.

His wife, Susan, hopped on one foot, pulling on a shoe. 'Gilbert,' she pleaded and then she went after him, at a run.

The young surfer, Ross, strode up to Martin. 'You told him about me? You *brought him here*?' His tone was incredulous.

'No,' said Martin, 'that's not . . .' But Ross was already on his way, following the other two. 'Your gynaecomastia, by the way,' Martin shouted after him, 'is caused by . . . oh never mind.'

As for Martin, as he stepped out into the bright sunshine, underneath the crisis there was the satisfaction of seeing the puzzle made again – complete. The HRT cream had wrought its effect, in different ways, on Susan Brading, on her husband and on her lover. The sun blinded him; he put up his hand to shade his eyes to see if he could see where the three of them had got to.

He was aware of someone tugging his arm, and of a voice mentioning his name. He glanced down to see the stout, sensible woman from before, the one who'd been introduced to him as something to do with the radio.

'. . . which is perfect timing!' Her voice floated up to him. A microphone was waved in front of his face; he didn't know why.

'Doctor?' she asked.

He was aware that everyone was looking at him, and now a sheet of paper was held out, which he was obviously expected to take hold of.

'So if we begin as usual with the junior competition?' The woman was prompting him, Martin realised. But he couldn't concentrate; he could see Susan Brading chasing her husband up the hill, and Ross chasing after her. He would have to follow.

And then he caught Louisa's one eye, warm and enquiring, and at her feet stood her juniors, all dressed as pirates also. It was the competition – and he was expected to announce the winners? In front of him was a table, with cups and certificates.

Susan Brading was on the footpath that tracked up the side of the hill. She was pulling at her husband's arm, but he yanked it free and quickened his pace, away from her.

Martin looked down to find a sweet-faced little girl standing there, expectantly.

Caroline could see that he was distracted, that he needed prompting. 'Doctor Ellingham? The junior prize. We're live on Radio Portwenn.'

There was a pause, while Martin observed that Ross, the young surfer, had caught up with Susan and her husband.

'Oh shi . . .' said Martin.

The little girl drew in her breath sharply and turned to her teacher to say something. Louisa ducked lower to catch her whisper, 'Miss, that man said the *s-word*.'

'No, he didn't, not quite,' said Louisa, as though it was a triumph for Dr Martin Ellingham to have stopped himself at the very last letter.

In a small kitchen on New Street, on top of the hill, old Mrs Barwood heard the new doctor say the s-word on the radio. She was too lame to walk down and join the celebrations.

Patrick Hawker, Captain of the lifeboat, had nipped home for a sandwich and was listening to the radio. He stopped chewing when the radio became silent, apart from Caroline's prompting, and then he heard it. The new doctor said the s-word.

Old Dr Sim, Portwenn's recently retired doctor, lived some miles away and had thought it proper not to turn up on Lifeboat Day, not before the new doctor had got his feet under the desk. He was listening to the festivities on Radio Portwenn, and heard it. He himself had never sworn in his life, let alone in public, and on the radio. He wondered what kind of doctor this new man could be.

Meanwhile, on the harbour side, the stunned silence of the onlookers was broken by a distant cry floating over from the footpath. It was Ross, who'd stopped, cupped his hands round his mouth and shouted, 'Oi, Ellingham!'

Everyone turned round to look.

Ross cupped his hands round his mouth again, pleased to have the whole village as his audience. 'You tosser!' he shouted.

There was a flash of light: the local news photographer caught Martin's frowning expression.

Night closed over Portwenn, and the emotional disturbance meant physical upheaval, too, and several people spent the night in unusual places, for various reasons. Mrs Susan Brading eventually slept in the spare bedroom of a friend's house. Ross passed much of the night travelling in a car or on foot, looking for her. Gilbert Spencer fell into a fitful sleep in his own living room. He couldn't face the bedroom.

Martin, as it happened, spent the night in his car – trying to sleep, at least some of the time. There was nothing else for it: it was dark outside, he was completely lost, his front wheels spun uselessly in the bog, there was an immovable granite rock behind his rear wheel, which he'd just bounced over, and he was in the middle of nowhere. For a while he listened to the radio. Every now and again he turned the engine on to warm up the interior of the car. Once or twice he got out and stood near the road, looking for any sign of life: car headlights, or a twinkling of lights from a house set somewhere in the hills. But there was nothing, and the safest thing to do was to wait for the five hours or so, until daylight came.

He'd spent the evening trying to track down Ross, but he realised now that he'd been deliberately misinformed, sent on a wild goose chase by friends of Ross. He wouldn't have been surprised if they'd been in the car that had driven straight at him, seemingly, and forced him to swerve off the road.

He buttoned his coat up to the neck and turned off the radio. He fumbled for the lever and tilted the seat until it was almost flat. He lay there, arms folded across his chest, closed his eyes and waited for sleep to come.

Instead he was pursued by imaginings, thoughts, and the ghost of himself as a child. He could see the circle he'd drawn with a stick on the beach: round and round he'd walked, watching how the tip of the stick ploughed up a trail in the virgin sand. And then his father's legs were there, running with seawater; and his father had invented this game: Martin had to run along the line he'd drawn, and his father had to chase him; and neither of them were allowed to leave the line because that was like falling off the edge . . .

And here he was, in the same village, a doctor, a GP. No, he thought, as his eyes flicked open to look at the car roof, he wasn't a GP, not really. The events of the past few days had proved it. The young surfer, Ross, would inevitably make a complaint. They all thought Martin had deliberately gone in there with Gilbert, to show him . . . What sort of person did they think he was? It was incredible. And yet the truth was, yes, those three did need to sit down together, all of them, to talk through what had happened. They were grown-ups, for heaven's sake. And yet they were running around like they were in the playground, hurting each other.

He closed his eyes again. No, he wasn't a GP. He wasn't any good at living in a village that was plainly too small for him. He would call his friend on the board, Chris Parsons, and tender his resignation. It was best to call it a day before it became an even greater disaster. He really was no good at people; he already knew that. The best type of patient for him was an unconscious one, lying flat, covered with a green sheet. The 'Under Offer' board had been telling him something, after all. He couldn't even deal with the surgery's plumbing system. He couldn't win the respect of the Practice Receptionist. His first three patients had ended up literally running away from him. The village of Portwenn was the china shop; he was the bull. The only person who seemed to appreciate his being there was that mongrel dog, which had hung around, night and day, until he'd dragged it to the police station yesterday.

The whole village – no, the next village as well, the whole of Cornwall, no doubt – would know about the debacle this afternoon.

He wasn't a GP.

Quite suddenly, out of the darkness, Louisa Glasson was sitting in the passenger seat next to him. The school teacher. He had the sense of being pulled up from the very depths to the surface. She was saying, 'You're not at all like I thought you were.'

'Hmm?' He levered himself up. 'Where did you come from?'

'I'm a GP,' she said. 'I'm your GP.'

Martin was aware she was teasing him, of course. But where had she come from – how had she found him? 'I went to the next village, where they told me Ross lived,' he explained, 'but he doesn't live there at all, he lives in Portwenn, above the gift shop, and I was driving back when I was run off the road by some lunatic . . .'

'I've come to help you,' said Louisa, leaning towards him, twisting around in the passenger seat. Her figure – her shoulders, breasts, arms, neck – became more emphatic, more obvious. She swept her hair behind her ear. 'That is, if you want any help.' Her voice was gentle, warm.

'I'm not staying in Portwenn,' he said. 'It's not really the place for me.'

'But it was the HRT cream, after all. You were right.'

'I know, but . . .'

She leaned over him and the curtain of her hair fell forward and made it darker even than night, and enclosed him. At the same time the knocking sound became louder, and Martin opened his eyes; daylight blinded him; and against the driver's window a knuckle tapped the glass.

There was no Louisa in the passenger seat. He was alone, cold.

He struggled to sit upright and saw that it was Portwenn's policeman, PC Mark somebody-or-other, who had found him. He recognised him from the police station, where he'd taken the dog. He pressed the button and the window slid down.

'Everything all right?' asked Mark. 'Apart from the burst tyres?'

'Yes, fine.' Martin levered the seat back into the upright position. 'Just enjoying a night in the car, in a ditch, in the middle of nowhere.'

'Picked a fine one.'

'Yes. That's what I thought.'

'Come on, I'll give you a lift into village, and then we'll get your car sorted.'

Bouncing along in the police Land Rover, it struck Martin that PC Mark Mylow was a bit like a plank of wood – a cheerful plank of wood, with arms and legs that moved, and a mouth that spoke.

'You missed the show at the pub last night,' said the policeman.

'I was making my own fun,' said Martin gloomily. 'What happened?'

'Gilbert got drunk and tried to kill Ross.'

'Sorry to hear that. Were you called on to intervene, in a professional capacity?'

'I took the view that a lobster is not a particularly lethal weapon,' said PC Mylow, proudly.

'Well, I suppose it's got the row over with,' said Martin.

'Not sure 'bout that. The old man says he's divorcing Susan.'

They drove on in silence. The walls zoomed past; the corners didn't seem to worry PC Mylow. No wonder he'd been run off the road, thought Martin, if everyone drove this fast. He didn't see how cars could ever get past each other in these lanes.

'You a bit unhappy with Portwenn, after all?' asked the policeman.

'I've antagonised half the village. I've buggered up a marriage. I've crashed my car. I don't think Portwenn is very happy with me, put it that way,' said Martin.

'I'm a bit unhappy, too,' said Mark.

This was an unlikely statement to hear from someone in a policeman's uniform.

'A bit . . . depressed,' added Mark, in a reasonable tone of voice.

Martin glanced at the other man. No doubt this was going to turn into a consultation. He decided to wait, and see what happened next.

'Doc Sim wanted to give me something, but I'm trying the homeopathic route,' said PC Mylow. 'So I know how you feel. God knows *I've* wanted to drive *my* car into a ditch sometimes.'

'I didn't drive into a ditch. Somebody came at me. And not for the first time since I've been here.'

'Ah,' said Mark, kindly, 'I've had that too. It's just like . . . everybody's coming at you.'

Martin was pleased they'd arrived at the surgery and he could escape the benign, all-seeing presence of PC Mylow. He climbed out of the Land Rover and slammed the door – but straightaway the dog was under his feet. The same dog. The one he'd taken into the police station two days previously, to report it as a stray and have it taken away.

PC Mylow was turning his Land Rover around to go back down the hill.

'The dog!' called Martin.

'I know,' said PC Mylow, shaking his head regretfully.

'I brought it into the police station,' complained Martin. 'I thought it was being . . .'

'It got out,' called PC Mylow from the side window of the moving Land Rover. 'It had a good lawyer.'

There was worse news when he stepped inside the surgery. There was the smell of underground caves, and splashing sounds, and the floor had a glittery look – and there was his mail, floating about – in six inches of water. The place was flooded. A thin waterfall appeared from the waiting-room ceiling. The plumber appeared, the father, Bert Large, as round as a cistern ball valve himself, looking reproachful as always, and in his broad West-Country accent he said the most obviously untrue thing, 'Everything under control. Don't worry.'

Martin felt like the water was up to his neck, not just up to his ankles. The village of Portwenn really didn't want him.

'Sometimes happens when we re-pressurise a system,' said Bert Large, sadly. 'But fear not. Completely normal.' His short legs paddled through the water.

Martin thought – a depressed policeman called My-low. A large plumber called Large. What was going on? He felt caught by a conspiracy of madness.

Martin snapped. 'Right, everyone out!' He might have been talking to himself. 'Will everyone just sod off?' he said.

A call came from behind him. 'Hello? Doctor Ellingham? Delivery. Medical equipment of sorts, looks like, by the label. Where d'you want it?'

Dr Martin Ellingham had come to Portwenn by accident, and it seemed that accidents and disasters pursued him relentlessly still, now that he was here. It wasn't surprising that he was turning into the worst version of himself that he knew was possible. After all, he knew the warning signs. First of all he had that feeling of looking down on other human beings, which was perhaps exaggerated by his sense of being in charge, of knowing more than anyone else what should be done. Also, he recognised that fatal ingredient: the habit he had of trying to pick people up and put them down where they ought to be.

Something was bound to go wrong.

He was in the pub with the first person he'd arranged to meet: Susan Brading. He made sure to buy the drinks, because he was the host of this occasion. He carried over the glass of white wine for her, and an orange juice for himself. 'So,' he said, and placed the glass in front of her, 'I just wanted to say, that I could have handled things better.'

Susan Brading rushed to take the blame. 'I'm the one who should be apologising. To you, and to Gilbert, and to Ross. Apologies all round, is the order of the day.'

'I understand that Gilbert wants—'

She hurried to interrupt him. 'A divorce, yes.' She added in a desperate tone, 'I've been such a fool.'

'Is it worth talking to him?'

'He won't talk. And to be honest, I can't face him.'

'And what about Ross?'

Susan shook her head wryly. 'Keeps calling. I told him it's all over – long letter, you know the sort of thing – but he won't *accept* it.' She sounded astonished.

'He doesn't seem the sort to bow out gracefully.'

Susan smiled. 'He's a boy. Today he thinks his heart is broken, tomorrow there will be good waves. He'll surf, he'll forget, and in a month or two there'll be a sultry nineteen-year-old who'll let him enjoy her breasts without giving him ones of his own,' she ended mournfully.

Martin cleared his throat. 'You're going to have to talk to both of them, you do know that?' He rose to his feet, lifted a hand in the air.

Susan looked in the same direction, to see her husband, Lieutenant Colonel Gilbert Spencer, appear in front of her eyes.

Gilbert stopped dead when he saw his wife was there, as

well. 'I said I'd talk to you, not her,' he called over to Martin.

'Gilbert,' began Martin.

'Darling,' interrupted Susan, 'let me explain, please.'

'You've found someone else,' said Gilbert in a sarcastic tone. 'No explanation necessary.'

'Don't be so pompous,' said Martin.

Susan was trying hard. 'It was nothing, darling, it was . . .'

Gilbert didn't believe that, and he was still trapped in trying to work out what had happened in his life over the past few months, just how often, and when, and how badly, he'd been betrayed. He said in an accusing tone, 'Were you with him – when his car was caught in the tide?'

'I hardly think—'

'Were you?' interrupted Gilbert. 'Because the tide takes . . . how long to come in?'

Susan could only bite her lip, and cast her eyes down, ashamed to be hurting him.

'So don't tell me it was nothing,' said Gilbert.

The empty pub was occupied only by the atmosphere between them, of hurt, and yet tenderness.

'I want to suggest something,' declared Martin. He knew exactly what he wanted to say – the most straightforward, obvious thing – and this was the moment when he must act, and say it. They were both looking at him, from either ends of the argument. He turned to Gilbert. 'You still love Susan.'

Gilbert wanted to say no, he didn't. But somehow he couldn't quite get it out.

'You love her,' insisted Martin crossly.

Gilbert shrugged.

'You do.'

He nodded, mute. It was a bleak place to be in, at the moment, loving Susan Brading.

'There you go,' said Martin. 'And she loves you. Problem solved.'

'You don't know anything about human relationships,' complained Gilbert.

'Darling,' Susan explained, 'I think the Doctor is just . . .' She stopped, because she saw Ross coming into the pub as well. She glanced at Martin. 'Oh no,' she mumbled, 'you didn't, did you?'

'Good grief, it's lover-boy.' Lieutenant Colonel Gilbert Spencer turned round, stiff-legged.

Martin realised immediately – this might have been a step too far. A mistake. None the less he carried on, 'The three of you have created this problem, so it will take the three of you to sort it out . . .' He sounded so perfectly reasonable. All it took was for everyone else to be as reasonable, too.

'Ross,' said Susan. But Ross wasn't listening. He was bouncing on his toes, rocking from one foot to another, glaring at Gilbert. Men are such apes, she thought.

Ross pointed at Gilbert. 'You had your chance with Susan and you blew it.'

'I'm going to punch your lights out.' Gilbert's hands clenched into fists.

'Hold on,' said Martin. 'We were having a thoroughly rational—'

'Go back to your garden, old man,' said Ross.

Gilbert swung a curled right fist, and it connected with Ross's cheekbone. It was strong enough to make Ross lose his balance and fall, but only for a moment; he scrambled to his feet. 'You get that one for free.'

'Come on, then,' said the old soldier, flushed with success.

Ross sprang forward, and at the same time Martin moved between them. Ross's punch was already on its way, and connected hard with the bridge of Martin's nose. There was the muted sound of damaged cartilage.

'Ah . . .' Martin was stunned. He cupped his nose, feeling the blood rush over his open mouth.

Ross saw the damage and it was as if all the anger had been let out of him. 'I didn't mean to do that.' He sat down wearily. 'I didn't mean to do that.'

In the evenings, it was as if the village of Portwenn sat on its own porch and kicked back, relaxed, in order to look out to sea. The light softened, and the 'opes' – the narrow alleyways that made the village like a warren – chimed with different noises: the calls of children back from school, fed already, and let out to play, the first gatherings of drinkers in and around the pubs, the scooter from which the baffle had been removed angrily buzzing up the hill, two-up. The shops were locked, quiet. In the harbour area, people who'd parked their cars began moving them, as the tide would be once more about to wash the beach clean.

61

Martin didn't have to find or buy any packing boxes; he could use the same ones that he'd recently unpacked. They were all neatly piled up in the living room. They still had the scrunched up newspaper inside them that he'd used to pack with. The only thing he'd needed to buy was a roll of tape. It came with a handy dispenser so he could simply roll it across the top of a box, twist upwards to make the cut, and the box was sealed. He packed up the kitchen equipment; he took the pictures from the walls; he sorted his books by size and packed them. Ten, fifteen boxes stood there, sealed with parcel tape.

Every time he knelt down, or lifted something, his nose throbbed with pain.

He began to slow down. He went to make himself a cup of tea, but found he had no kettle. The mug dangled uselessly in his hand. He was standing in the reception area of the surgery, looking out from the window. The estate agent's sign stood there, confident, brightly coloured in the sunlight. 'You win,' he muttered. A second later, he wondered if he'd actually said those words out loud – or had it been only a thought? He went into the kitchen.

The dog gazed up at him with its obsequiously friendly eyes. Horrible thing. 'Get out!' he shouted. 'Never. Ever!' He felt insanely angry. The wretched thing just continued to smile at him.

He went to the sink and turned on the tap: clean, cold water came out. He filled the mug and drank.

It was quiet. Until now the place had been filled with the

noise he himself was making: the thump of books piled up, the jangling of cutlery being wrapped, the harsh buzz of the parcel tape as it came off the reel, the sound of his own footsteps; but now it was as if the house silently waited for him to leave.

He went back to the window, treading softly, as if the silence demanded to be preserved. Outside, he saw sunlight on the paved area in front of his house, and then, beyond the edge of the cliff, the sea. He remembered his thought from the train about Cornish light: the air, here, was washed so clean, the light travelled through it more fluently and elegantly.

He took another swallow of water.

He remembered the gang of girls, the Bevy of Beauties as the village described them. What had they said, yesterday? He'd been walking back down the hill and he'd heard them call out, as they'd clattered past, 'Doctor, Doctor, guess what, I'm growin' breasts,' and one of them had lifted up her T-shirt. 'Call those breasts, girl?' another one had shouted, and another, 'Shut your face, they never are,' and the first one again, 'Bigger 'n yours, love, that's for sure . . .'

And Elaine – he remembered her goodbye to him. In this very room. There was her desk. She'd picked up her few personal things, and she'd been standing there with that insolent look, hippy clothes full of colour and life, and she'd said very politely, 'Thanks for everything.'

'I haven't given you anything,' Martin had replied.

'Oh no, so you haven't,' she'd said.

She inclined always towards sarcasm, thought Martin. But there was something about her. Was it – the way she'd decided to make an assumed over-confidence the answer to a lack of confidence?

He put down the mug. The slight thud as it made contact with the desk sounded very loud.

It came back to him – his talk with Aunt Joan. She'd frowned, and he'd felt that debilitating smallness, uselessness, that her disapproval always brought out in him.

'What did you expect, coming here?' she'd asked, her grey hair all anyhow around a stern expression. 'Crab sandwiches and cream teas and a clear blue sky?'

Martin's hand had instinctively cupped his broken nose. 'I was hoping for a slightly more hospitable environment,' he'd said.

'Rubbish,' she'd replied quickly. It was easy for her to be rude. 'If you want a chocolate box village, try the Isle of Wight,' she said. 'This is a real place.'

He wondered why Aunt Joan thought the Isle of Wight wasn't a real place.

And then Aunt Joan's expression had changed. She took a step closer, and now it was as if she were looking through him, to a place a long way off. 'You know,' she began, and usually she spoke abruptly, quickly, and moved on just as fast; it was uncharacteristic of her to pause, to search for the right words. 'You know,' she'd started again, 'I often worried, when you stopped coming down for the summer, that you might have felt you weren't welcome.'

'I can't remember,' said Martin truthfully. 'I think . . . I thought it just wasn't convenient anymore.'

Joan's mouth tightened. 'You know he wouldn't send you, don't you?'

'Dad? No, I didn't know. Why not?'

'It doesn't matter now. It was a long time ago. I just wanted you to know, you were always welcome here.' And now she seemed not, after all, to be looking through him, to a time long ago, but instead to be looking right at him, with an intense, familiar love. '*Are* always welcome,' she finished.

So he had been right, thought Martin. Something had happened, all those years ago. The wrong words had been said, or the wrong thing had happened. And perhaps Aunt Joan had been the one person who'd loved him, and she'd been taken away.

He heard the familiar panting of the dog, and turned to look at its disease-laden mouth, hanging open. He was going to have to kick it, to get it out of there. The dog slumped onto its front, allowing its paws to slide forwards. It gave a groan, and started panting again, and then lifted one paw and wiped it over its ear.

Martin frowned and went to his bag. He fetched out his otoscope and switched it on. The beam of light played over the dog's fur. Following the examination, Martin diagnosed an ear infection. Prescription would be some antibiotics. And then it could go away and bother someone else.

And then Martin remembered Louisa Glasson, and her attempt, during his interview, to keep him away from here, from her village. He had sensed, in her, a love for the place and for its inhabitants, especially its children – as he had been himself, once, a child in Portwenn.

But he didn't belong here, as she plainly did.

He found himself in the bedroom, without realising quite how he got there. Half-a-dozen shirts were folded over his arm. Standing in front of him was the wardrobe, which had remained locked during his stay because he couldn't find the key. Sombre, motionless and immovable, the wardrobe was animated only by his own reflection in the oval mirror, which in the gloom looked like a portrait in a Victorian photograph album – and it gave him the idea that he *was* the wardrobe, and locked inside him was the unknown but empty space that meant he would always be alone, and no one could find the key.

Somehow, even to be among the many people whose children were the responsibility of Louisa Glasson, school teacher, made it important to stay.

He, too, had a duty to the place, which he'd only just shouldered, surely – and here he was shrugging it off almost immediately. The French for duty was *devoir*, which also meant in English, *must*.

2

Martin slept, as did most of Portwenn; only a few people rose before the first slivers of dawn warmed the village's streets and burned off the mist that hung over the sea. The boats bobbed in the harbour, and the baker and the milkman and the newsagent were already at work.

Marianne Walker lifted back her puffy thirteen-tog duvet and sat up, her feet searching for slippers. She checked all around her body for the usual ailments: headache, yes; indigestion, yes, but it had been bad enough at midnight to wake her. Trapped wind, as usual. She feared the terrible, long detonation she'd shortly make might wake the neighbours. She would be the one person certain to attend the new doctor's surgery this morning.

In his whitewashed cottage on Meard Street, Eddie Rumbold had already been up for an hour, and he'd found his teeth and popped them in. Now he could talk to his wife, Joan, about her ailments: she had high blood pressure; she had a low-functioning thyroid; she had bones that were brittle as twigs. He murmured the same old lines, looking at the chair where she habitually sat, from where she could look out of the window and see the roofs of the houses below, and yet she could turn her head the other way, and see the television. But he didn't receive any reply; not for six years had he had a reply, because Joan had died that long ago. He didn't count himself as lonely because, after all, he talked to her still. He would go down to the new doctor's surgery, later, to discuss his wife's complaints.

Toni Black set out with her rolling, flat-footed gait, down the steep-sided Fairland Road, to visit her daughter-in-law and give the grandchildren their breakfast, which allowed her daughter-in-law to leave for work in Bideford, miles away. In her mind she welcomed the challenge: the village had a new doctor who was single and male and capable of stepping over a piece of straw, and therefore became at a stroke one of the most eligible bachelors in village, even without taking into account that he was an actual professional. Slap, slap, slap went her slippers down the steeply sloping hill. She had a list of brides as long as her arm. But first she needed to have a good look at him, and judge what sort of girl might do.

Dr Martin Ellingham had had a dream, that night, that a prick of blood appeared on the back of his hand. The dot of red swelled until it was the size of a berry, when the surface tension broke. Instead of running across his skin in one direction, the blood took off in different directions until it made a star shape, and it leaked from his body too fast. He could feel a draining sensation – exactly like fear – and then panic. He woke up. There was no blood.

He was in his new house: it was the first day with a schedule of patients who had booked appointments with the Practice Receptionist, Elaine. He'd taken a saw to the estate agent's sign.

He would realise afterwards, when the day was finished, that he'd never sacked anyone before. It was because of the biscuits, but it was mostly to do with one missing digit from a phone number.

As might seem appropriate, the brass plaque had arrived and was fitted to the right hand side of his front door. It was engraved with his name and qualifications: Dr Martin Ellingham, MB BS FRCS. It was shined to a high gloss: he could duck down and see his own reflection: the white shirt, the tie, and the jacket lapels. Dr Martin Ellingham, Portwenn.

He had made the decision years ago always to wear a suit at work; and while it seemed more incongruous in this village than in London, it invoked the psychological power of a uniform, and this was the uniform he'd chosen.

He was outside his open front door for another reason, other than to admire his own name engraved on a brass plaque. He bent down and patted his knees. 'Come on,' he commanded. Perhaps today of all days this wretched dog would leave the house without his having to lose his temper.

The dog sat there in the hallway, looking friendly.

'Come on,' repeated Martin. 'Out you come.'

The dog wagged its tail. It wasn't going to budge.

Martin had enough experience of this particular dog to know it was not going to do what he wanted. Instead he had to walk back into the house, take hold of its collar, and pull, which the dog objected to by attempting to remain sitting down even as he dragged it outside. And then Martin quickly turned, dashed back into the surgery and slammed the door.

It was done: the dog was evicted.

There, in the entrance corridor to his new surgery, a thought struck him: the dog had something wrong with it, an ailment. Suddenly Martin, the most rational of men, was afflicted with the ridiculous notion that the dog was the reincarnation of a patient who had died, and who had come back for correct diagnosis, for proper treatment . . .

These kinds of thoughts weren't helpful. This was a doctor's surgery, re-fitted. The equipment clean and new.

The front door opened and Elaine appeared. Every bit of her clothing was a different colour. Bangles chink-chinked on her wrists. At the centre of pools of make-up, her eyes, he realised, had the tawny colour of a bird of prey, and certainly she needed to be queen of all she surveyed. Her insolent gait, Martin thought, was indicative of . . . And then he saw that, at the same time as she came in, slaloming around her legs came the dog, happily bounding indoors.

'The dog, mind the dog,' shouted Martin, but it was useless.

'I'm buying the biscuits in the supermarket, right?' began

Elaine as if she was continuing a conversation they'd already started, 'and this bimbo won't let me through on six items or less. "Sorry, six items or less!" she says, you know the type, all blonde with three-inch nails, and yes, I had twenty packets, but *all the same*, d'you see, so it was only *one* thing, wasn't it?' She handed him the receipt. 'That's for petty cash,' she said.

'Hang on,' said Martin, 'and all these biscuits are for—?'

His question was cut off by the sound of the door being opened: his work had begun.

During the morning, Martin began to see how it was: there were many more people in the waiting room than he actually saw as patients; and each of these people was given a cup of tea and biscuits. There was a buzz of conversation, whereas most doctors' waiting rooms were quiet places. Elaine had taken it on herself to run a kind of social centre. Even the patients he did see didn't have much wrong with them; it was more that they wanted to chat, and Martin began to realise, as the morning wore on, that he'd become part of the café society, too. It was obviously how Doctor Sim had run the place, and everyone assumed he would run things in the same way.

But he *wasn't* Doctor Sim, and if there was one thing in the world that Martin couldn't do it was small talk; it was like breathing in poison gas for him. And it was an injustice, also, that buckets full of biscuits and gallons of tea were being eaten and drunk at his expense. He didn't want to encourage hypochondria. He felt a tide of anger rising

71

fast, and when that happened he simply did what had to be done.

'Right,' he called out to the waiting room. Everyone fell silent and turned to look at him. 'Is there anyone here,' went on Martin, 'with a genuine medical complaint, who seriously needs to see a doctor?'

He was aware of Elaine's jaw hanging open, and then it snapped shut, and her expression was one of calculating disapproval.

From among his audience he saw a single hand tentatively raised, but when Martin looked in the man's direction, the hand went down again.

'Thank you,' called Martin. 'And goodbye. In your own time. Thank you very much.'

Elaine was offering him a steady glare. She was the attraction, of course; he realised that.

People filtered out; and he watched them go. Most wouldn't look him in the eye; they were ashamed or amused, like children. There was one man, though, among the younger ones at fifty or so years of age, who held Martin's gaze quite easily, and, as he went past, he opened his mouth and a hoarse voice came from somewhere. Martin didn't catch exactly what was said, only that it was something about not listening, or not lasting . . .

But neither what had been said, nor the tone of voice, was of any concern to Martin. It was the strained hoarseness that he'd noticed. He stepped forward and called to the man's retreating back, 'How long have you had that cough?'

The man was called Roger Fenn and three minutes later he was standing in the consulting room and Martin was holding a stethoscope to his chest, and afterwards examining his neck, and the inside of his mouth.

'You think if you're professional, they'll appreciate you,' said Roger, who considered this examination a waste of time. 'They won't,' he added.

Martin didn't hear. He was concentrating on the information coming through his fingertips as he pressed lightly against the man's neck. 'How long have you been hoarse?'

'Twenty-five years. From shouting at ungrateful pupils. Before they got rid of me.'

Martin sat his patient down, twisted the end of his torch, and shone the light into his mouth. There was a period of silence.

Roger Fenn could hear the doctor's breathing, as he leaned close to him. When the torch was taken away Roger asked, 'What's with the full MOT? Just the same old cough.'

'You have a lump in your neck.'

'That? It's nothing. Had that since I was a boy.'

'I don't think so,' said Martin. 'I'm going to refer you. There'll be a biopsy and we'll take it from there.'

'A referral? Great. Otherwise known as "covering your arse".'

'No, otherwise known as providing specialist treatment.'

'You ever noticed how nobody makes it their business to know anything anymore? It's always pass the buck.'

'In cases like this it's appropriate to investigate further

before making a diagnosis.' One of the advantages of being prickly himself was that Martin didn't particularly mind when other people were prickly.

'Nothing for the cough, then,' muttered Roger.

'Nothing for the chip on the shoulder either, I'm afraid,' said Martin.

That was enough for Roger. 'Now who's having their time wasted? Stuff your referral.' And he was gone.

Martin watched the surgery door close. Why couldn't patients simply lie down, cover themselves with a green sheet and not say a word?

He was stopped from even thinking about going after Roger Fenn by what happened next: Elaine came in, casual as ever, and plonked a piece of paper on his desk. 'What's this?' he asked.

She replied as if to someone mentally retarded, 'It's a *message*?'

He read the slip of paper a second time. 'Roy or Steven.'

'Boy of seven?' said Elaine, rolling her eyes. 'Doc Sim could read my writing. Stomach pain.'

'Temperature 104? Could be appendicitis. What's this name?'

Elaine leaned over to look at her own handwriting. 'Robson. Could be. Or Johnson?' She pleaded with him, 'Well the mother was hysterical wasn't she, like no kid's ever had belly ache and a temperature.'

Martin felt a cold dread invade the room. 'A child can die of appendicitis.'

Elaine felt the same dread, and the blame for this began to gather around her, specifically. She felt ashamed, but wasn't ever going to admit it. 'Look, I didn't worry so much about the name because I knew you'd straightaway call the number, see?' She pulled the message out of his grip and dialled the number, and handed him the handset.

Martin listened to a recorded voice saying very calmly, 'Number not recognised. Please check, and dial again.' He did as he was told, and heard the same automatic response. He put the phone down and looked Elaine in the eye. 'Number not recognised.'

'No, that can't be . . .' The dread had become stronger; and, mixed with blame, it made her doubly ashamed.

Martin said quietly, 'There's a sick child somewhere, but you didn't get the telephone number, let alone the name. I suppose we could get the name from the obituary.'

'Maybe we could just . . . we should . . .' But she was defeated.

'I think you should look for another job.'

'What? Just because . . .'

'Because,' Martin interrupted, already preparing to leave, 'you are the most incompetent person I have ever had the misfortune to encounter. And your incompetence might now end up costing somebody their life.'

He picked up his medical bag, opened it to check it was in order, snapped it shut. 'You're fired,' he said, and walked out of the building.

He could almost as quickly walk, but he might need the

car with him and he could park right by the school gates. He took off quickly down the hill, passed the mouth of the harbour, and twenty seconds later he pulled up outside the school and was out of the car even as he pulled out the ignition key.

Minutes later, he was facing Louisa, in the corridor outside her class room. 'Seven years old,' he said, 'name could be Johnson or Robson.'

'Nobody in my class.' Even as she was saying it, she was already walking. 'We can ask Richard.'

Martin followed, but suddenly she stopped in her tracks and turned. 'Bobby Richards,' she said with certainty. 'Bobby was sick yesterday in the playground.' She headed down the corridor in the opposite direction, breaking into a trot.

In the school office, Louisa was deft, quick. In half a minute she was on the phone to Bobby's home.

Martin listened impatiently to her end of the conversation. 'This is Miss Glasson from the school. Just checking up on Bobby?' He watched her listening, and he could hear the high-pitched scratching sound of the voice at the other end. 'Oh dear,' came Louisa's reply. 'Well, I'm sure the doctor will . . .' Martin snatched the phone from her. He noticed Louisa's hurt, but didn't have time to apologise. 'Mrs Richards?'

'Yes,' came the anxious voice at the other end.

'Doctor Ellingham here. Is his temperature still elevated?'

'It's 104, the last time, which was—'

Martin interrupted, 'Can I have your address?' He

listened, and wrote it down. The trouble was, he didn't know where it was; he was new here . . . 'Thank you,' he said. 'I'll be with you in fifteen—'

Louisa interrupted, 'Half an hour.' She was writing something down, as well, fiercely concentrating.

'I'll be with you in half an hour,' he said. He lifted his head, and drew breath to ask Louisa for directions, but he didn't say a word, because something happened, then, that was so perfectly efficient that it was strangely moving. It didn't matter that he'd snatched the phone from her; it didn't matter that he'd interrupted her class; it only mattered that the expression on Louisa's face was one of urgent concern for the sick child; and there – she was already holding out a piece of paper for him to take. 'Map,' she said.

She'd shaved two minutes off the response time. He hadn't had to ask.

Louisa wandered back to her class room, but she felt out of sorts, almost as if she'd been abandoned. She put it down to the fact that it was because she wanted to be with the boy, to see it through rather than be left behind. And yet, curiously, the feeling persisted even after they'd found out that Bobby Richards only had a dose of tonsillitis and wasn't in danger, after all. She put it down to the fact that it was the emergency itself that had attracted her, made her want to stay close . . .

The near-miss did have one other consequence, which slowly became evident to Martin over the next day or so. It was odd, and it took him a while to realise what was going on. He first noticed it when Bobby Richards's older sister, a girl whom he recognised from the Bevy of Beauties, had refused to make him a cup of tea during his second visit to check up on her brother. The second time he noticed was at lunchtime, in the Port Café. He got a table all right, and the waitress, a young girl called Jade who he knew was a friend of Elaine's, came over, flipped her notebook, and stood ready to take his order.

'A mineral water, please, and the pasta. Thank you.'

'Pasta's finished,' said Jade.

'Ah. Never mind. What's the soup?' asked Martin.

'Soup's all gone,' said Jade stoically.

Martin had to go back to the menu, now. 'Chilli con carne?' he enquired, beginning to realise what was going on.

Jade shrugged. 'Sorry.'

'And the pasties are finished, of course,' he said abruptly.

Jade raised her eyebrows.

'You're a friend of Elaine's,' said Martin.

Jade simply stared at him.

Martin rose to his feet. 'I see.'

The third time it happened was at the petrol station. He'd pulled up at the pump; he'd inserted the nozzle and he waited for the display to return to zero and the pump motor to switch on. And he waited. He squeezed the nozzle, just to test it, but there was nothing. He looked over at the cashier's window and waved an arm, gesticulating at the pump. She looked blankly at him, and shook her head slowly.

Martin had had enough. He walked in, and strode as calmly as he could to the cashier's desk. Yes, the girl was about Elaine's age; he ducked forward to read her name badge. 'Pamela,' he said.

She looked at him steadily, her jaw moving the chewing gum from one side of her mouth to the other.

'You and I both know what's going on, here, don't we? But if you'd just let me have some petrol, I won't tell anyone.'

'Sorry?' said Pamela, in an insolent tone of voice.

'I get it, OK?' He smiled at her, graciously. 'I get the message. Friend of Elaine.'

'Who's Elaine?'

Martin felt his usual quota of impatience. This behaviour was so childish! He'd had every right to fire Elaine – it was important, for the sake of the village, that she was fired. Getting rid of Elaine, suddenly, was the equivalent of saving people's lives. Didn't the inhabitants of this godforsaken place understand that?

Another driver turned up and stood next to Martin, and said, 'Number three, please.'

'Twenty-five pound fifty,' said Pamela, with a sniff, and a glance at Martin.

The driver took a Mars bar from the display at the counter. 'And one of these. Ta.'

Martin's impatience had already turned to aggravation, and now it turned to anger. 'Pamela, let me paint you a picture.' He was probably shouting but he didn't care. 'It's snowing outside. You're about to give birth to your fifth child in three years. Your waters break. You're frightened. You're alone – because your boyfriend is rotting in Borstal. And you ring good old Doctor Ellingham, the one person within a radius of a hundred miles who can help you. But guess what? I say . . . I say, "Sorry, Pamela, I don't do births."'

The driver standing next to Martin was leaning back as though a terrible smell had suddenly afflicted him. 'You all right, mate?'

'No I bloody well am not,' said Martin.

'Ah, you must be Doc Martin,' said the driver. He leaned forward to key in his pin number.

Pamela piped up, 'There's no more petrol, because the tank's empty.'

Martin was incensed. 'Then what's he put in his car? Horse urine?' Martin plucked the Mars bar from the driver's hand and held it stiffly under Pamela's nose. 'Oh I'm sorry, you can't have this Mars bar, not unless you give Elaine her job back, because God forbid you should do anything to upset this village of the damned.'

'We – don't – have – any – petrol,' said Pamela, as if to a mentally retarded person.

'So what's *he* just bought?' Martin climbed higher than ever on his high horse. 'Hmm?' He'd got her now, cornered. What silly answer could she possibly come up with? He hurled the Mars bar behind the desk, where it hit the cigarette display and dropped to the ground.

'That would be *diesel*,' said Pamela calmly, 'that he just bought.' She took a fresh Mars bar from the display and handed it to the driver. 'And a Mars bar,' she added. 'Which comes from outer space of course. Like you do. Obviously.'

For some minutes Martin sat in his car and waited for his pulse rate to drop. He did actually mind that he'd made such a fool of himself. But it seemed part of the way that this village, Portwenn, well – the people here sort of *got in his way*, if truth be told. Maybe all people, everywhere, got in his way.

He stared out of the car windscreen. What bleak places petrol station forecourts are, he thought. The advertising hoardings, the cheapest possible manufacture of the building itself, and the awning. The rows and rows of sweets and crisps inside. Guzzling. He remembered that word from comic books in his childhood. Desperate Dan guzzled burgers and sausages. Here, in petrol station forecourts, we guzzle fuel, Martin thought, and we guzzle chocolate, and crisps, and fags and booze, and the tarmac is stained and the lottery tickets clamour for attention and . . . even in such a beautiful place as Portwenn, thought Martin, the petrol station forecourt was like the plughole of human guzzling.

He switched on the ignition. The fuel needle wasn't quite in the red; he had enough miles left. He was still angry.

Martin should have left his car and walked home; it was because he was so drunk on humiliation and annoyance, that he dinged Roger Fenn's car, just a touch, on the exit road.

Both drivers climbed out of their vehicles.

Roger Fenn said in his hoarse voice, 'Driving with your eyes closed?'

'Mr Fenn,' said Martin. It seemed like a good thing from now on to say as few words as possible and not to accuse anyone of anything. 'I was on my way to see you.'

Roger Fenn leaned over the front end of his Peugeot. There was a white scratch visible through the blue paintwork. 'Great,' he rasped, 'look at that.'

'You didn't want to be referred,' said Martin, 'so I thought I ought to give you my opinion.'

Roger coughed. 'I don't want your opinion,' he said. 'I've got some cough syrup. So, thanks, but go and drive into someone else.' His voice was a coarse sawing back and forth across his vocal cords.

'Mr Fenn, there's a high probability that you have a cancer of the larynx. You'll require surgery and may well lose your voice. You may not care about that, but unfortunately I'm paid to.'

Roger stood there, silently; Martin watched his words sink in. The cars stood nose-to-nose, and Martin and Roger Fenn were face-to-face; all the hostility in Roger's expression turned to shock.

The first thing Martin did when he returned to the surgery was to arrange for a laryngoscopy to be performed on Roger Fenn; and, not only that, he fought for it to happen the next day. 'He's a smoker,' he shouted down the phone, 'and he has a lump in his neck. What more do you want, the tumour to come out and wave?'

His slamming-down of the phone – the clatter, and the light concussion of its ring-tone hanging in the air – served to emphasise how completely empty was the surgery. Dr Martin Ellingham was alone. He listened carefully into the silence; all he could hear was the calm panting of the dog, which he'd tied to the radiator in the vague hope that if the plumbing went wrong again it would drown. And the drip of a tap reminded him of the plumbers, Large and Son.

There was no Elaine; there were no patients. A memory came to mind: the waiting room filled with mostly elderly men and women drinking tea and eating biscuits. Strangely, following his sacking of Elaine, the appointment book had emptied. He'd answered a series of phone calls, and after each one he'd struck out another name in the appointments book, which now contained two pages of crossings-out, and acres of empty pages.

The next day, it was still just Martin and the dog, in an empty surgery, when the return call from the hospital broke the silence. Martin was fighting with the shrink-wrap surrounding half-a-dozen cans of Winalot. 'I mean, why do they make it like Fort Knox to get into these things?' he said out loud. Or maybe he was talking to the dog, which waited anxiously, bumping into Martin's ankles. Martin fetched a knife and stabbed at the shrink-wrap, which only punctured if he used all his strength. 'If you were a little old lady,' said Martin to the dog, 'how could you possibly get into any kind of food? You'd starve!' He tried to tear the punctured shrink-wrap, but it wouldn't. He had to saw at it with the knife, and eventually he bullied one can – pushed and pulled and wrenched – until it squeezed out. The ring pull at the top took a bit of work, too, and by the time the phone went his hands were covered in Winalot, he had paw-prints all over his shirt, and he was in no mood . . .

'Portwenn surgery,' he said into the phone. He could wipe down the receiver later.

'Doctor Ellingham?'

'Yes.'

'Richard Edgerton here, ENT.'

'Ah. Thanks for coming back so quickly.'

'I have the histology here for your patient, Roger Fenn.'

After he'd put the phone down, there was no other patient to delay him and so ten minutes later Martin steered the car up through the narrow streets of Portwenn and onto the top of the cliff. A couple of miles later he turned downhill again, into the space in front of Roger Fenn's barn conversion. When he was out of the car Martin paused, because he could hear music. He waited for a while, and listened. The voice was Roger Fenn's – hoarse, bluesy, with a touch of belligerence in the tone, yet it sounded full of quiet wisdom. The instrument was an electric piano? Martin wondered if it was a recording, or was Roger in the house, singing? He lifted his finger to the bell-push, but didn't press. It struck Martin as wrong, to stop the music. He didn't want to go inside. He wished he wasn't here.

He tried the handle and it gave way; he walked into the

house. He registered certain things: A framed album cover. Pictures of a band on the road. An acoustic guitar with a fat leather strap, propped carefully in a stand. There was a row of class photographs taken outside the school building in Portwenn, and when Martin leaned closer, expecting to find Louisa, instead he saw pictures of Roger Fenn, more or less as he looked now. He remembered – Roger Fenn had been the music teacher at the school but he had been forced into redundancy, and Louisa Glasson had been hired to replace him.

Martin followed the music, which became louder as he walked through the house. He came to a room full of daylight, with a breath-taking view over the top of the cliff, out to sea. At the same time the music stopped; Roger Fenn sat at the electric piano, his fingers stilled, knowing that Martin's driving up here, without warning, meant it was bad news.

'Don't stop on my account,' said Martin.

'You lost?' Roger's voice was worse. 'Looking for children to frighten?'

Martin gestured at the pictures on the wall. 'You used to be in a band.'

'Gave it up,' he rasped, 'for something more sensible. That would see me through. Guess what. To a nice safe retirement.' And then he added, 'What do you do . . . when you're not working?'

It wasn't a question that Martin had ever considered. He sounded confused. 'I'm always working.'

'And there was me thinking . . . this was a social call,' said Roger.

The sunlight strengthened, and filled the room with light. Outside, a hundred yards beyond the house, the cliff made its near-vertical leap to the sea, and the waves worked away, worked again, to polish the boulders, and move the sand from one place to another, as it had done for countless years.

In the room filled with light, the two men were curiously still, motionless, for a long time. Only a few words were exchanged between them, and then a handshake.

When he'd returned from seeing his one patient, Martin parked the car outside his surgery, walked in and shut the door behind him. He was alone again. All the equipment was new, in place, ready to use. He'd gone through the filing system, and the notes were in pristine order, with new coloured tabs.

When the doorbell rang, Martin felt a surge of optimism; after all, he was a doctor; other people *would* fall ill, or have accidents. He would be needed.

He opened the door to a delivery driver – a van was pulled up on the slope outside the surgery.

'Caterin'' packs, tea and coffee,' said the driver, putting a box down on the doorstep and returning to his van. He laboured back, partly obscured by the next box, his bandy legs hinting at a lifetime of lifting. He dropped it with a thump, dug out the paperwork and a pen, and held them out for Martin's signature.

'I didn't order this,' said Martin.

'You Ellingham?'

'The person who ordered this no longer works here. Take it back please.'

'Can't do that,' said the driver calmly.

'Yes you can,' said Martin. 'You've got a van and everything.' Something in his tone of voice sounded a bit like Elaine's.

'Can't take it back,' explained the driver, 'until you accept delivery.'

'Oh, of course,' said Martin. 'Silly me.'

'It's not rocket science,' said the driver in a kind voice. 'You accept delivery, then you get a returns number, then you arrange a time to have the package, or packages, picked up.' He added happily, 'And then I come back and collect them.'

'You do?'

'Yes. Mind if I use your loo?'

'By all means.' Martin stepped aside, and the driver with the bandy legs walked into the hallway. Martin pointed the way.

When the driver came out of the loo, he was disconcerted to find Martin waiting there.

'That took a while,' said Martin, frowning.

'What?'

'Poor urine flow,' said Martin.

'You what?'

'Especially if there's any discomfort,' Martin persisted, 'you should have your prostate checked.'

87

The driver was making for the door. 'Blimey, I . . .'

'It could be enlarged. I could check it for you. I'm a doctor.'

The driver could see daylight and headed for it. 'What, you mean up the jacksie? No fear.'

'It won't take a minute.' Martin was calm, professional.

'Not on your life,' the driver threw over his shoulder.

Martin was going to make one of his habitual attempts to abandon the dog, but when he stepped outside his door, with the dog on the leash, he looked down on the village of Portwenn, which grew up the steep slope on the opposite side of the valley, and he turned the other way, to avoid the village that seemed so determined to avoid him, and walked the few more yards before the lane turned into the footpath, and he could be alone on the cliff top, behind which the sun set, sending golden rays to split between a few clouds that were left over. He plonked one solitary foot in front of the other, each of them shod in brightly shining black leather shoes, an unlikely figure in his suit and tie, too tall, too lonely in this new job, with a stray dog the only living creature to accompany him – and even that, a creature he was trying to get rid of.

Even his patients – those he'd actually helped to mend – didn't like him. Yesterday, he'd walked the dog past the school – idly hoping to tie it to a railing, or find someone who actually owned it – when a football smacked against the fence and there, on the other side, was Bobby, the child who hadn't had appendicitis, after all. 'Bobby,' said Martin. 'Good to see you looking better. Tonsillitis gone?'

'I don't like you,' said Bobby through the wire.

'Well that's OK, because I like you,' replied Martin.

'You were mean to Elaine,' shouted Bobby. 'All my sisters say you're the W-word, the T-word, and the P-word. And the Z-word.'

'I don't think I know the Z-word,' said Martin.

'It's a word,' replied Bobby and kicked the football hard against the fence, which gave its harsh rattle.

His only supporter and companion was the dog, but the dog wasn't a follower he wanted. He'd already taken it once to the police station, but it had reappeared, and now he had a better idea: he'd take it further away, out to his aunt's house; she'd offered to give it a temporary home, and find it a new one.

Aunt Joan shared this trait with her nephew Martin: they both of them went straight to the point; there was nothing else worth saying. 'Maybe it wasn't exactly a wise thing to fire a perfectly good receptionist,' she said.

'Elaine, perfectly *good*?' Martin slapped his thighs and called the dog over to the kennel. The dogs lived outdoors on Aunt Joan's farm. 'She made appointments before I even opened, she printed prescriptions so inaccurate as to render them potentially lethal. I had to . . .'

Joan interrupted, 'But didn't you check them?'

' . . . I had to go to over to the *school* to trace a child with suspected appendicitis because Elaine couldn't—'

'That boy had a sore throat. Come on, Marty.'

'Elaine wasn't to know that.' The dog didn't like the look of the kennel, and Martin was fed up with slapping his thighs like a pantomime prince, trying to get the dog to move. 'Here. Come on. Come here.'

'Everyone makes mistakes,' said Aunt Joan.

'But she can't admit them,' said Martin. 'She meets any complaint with a complaint of her own, and any suggestion or instruction with a suggestion or construction of her own.'

'Construction?'

'Instruction, you know what I meant.'

'Of course when you make a mistake, Marty, you roll over and ask for your tummy to be tickled.'

The insanity of this remark, so haughtily delivered, added to his frustration at the dog. 'What the *hell* is the matter with this animal?' he shouted.

Joan calmly walked forwards. Her brisk no-nonsense voice uttered a simple command, 'Come,' and she slapped *her* thigh, and the dog followed her, and walked into the kennel, and Joan closed the kennel door.

'What . . . how?' began Martin. 'I did that,' and he slapped his thigh in the same way.

Joan was already heading into the house; Martin followed.

They shared a pot of tea and exchanged their news; and when Martin left his aunt's farm, his car was a solitary silver dot that moved along the cliff tops, around and down, and up and over, the great spread of the Atlantic ocean glistening on one side, the ancient landscape of Cornwall folded into hills and valleys on the other side. Abruptly, for no apparent reason, the silver vehicle stopped, its nose diving sharply, before it rested at a standstill, engine at tick-over.

Inside the car, Martin had had a fright – he'd seen something move in his rear-view mirror – something inside the car, on the back seat, something alive. Hairy. He swivelled sharply, and looked into the panting face of the dog.

Louisa Glasson did what she always did when she visited a hospital: she looked at the seams between the glass and the window frames, between the door and the wall, and the walls and the floor. As was normal in a modern hospital, the blue hard-compound linoleum, when it met the wall, carried on and climbed up the first six inches. But the state of the seam between the two told you everything about how well the hospital was cleaned and maintained. It should be clean, neat and undamaged. She walked onwards; the blue plastic underfoot had just the right quality of dry cleanliness. She came to the first pair of swing doors: where the door frame was fixed to the wall was dead straight, with perfect paintwork. Where the door handle was fixed on, there was no tell-tale grubby tidemark.

She never did this in people's homes, she thought. It was something to do with being in a hospital. Cleanliness was part of their profession. And Louisa, with all the charm she could bring to bear on the subject, expected people to be professional.

She was at Treliske Hospital in a professional capacity. She was heading for a tricky encounter, but she wouldn't let the difficulty stop her. Roger Fenn's bitterness was understandable, and the fact that it was directed specifically against her made the visit daunting. But to do the right thing created its own pressure, a bow wave, and it carried her before it, strongly.

She knew which colour-coded signs to follow because she'd visited before. She found him in exactly the same place: in bed, pillows supporting his head, wearing pyjamas, the drip feed to the canula in his arm, the curtain half drawn across. She saw first of all the bump made by his feet, and then the book propped up on the white sheet, and then his face, relaxed and unaware of being observed. One step later and he looked up to see her: his expression tightened; the book flopped down. 'Again?' he said as she drew near. 'We don't speak for a year and now it's twice in two days. I must get cancer more often.'

She sat carefully at his bedside. 'I can't stay so long this time. I—'

'Yes, of course, you have my job to go back to.'

His comment sponsored in Louisa a sense of her own good luck, and his bad luck, which after all was just what he'd intended, but she had no answer for him. She turned the bunch of flowers in her hands and looked around for a vase to put them in, but there was none. 'So,' she said. And a while later she said something that was true, but would be difficult for him to hear. 'Everyone at school sends their love.'

'Really?' asked Roger calmly. 'Last time they sent their love, it came in an envelope with a P45.'

Louisa knew then, for certain, that Roger must think about the school every day, and he must have ill feelings about it every day, and this knowledge made her uncomfortable. Surely they both wanted to change the subject. 'So did the surgeons say exactly what they were going to do today?'

Roger's dislike of his surgeon swept away all his dislike of the school, and of Louisa. It was like he talked to himself. 'I don't know. The guy makes Ellingham look positively tame.'

'And still no sign of Martin?'

Roger shook his head. 'No.'

Louisa was angry: if her sense of professionalism demanded she was here, how much more powerfully should Martin's conscience have brought him to his patient's bedside?

Roger noticed Louisa's coldness. 'Why should that bother you so much? Why would I want to see him, anyway?'

'Maybe he could explain to you what's going on.'

'It's clear what's going on. I've been pushed out of my job an inch before I qualify for a pension. And minutes before I'm due to lose my voice forever, I find myself having to have a nice friendly chat with the woman who replaced me.'

'Roger, I'm so sorry, but—'

'If you want forgiveness, try a priest.'

Louisa felt the impulse to reach forward and pick up his hand, but at the same time she imagined how he would snatch it away, and so she resisted. Instead she made a decision: that her visit was a worse thing, for him, than if she had not visited. It was wrong to have come. She started to try and think of the right words to allow her to leave gracefully. Go, said a voice inside her head.

At the same time as Louisa was standing up, Doctor Martin Ellingham arrived at the hospital. He steered his Lexus around the rows of cars, looking for a space in the public car park, but there was none. Cars were even jammed up on the verges, and adding themselves to the ends of rows where no lines were painted.

He drove into the staff car park, and aimed the car into a space marked 'Reserved Brownlow'. He climbed from the car and walked into the hospital. He thought it polite to leave his car keys at the reception desk, just in case his car needed to be moved. He approached the desk and said, 'ENT, please.'

'Second floor.' The receptionist had a pony tail, which swung behind her. She looked efficient.

Martin thought he might offer her a job. He put his car keys on the counter and said, 'I've parked in the spot reserved for a certain Mr Brownlow. Here are my keys in case someone needs to move my car.'

She asked, 'And you are?'

'Dr Martin Ellingham, Portwenn.'

'You're a GP?' Her tone was of disbelief.

'Yes,' said Martin. 'And you're a receptionist.' He started to walk off, but she hadn't finished.

'Excuse me,' she said, 'but you can't park in the staff car park.'

'I have to talk to a patient.'

She was furious, now. 'Is it me, or do you not understand plain English?'

'It's you,' said Martin in a slow voice. 'Look, we both know this is going to end up with me walking down that corridor. I'll just save us some time.' Martin carried on.

The Treliske Hospital in Truro was mapped with corridors, which intersected at right angles, and it happened that as Martin swung into one section, at the other end Louisa Glasson turned the corner and disappeared; he unwittingly saw the tilt and sway of her skirt, and a brief view of her profile, but she was too far away for him to recognise her, or even to be curious as to who she might be, obscured as she was by other figures who trawled slowly along in both directions – staff, and patients, and visitors. And Louisa herself walked out of the hospital with the misplaced sense of injustice that Martin hadn't bothered to visit the one patient left to him. She carried that injustice, and added the whole weight of it to that side of the scales that measured all that was wrong about Dr Martin Ellingham.

Roger Fenn stared at the familiar white paint of the hospital ceiling, not a blemish or a cobweb on it, thinking how he had been wrong to reveal to Louisa his long-standing bitterness over losing his job. The tube in his arm, the curtain hanging on its rail, the window offering its square of blue sky, which he wasn't allowed to walk under, and the rasping sound of his voice as he'd spoken to Louisa, all this, in its effect, was like a wounding of him, and added to the sense of hurt. And he'd lost his temper. He closed his eyes, to make the hospital go away.

Martin approached Roger's bed, and noticed the black line drawn in a curve around the site of the lump in his neck. 'The surgeon's been in?' asked Martin.

'Yeah.' Roger opened his eyes and pulled himself up on the cushions. How bony and weak his limbs seemed. 'The surgeon's been in,' he rasped, 'and before I met *him*, I thought *you* were a smug bastard.' He was going to miss swearing, if he lost his voice.

'If the squamous cells haven't spread, the voice might be saved.'

'Yeah, yeah. He said that. If the squamous cells haven't spread, the voice might be saved. *The* voice. It's not *the* voice.'

'Your voice, quite right,' said Martin. 'My former pro‑fession is populated by arrogant overpaid men with God complexes. But then, I do tend to see the good in people.'

'That why you switched to being a GP?'

'No, I switched to being a GP because I get on so well with people.'

Roger choked, and fleetingly, in his mind, the obstruction to his laughter being there, in his throat, felt like a sign, a message to him, but he didn't know what it could mean. In any event, he'd wanted to laugh.

Martin watched the same featureless square of blue in the window. The outside world seemed a long way off. 'No, I left surgery because . . . I have a heightened emotional reaction to certain events.'

Roger Fenn knew he'd been handed something unusual, with this confession by Martin. He didn't want to say anything. He wanted to wait, like one might sit quietly in order to catch sight of a rare creature. But nothing came. Eventually Roger said, 'Heightened emotional reaction. You're in medical-speak again.'

'Panic attacks,' said Martin. 'Sometimes I have panic attacks.'

'What kind?'

'Palpitations, sweating, chest pain, breathlessness . . .'

'No, I mean what brings them on?' Roger was happy in this conversation; it was easy suddenly.

'Smells,' said Martin. 'The smell of cauterised flesh. Blood. The iron smell of it. Sometimes just the sight of it.'

'Not so good for the career.'

What a long sequence of events, thought Martin, was contained within Roger Fenn's short answer. Not so good for the career, indeed. It had led him from all the way up there, down to here: a GP with one patient in a village that didn't want him. 'I used to have the Midas touch,' said Martin. 'I couldn't look at a body on the operating table without fixing it. Then one day in the middle of the most routine procedure, I suddenly thought – with the flesh parting under my knife – this is someone's sister, someone's wife, or mother. This is not anonymous. *Not* routine. And then' – he snapped his fingers – 'it was gone.' He looked away from the window, and directly at Roger. 'I was up there on the high wire and I made the mistake of looking down. Haven't operated since that moment.'

They watched as an elderly woman limped into the ward, putting down only the toe of her left foot. Her vest hung at an angle. She sat with deliberate slowness on the bed opposite.

How many other people had lines drawn on their skin where they were about to be cut, Roger wondered. Like dolls returned to their makers. He looked at Martin, and the two men held each other's gaze comfortably; they both realised at the same time that they'd agreed, for a moment, to become friends.

Roger Fenn said, 'You might want to keep it quiet, that you panic at the sight or smell of blood.'

Martin nodded. 'Yes,' he said, shortly. 'After all, I'd hate the village to fall out of love with me.'

Roger smiled at Martin's frown. 'Secret's safe with me,' said Roger.

'It's not like you're going to be able to tell anyone,' said Martin and drew his finger across his throat.

Hang on, thought Roger, that was two, three jokes in a row – not bad going. He felt the smile come yet again.

'Had any family in?' asked Martin.

Roger shook his head. 'Decided not to call my daughter.

She stopped needing me a long time ago.' He grimaced. 'You know. She has a TV of her own.' After a while he asked, 'You got anyone?'

Martin shook his head. 'Only child.'

'Parents dead?'

'Costa del Sol. Golf.'

'Nice.'

'We don't speak.'

'That's because you're a miserable bugger.'

Martin nodded.

'Look at us,' said Roger, rubbing an inch of sheet between his fingers. 'What's the collective noun for a group of miserable buggers?'

Neither man looked at the other one; and the intimacy between them suddenly disappeared.

Louisa Glasson, despite herself, rehearsed what she was going to say to Martin, even as she drove back to Portwenn. She would simply walk up to him, and say it. Her lips moved as she drove along. 'Martin, don't you think you should have *visited* your one patient in hospital? Don't you think' – she changed up to third and zoomed forward – 'that a man who is going to undergo cancer surgery deserves . . .?' She felt the white lines thump against the tyres as she took a corner too fast.

No, she ticked herself off – she mustn't rant. It would be better just to speak in a quiet, authoritative tone. She eased her foot off the accelerator and settled at a steady fifty-five. 'Martin, I think it would have been advisable for you to have visited Roger Fenn in hospital before his operation.'

She came to the top of the hill. The descent into Portwenn was always a bit like starting down a toboggan run. She glanced across the shining expanse of the bay to where the doctor's surgery stood, on its own, on the opposite side. It looked blank, unused, still.

It was all very well practising what she would say, but when would she next see him? She thought about where she could go, to make sure she bumped into him. She could simply go up to the surgery. Or, he'd taken to walking that dog along the cliffs – she could make sure to go up there, too. What about the wedding – would he be at the wedding on Saturday week?

She parked the car and let herself into her house, and went straight out the back onto the little balcony that overlooked the harbour. She sat with a thump on the cane chair. If she threw a pebble from here, it could probably clear the other houses and land in the sea, eighty feet below.

She folded her arms and stared across the bay at the doctor's surgery. Yes, it had the unmistakeable air of an empty house. Martin was probably away, eating in some fancy restaurant, or swooping about in his oversized car. Had he given even one thought, she wondered, to Roger Fenn?

She stood up abruptly and went inside. In the fridge door stood an open bottle of Devon's Sharpham wine, and she was going to pour herself a glass on her balcony and sit in the sun.

When she set the bottle down on the table, she saw that, by mistake, she'd brought out two glasses.

3

In the Fish Market, the stainless steel surfaces were sluiced and ice was poured from buckets; they lifted the gaily coloured hatches at 5am. Portwenn's radio station started at 8. The school building began to echo with voices at 8.30 and went suddenly quiet, all the children standing in rows, at 9am. Large and Son, the plumbers, were already on site by 8am – the father gladly and the son – reluctant. Gilbert Spencer lifted a handful of his vest and used it to wipe the toothpaste from his mouth – an old army habit. Police Constable Mylow leaned over a booking form and wrote left-handed, his arm curved around in an embrace of his handwriting. Two small rows of cars slowly lined up on the beach, and, in the café, only the corner table next to the toilets was empty. Portwenn, in the brightening sun, glued itself to the cliff.

And Caroline, sometimes nicknamed Radio Caroline, sipped her first glass of wine. She was up to a bottle a day, before 6pm. Her friends warned her, sensing the abyss that awaited anyone who took a wrong step.

As it happened, Martin was going to come into contact

with Caroline that morning. The community radio station was housed in a sound-proof shed tacked onto the side of the Bay Hotel, and this morning the guest on its morning chat show, Dr Martin Ellingham, sat stiffly, waiting for the music to finish, his collar a sharp white band against his neck.

Opposite him, at her habitual desk, sat Caroline. 'Today's Portwenn Personality Playlist is brought to you by our featured guest this morning, our new GP, Doc Martin.'

'Doctor Ellingham,' Martin corrected her. 'Or Martin.'

A man was waving at him through the glass partition. 'What?' he asked. The man waved frantically, again. He realised he was being asked to speak into the microphone, which stood like a cactus on the desk between him and this woman, the interviewer . . . what was her name? 'Oh, right.' He leaned forward until he was close to the microphone. 'Doctor Ellingham,' he repeated, 'or Martin.'

Caroline nodded and her eyebrows popped up. She glanced down at her notes. 'So, Doc, you gave up your life in London, and your career as a brain surgeon—'

'Vascular specialist,' said Martin.

'To be our GP here in sleepy old Portwenn.'

'Yes.'

Caroline waited for a beat, and when nothing came, she nodded, and then waved her hand in a little circle; she was encouraging him to speak. This was a talk show; he was the guest.

'Yes, Caroline,' said Martin.

'What made you decide to do that?'

'I wanted to move.'

'What were your first impressions of our lovely village?'

Martin tried to remember the day he'd first set foot in Portwenn. 'Windy?' he said eventually. He was sure it had been gusting.

Louisa couldn't hear the broadcast because she was cycling through the village. Other inhabitants of the village, who hadn't yet encountered their new doctor, wandered closer to their radio sets, and touched the volume controls to hear more easily. The long silences and the obvious anxiety of the show's host were like a magnet, drawing them into the void.

'And the people?' asked Caroline.

'The people?' came Martin's voice, after a while.

'The people of Portwenn?'

'Oh. Yes. Of course. You mean, first impressions?'

'Well, yes, if you like.'

'They seemed . . . alive and well,' said Martin.

'And how about your personal life, Doc? Ever been married?'

'No.'

'Engaged?' said Caroline.

'No.'

'A trail of broken hearts then, I bet, in London?'

'No,' said Martin, frowning.

'Oh, I see.'

'Look,' said Martin, 'are we live? Because I need a pee—'

Caroline interrupted, and spoke cheerfully about guests always running out on her; and she put on a record to cover the gap. 'Do you think you could hurry up?' she said in a quite different voice.

'What?'

'This record finishes in two minutes and twenty-one seconds and I'm not putting out two in a row. This is meant to be a talk show.'

Martin had to bend low for every doorway in this village, and to leave the radio shack was no exception. He went into the Bay Hotel and sought out the Gents, and inside he found two of his listeners.

'Ah, Doc Martin.' Bert, the older Mr Large, of the celebrated Portwenn plumbers, Large and Son, was standing at the urinals, but only to replace the pipe work and the automatic flush. His overalls strained around his stomach.

Al, young and slender, was under the sink with a wrench.

Bert waved at his son, Al. 'Doc, you're from London, tell young Bill Gates here that computers are one of those fads.'

'Dad,' complained his son from under the sink.

'Computers are one of those fads,' said Martin baldly. 'Now out of the way, I need to pee.'

'Out of commission,' said Bert, proud of his handiwork. 'Try a cubicle.'

Martin took one stride to the nearest one and pushed at the door.

'Ooop,' said Bert. 'Out of order, that one, too.' Every now

and again he'd adjust his stomach as if it were a rucksack he was carrying in front of him.

Martin ducked back out and stepped to the next cubicle.

'Not that one,' said Bert.

Martin moved to the last cubicle and looked at Bert.

'What you waiting for, go on then.'

Martin went in. He could hear the change of tone in Bert's voice as the latter talked to his son. It was the low, grumbling tone used by family members when very ordinary things were being discussed. 'You're stopping with me until you've learned the trade. That's the deal.'

'It's not that different from plumbing. Circuits. Logic.'

'I promised your mum. God rest her and all that.'

'Promised her what?' came Al's voice from the under the sink. 'That you'd stop me having the career I want?'

Bert could see his son's Adam's apple moving. 'That I'd see you right.'

Martin came out of his cubicle and headed for the basin to wash his hands.

'Oop,' said Bert. 'Sorry Doc, no water.'

'Oh.'

'It was only a number one, weren't it?' said Bert. 'Don't need to wash your hands, doesn't count.'

'I'll inform the medical community,' said Martin on his way out.

Back in the radio shack, the record was just about to end. 'D'you think you could give more than one-word answers?' Caroline put in quickly as Martin took his seat. 'After all, it's a chat show?' When the indicator light came on she gritted her teeth and asked, 'I have with me Doc Martin, I'm pleased to say. Now then, Doc, am I right in thinking that you spent a summer or two in Portwenn as a young boy?'

'Yes,' said Martin.

'With your Aunt Joan?'

'Yes.' As he heard the syllables come out of his mouth one at a time, each question annoying him and each answer annoying her, two words sprang to mind, *Vanity Fair*, because the title of the famous literary work lent itself to a summation of what the media, radio and television, was – a vanity fairground. He and Caroline were going round and round.

After it was finished he felt confused and couldn't remember where his car was parked. There was the plumbers' van, Large and Son, and he saw his car next to it, although he could have sworn it had been in a different place. As he approached he overheard the meandering tones of complaint in which family arguments were always conducted.

'Over my dead body,' said Bert, leaning down to pick up tools.

'I've got a place and I'm going to college,' said his son, Al.

'You're staying here where I can look after you.'

'I don't need looking after.' Al slammed shut the back of the van.

'I promised your mum . . .'

'Oh, mum – you always wheel her out when you're losing an argument.'

Bert pushed his hat back and forth to scratch his head. 'How you going to pay for it, then?'

'I'll think of something,' said Al.

'Well good, because you'll get nothing from me.'

Al shouted, 'I don't want anything you can give me. I don't want a life fixing toilets.' He couldn't face riding next to his father in the van; the thought of being near him, of watching him crunch the gears and wobble the steering wheel, his little whistles and sighs and murmurs – all this made Al's skin crawl. Instead he took off, walking fast.

Bert watched him go. He swayed from foot to foot and rubbed his mouth with the back of his hand. He caught Martin's eye and judged the new doctor to be too tall, too fast moving, too well-dressed and clever, and surly. He held the other man's eye and said, 'And you can shove it, too.'

Martin had relented and given Elaine her job back; and when he returned to the surgery that morning she was already there: the same plaited hair but this time with beads woven into it, the same hippy-chic clothes, and it was as if every limb of her body was sulky in its own, distinctive way: the leg she was standing on, the other leg that wagged from side to side, and the hand on her hip was confrontational, and next it was her jaw, chewing gum, that was insolent, and then her eyes rolled back, and finally it was the almost inaudible 'Sttt . . .' that came from her mouth, before her attitude came round full circle and she rested her weight on the other leg.

'Elaine,' he said. 'Welcome back.'

'Doc.'

For the second or third time they went through some ground rules: appointments, filing, and telephone procedure. The silent piece of knowledge in the room, at this moment, was that in return for giving Elaine her job back, he had been served lunch in The Crab and Lobster, and he had a string of patients queuing up.

Martin went through to the consulting room and sat stiffly upright in his chair, hands folded on the desk. Was it the right thing, to have brought Elaine back? It seemed like he hadn't had any option. Events . . . Elaine herself.

He was aware that his mind was populated with people, crowds of them, mostly patients, while the room he was in, and the house he lived in, was empty, with only his own breath disturbing the air, and medical equipment standing ready. At this exact, banal moment, he sat up sharply, in order to fight off a dizzy spell. He stood and walked a few paces, and back.

The nameless, causeless attack of anxiety abated; he pushed it aside with practical concerns. A few seconds later he no longer remembered what had driven him from his chair.

He washed his hands. He had patients waiting. He watched his fingers writhing together to make foam. He rubbed at the tip of each finger and thumb, especially around the nails – vulnerable area.

For no reason the two words repeated themselves in his head – vulnerable area – and lost all their original meaning.

While Martin prepared for his first batch of real patients in the surgery, on the other side of the village, on the west-facing slope, Louisa Glasson was in the whitewashed converted chapel, looking for a pile of Year-Six English marking. She moved along shelves, looked under books and papers, opened and closed drawers. She'd dumped it in here and someone had moved it. 'You should go see the doctor,' she said to her colleague, Jean. 'You do look pale.'

'I'll be all right,' said Jean. She clutched a bottle of mineral water in her hand. 'Did you hear him on the radio? Doc Martin?'

'Not really, only caught a bit of it when I was walking down at the front.'

'Very cagey about everything, he was. No hint of a love life.'

'Really?'

'Can't think what you must have seen in him, at the interview?'

'Don't blame me,' said Louisa. 'At the time, only one of my eyes was working.'

'Oh, I thought you quite liked him.' Jean swigged from her bottle.

'He was fine,' said Lousia, still hunting for her papers.

'What are you after?' Jean asked.

'My Martin,' said Louisa. 'Marking, I mean. My Year-Six marking.'

Both Louisa and Martin were invited to Elaine's father's wedding; she counted it as the next time she would see him, to be able to tear him off a strip about Roger Fenn.

The irony was that although Martin was going to attend the wedding, Elaine herself refused to go on the grounds that her father's new wife carried around a small dog in her handbag.

The father was mournful about it; and Martin made an attempt to persuade Elaine to go – but she refused. For the bride, the dog in the handbag was the most important guest; for Elaine, it was a symbol of all that was wrong with her father's choice of new partner.

Everyone else was transformed by their smart clothes; for Martin it was an immaculate dark suit as usual, so he looked just the same. While he waited with the other guests around the door of church, Elaine's father's description of her sounded in his head, 'Difficult girl, she is . . .' She was a glaring absence – the bridegroom's daughter.

Louisa arrived, dressed in an outfit that was summer itself, but her face was like a cold rain shower. On walking up the path to the church, she passed right by Martin as if he didn't exist. She was cross with him, for some reason. Underneath the immediate sense of mystery and injustice – what on earth had he done? – Martin felt a strain of pride; he can't have done anything wrong, because he never did, or very rarely. He followed her into the village church, which was packed full on either side of the aisle. He caught up with her just as she was taking her seat. 'Have I done anything to offend you?' he asked.

'It's what you haven't done,' she hissed.

'That narrows it down,' said Martin, but the wedding march drowned out his words.

The usher urged him to sit down in Louisa's row; and she was forced to accept that he must sit next to her.

'I can't believe you didn't visit Roger in hospital,' said Louisa. 'He didn't have a *clue* what was going on and—'

'OK, wait a minute—' But Martin was stopped because a woman in the row in front, as if she were an owl, swivelled her head right round and stared at him.

When the bride walked down the aisle, the little dog was carried in a different, more glamorous handbag, and the wedding started – but then there was a stir, as people looked back at the opening door of the church; and a murmur of approval travelled from the back of the building to the front, so even the bride and groom turned round to see what it meant – Elaine stood there. She had turned up, after all. The ceremony continued on a note of luxurious approval and family solidarity.

After the service, and with the guests milling around outside, with confetti on the ground and photographs being taken, the argument between Martin and Louisa picked up again. They were among a group of people gathered around

Roger Fenn, who was unable to talk much but who gestured instead.

Martin strolled over. 'Roger, good to see you.'

Louisa was sarcastic. 'Don't you think it's a bit late for the concerned routine?'

'What?'

'When you have precisely one patient,' said Louisa accusingly, 'I'd have thought you'd want to visit him in hospital.'

'Hang on a minute . . .'

Roger Fenn cleared his throat. It looked like he wanted to speak.

'Don't!' Louisa put a hand on Roger's arm. 'You don't have to say anything.'

Roger signalled that he was going to. The words came slowly, in a hoarse whisper, one after another, but Roger was smiling. 'He did. Visit. Depressed the hell. Out of me.'

'It was mutual,' said Martin.

In the sunlight, with the churchyard basking in the atmosphere created by the slightly dotty affection between a middle-aged man, Elaine's father, and a woman with a dog in her handbag, everyone inhabited the same general mood of optimism and good humour, except for Louisa, who now felt like an outcast, and it was her own fault.

'You could have told me,' she said.

'I tried, but that woman . . .'

Louisa's exasperated, ashamed expression often, in the

days afterwards, visited various people's memories, as one of the prettiest pictures made by anyone during the afternoon.

At ten minutes to two, Martin, pursued by the dog, walked up to the top of the cliff and he sucked in the fresh air and the view of the ocean.

Half an hour later he returned to the surgery, and as he went into the waiting room he heard Elaine say into the phone, 'No, just no, Greg, OK? Don't you see . . .' – but when she saw him she abruptly changed her tone. 'So that's Thursday, at 12.15, then? Thanks very much.' She plonked down the phone.

'Perhaps we'll meet Greg one day,' said Martin, because he wanted to point out to her that he'd noticed her deception, and he didn't mind if the patients seated around the edge of the room knew it, either.

'God, why?' said Elaine scornfully, and then she said matter-of-factly, 'You were rubbish on the radio that time, by the way.'

'Thank you,' said Martin. 'Appointments?'

'Machine doesn't work.' She batted the new computer on her desk. 'It keeps saying I can't do what I want to do.' She handed him a handwritten list. 'There you go, instead.'

Martin took the list and read the name at the top. 'Ricky Willow?'

A boy and his mum stood up, and together they walked through to the surgery.

'So, Ricky,' began Martin when they were all seated. 'What's the problem?'

The boy started to answer but his mum rode over the top of him. 'His bottom. It's the runs,' she said and her eyes bulged.

'I see,' said Martin. 'Diarrhoea. How long has this been going on?'

Martin had aimed his question at the boy, but the mother again answered for him. 'Two days.'

'You taking plenty of fluid? Do you have a fever, or any headaches?'

'It's just his bottom,' said the mother. 'He holds it in too long.'

Ricky, the boy, had turned rigid with embarrassment.

'Could be something you ate,' said Martin, 'or it could be a viral infection. Take some rehydration salts and give it a couple of days.'

'Can I go back to work?' The boy's voice was intense, quiet.

Work – what type of job could such a young person have, wondered Martin.

Mrs Willow said proudly, 'He's a lifeguard at the leisure centre, see.'

'Ah, said Martin. 'Well. Perhaps you should make sure you're better before you go back to your poolside duties. Any problems, come back and see me again.'

Mrs Willow looked as if she'd been short-changed. 'Not going to check his bottom?' She swayed in her seat and turned to her son. She made a quick, aggressive gesture. 'Show him your bottom.'

Martin rescued the boy. 'An examination isn't necessary,' he said.

Mrs Willow brought her handbag onto her lap and rootled through it. 'You'll be wanting,' she said, and pulled out a glass jar containing a sloppy dark fluid, 'to put this in for testing I expect.'

For the first time in Portwenn, Martin felt the beginnings of a working life begin to wear a groove into the passing of his time here. The appointments clicked away, and he tried either to make up time, or give more time, according to the nature of the complaint and the character of the person concerned. He felt the presence of Elaine out there in the waiting room, more familiar with her job than he was with his, and the sleekness of their matching desktop computers satisfied him. The instant a person appeared through the surgery door Martin was measuring: height, weight, age, sex. Breathing. Their gait as they walked over to the chair, their posture, eye colour and brightness, skin complexion and condition, lips, condition of hair, teeth. Even as a person began to speak he was racing ahead to see if he could at least guess from which family of illnesses their complaint might come; and to have symptoms described to him was the equivalent of having differently cut out shapes put on the surgery table, and he must join them up to complete the puzzle, see the whole picture.

Elaine's departure at the end of the day left him alone in his new dwelling, and the surgery fell silent. He could do anything he wished and the freedom oppressed him. The lack of demand on his patience, on his skill, struck him as an unbearable lightness. Wasn't there a book . . . ?

He found himself washing his car. He should buy some - thing smaller, he thought, as he laboured at the glossy sides of the Lexus, something that would be better suited to the lanes and . . .

'Hello,' came her voice, and he didn't have to think who she was, and he stood quicker than he would have done for anyone else. The sponge in his hand threw out a spray of water that caught her. 'Hello,' he said. He stood there, tall as a mountain. There was something shameful, he thought, about washing a car.

Louisa brushed the water drops from her clothes. 'It's OK, I have lots of Prada,' she said.

'Oh.' Martin stood uselessly, looking.

'Designer clothes?' said Louisa, having to work her way into a conversation.

'Yes.'

'Of course this isn't actually Prada. It was a joke.'

Martin was confused because a demand had been made that he try and do something which he knew in advance he couldn't do: small talk. 'Yes, I see.'

'Anyway,' said Louisa, 'I thought I should apologise. That time with Roger Fenn. I felt that he needed looking after and

. . . I suppose I felt guilty about his . . . about the whole retirement thing.'

'You mean you were annoyed with yourself, and you took it out on me?'

'Hey!' Louisa felt like she'd been poked with a stick, but she saw in his expression only a genuine enquiry, such as a child might have for an insect crawling on the ground. 'Well, excuse me,' she began.

'No, no – I thought that's what *you* were saying.'

'Oh, yes, I suppose it was.'

'So – not my fault then? I visited him OK?'

'Not your fault.'

'Good.'

'Yeah.' Louisa was hoping for Martin perhaps to say a word or two and ease them both into a conversation. Instead she had to try. 'I've just been to the pub,' she said eventually.

'I've been cleaning the car,' said Martin, stupidly holding the sponge.

'The pub does good food,' said Louisa.

For a moment Martin thought she might be talking in riddles, because her voice had that curious flat tone to it. 'I cook for myself,' he said, and he realised that he, too, sounded like this. And then, with dread, it dawned on him that this was small talk.

'And drinks,' added Louisa. 'The pub does drinks.' She'd never had to work so hard to cover ground, make a date.

'I don't really drink lager,' said Martin.

It was getting ridiculous. She suggested in a very certain tone of voice, 'They've got a good selection of wine and whiskies.' She caught herself talking more loudly, as if to a deaf person.

'Really.' Louisa knew what Caroline had felt like, trying to get him to talk on the radio. She also was ready to give up. 'Maybe we'll bump into each other there, one day.' She was already walking away.

'I've got an idea,' Martin called after her. It frightened him that she could just go, of her own free will. 'Why don't we meet for a drink?'

Louisa stopped. She liked that bit – the fact that he'd said, '*I've* got an idea.'

'OK,' she replied.

'Wednesday, 7.30?'

And Louisa had to ask, not only because she was genuinely curious, but also, if his answer was no, then he'd definitely be on the autistic spectrum. 'You did know, didn't you, that I wanted you to ask me that?'

Martin said, 'Yes, I did.' He held her gaze for a while, as her curiosity and friendliness turned to something else, a kind of blankness that he found difficult to judge: it was as if she were looking beyond him or through him, to some - thing or someone else.

In any event when she smiled again it was easier. 'See you, then,' she said and turned away and walked down the hill.

He watched her go, and was conscious that she'd be aware of his watching her – the way the shoulders reduced in width, evenly, to the waist, from which point the hips flared out. The skirt swung as her legs moved. The neat shoes and the careful steps, the pony-tail of long dark hair that hung between her shoulder blades. She bobbed along, as each step took her further down the hill towards the village. He expected her to turn around. The more distant she became, the more she appeared dainty and light on her feet.

Standing next to his car with an enormous yellow sponge in his hand, Martin felt oafish and too large for the picturesque village laid out beneath him. Every door lintel, every street, every shop entrance or passageway was too small. He must duck his head to pass from one room to another; if he met someone in the street he felt like he was blocking it. There were passageways in this village that he couldn't walk down without scuffing both his shoulders and leaving whitewash marks on the sleeves of his jacket. Sometimes his foot would seek out the next step in one of the steep alleyways to find the tread was too narrow, threatening to pitch him forwards.

He wondered where Louisa lived, and with whom. The village was a system, a flow of energy and livelihoods and relationships, and the machine was self-winding, and invented itself anew every day, the memories laid down in drifts, usually the same memories with minor variations, created each day. And yet without thinking about it, or being aware of it, he had separated off Louisa and given her a different sphere, outside the influence of the machine.

As for Louisa, while she strolled back down to the village

she rehearsed what would happen if they met for a drink in the pub. She would saunter in and his big frown would switch on. She would unhook a bag from her forearm and rest it on the table. The dreaded small talk would stop him in its tracks. It would be her job to prevent the paralysis; she would only say exactly what she thought, immediately. And he must talk about work; it was the only way in which his relationships with people could function. She sensed in him a towering personal loneliness – but it was as if he didn't know it was there, himself.

That night, Martin had a recurring dream in which he was trying to perform life-saving surgery with a rubber scalpel.

Martin came downstairs to find one or two patients waiting and the sound of Elaine's voice, affronted by some indignity, on the phone. 'Well then, get something from the chemist and go to bed. No, not really. You can't see Doc Martin with just a belly ache.'

She looked up to see Martin enter the waiting room, and she rolled her eyes, popped her hand over the mouthpiece and said conspiratorially, 'Can you imagine?'

Martin frowned. 'I'd like a word, please, Elaine.' There was a warning tone in his voice.

Elaine said into the phone, 'Look, I've got to go.'

'Please take the caller's number. And name. Accurately,' he said meaningfully.

In his surgery, Elaine was back on her stroppy high horse. 'Now what?' she asked.

Martin was angry. Once again it felt dangerous to have Elaine as his practice receptionist. 'It's not your job to give medical advice down the phone.'

'It was a belly ache,' said Elaine. 'That's not medical advice, that's common sense.'

Martin placed a hand over his chest. 'Can I please decide who comes to my surgery?'

'No.'

'No?' Martin was confused.

'If they've got belly ache or diarrhoea then I have them wait. If they've got something serious I get them in straight-away.' She was proud of her management of the patients.

'I'm familiar with triage,' began Martin.

'I want an apology,' said Elaine boldly. 'If it weren't for me, you'd have had a dozen diarrhoeas since yesterday.'

'*How* many?'

Martin cursed the monumental stupidity of Elaine. The mind-numbing irony of it visited him again: if he didn't employ Elaine he wouldn't have any patients; but if he did, her slapdash incompetence risked killing them all.

Martin tried to call the Portwenn pharmacy, but it was engaged. He left his surgery and walked there. In the steep-sided village with the tiny streets and cottages, it felt like he could reach it in two strides.

Mrs Tishell, the pharmacist, swung round to greet him when she heard the tinkle of the bell. The neck brace gave her the movements of an automaton. 'Ah,' she said. 'Doctor Ellingham, I've been waiting for you.'

Martin felt dread. 'Oh – why?'

'Well it's the usual thing, isn't it, for a new GP to pay a courtesy call to his pharmacist?'

'Oh I see – yes, well, I meant to come in earlier, but . . .'

'I bought a cake, to welcome you. It got a teeny bit stale, I'm afraid, so I had to feed it to my cats.'

'I'm sorry. It wasn't very professional of me.'

'No, I'm sorry I assumed . . . have you got time for a cup of tea?'

'Well, no, I'm sorry, I don't have time, but I need some information.'

Mrs Tishell was excited. 'Oh yes. Down to business. Of course.'

'Have you noticed an increased demand for diarrhoea remedies?'

Her eyes gleamed. 'You could even say there's been a bit of a run on them.' She watched for her joke to have an effect, but the new doctor hadn't even seen it go past, which was a shame.

'How many?' asked Martin.

'Over the last several days, maybe twenty or thirty people?'

'Damn,' said Martin.

Mrs Tishell felt the blame settle on her. 'I should have informed you. I'm sorry. I should have been more alert.'

'Don't apologise.'

'I'm sorry,' repeated Mrs Tishell.

'D'you remember any names?'

'Yes. Some of the locals.'

'Could you give me a list?'

'I could.' Mrs Tishell smiled and slowly found a pen and a sheet of paper. As she did so, she threw affectionate glances at Martin. 'Judging by your recent prescriptions, you seem to be aware of reports of adrenal crisis in inhaled corticosteroids.' She lowered the pen to the page and began to write.

Martin was impatient. 'There have been cases of adrenal suppression, yes, after excessive doses of fluticasone.' He made it sound like it was her fault.

Mrs Tishell carefully wrote out the third name. 'So you've taken care,' she said admiringly, 'to ensure dosages below 400 micrograms per . . .'

Martin interrupted, 'I like to remain current. I find I kill fewer patients that way.'

She wasn't perturbed by his tone of voice; rather she seemed to enjoy the shock, like taking a cold shower. She picked up the list and beamed. 'It's so nice to have a doctor to talk to again.' And she confided, 'Doctor Sim and I could chat for *hours*.'

'Mrs Tishell—'

'Oh, hold on, I've just remembered another one.' She bent over the list again and began to write. 'When the quarterly MHRA bulletin comes out maybe we could get together over a pot of tea, and discuss it?' She held the completed list close to her breast and smiled at a frowning Martin. 'I could make sandwiches,' she suggested, and with a peculiar intensity she asked, 'Do you eat tongue?'

Martin didn't really hear what she was saying and was therefore confused; he only wanted the list and to leave and he couldn't understand why something else seemed to be going on. He took the list. 'I have to go,' he said. It was as if the words jumped from his mouth without his say-so.

Mrs Tishell watched him leave. 'Sorry,' she said to his retreating figure; and she realised that she'd tried to be professional, in a way, but she so very much *hadn't* been professional, after all. 'Sorry!' she called more loudly, and wrung her hands, watching Martin disappear through the glass door.

As he left the pharmacy, Martin was stopped by a woman he didn't know. 'Are you Doc Martin?' she asked.

'Doctor Ellingham,' he corrected her.

'I'm worried about my daughter, Emily.' A great draught of air caught in her throat. Anxiety made her breathless. 'She's got a terrible tummy bug. I called the surgery, but the girl said you wouldn't see her.'

'I will see her. Later today. Can I take your name and address?' Martin added them to the list.

'Because she's never ill,' went on Mrs Braithwaite as they walked along together. She had to run, from time to time, to keep up with him. 'Strong as an ox. Swims for the county.'

'Then she'll probably bounce back quickly,' said Martin. 'I'll telephone you this afternoon.'

They went their separate ways – Martin in a hurry. But after two strides he stopped and turned. 'Mrs Braithwaite?' he called.

She wore a troubled look. 'Yes?'

'Does Emily swim at the leisure centre?'

'She *lives* at the leisure centre.'

This was the difference between surgery and an ordinary medical practice, thought Martin. As a surgeon he was like a car mechanic: elbow deep among the tubes and valves and circuits, mending faults. Servicing and repair work. As a GP, it was this puzzle: he was given one or more symptoms, and he must cast around and find the causes, and therefore make the diagnosis, and fit the puzzle together. He could already feel the intense excitement of this – and began to feel the familiar pull, of being addicted to his work. Speed was important now: if he called a sample of the people on his list and asked them if they also used the leisure centre, he would have his answer.

Three phone calls – and three people said, 'Yes . . .'

An hour later Martin was in the leisure centre's pump room, accompanied by the Centre Manager, Bob Thomas, a track-suited man in his mid-thirties with a smart, sporty stride and an efficient manner. There was the watery, acid smell of a public swimming pool, but more intense. The room hummed.

'Everything's fine. I'll show you,' said Bob Thomas.

'The evidence shows us the pool is infected,' warned Martin. The last thing he wanted was an over-confident manager protecting his reputation.

'Properly chlorinated, filtered,' said Bob Thomas. 'Got all the records. Everything up to date.' He picked up a folder.

'Cryptosporidium parvum is a parasite, resistant to chlorine,' said Martin.

'Nothing wrong here, mate.' Bob Thomas leafed back a page and shook his head slowly, as if demonstrating how to say no to a child. 'Perfect pH. Right concentration of chlorine.'

Martin could not waste time. 'You need to close the pool, shock-treat it, and replace your filters.'

'What? Have you any idea? Who the hell do you think you are?'

'I'm a doctor with dozens of sick patients.'

'I'm asking you nicely to leave.'

Martin did leave, but not entirely. He swung through the male changing room, ignoring the slow-moving figures drifting in and out of the changing booths, until he stood at the poolside. He was fully dressed, and felt uncomfortable. The sound of children playing in the pool echoed loudly off the walls and ceiling. 'Can I have your attention please?'

It was as if he wasn't there.

'Excuse me?'

One or two children nearby looked at him and laughed; and one boy was bobbing up and down and staring at his friend with mad eyes. Martin felt a rush of the familiar frustration: people weren't doing what they were supposed to be doing. He shouted as loud as he could, 'Will you please listen!'

All motion in the pool slowed down, and stopped. The echoing sounds of human voices turned to silence, leaving only the light roar of the air conditioning. 'My name is Doctor Ellingham,' announced Martin. He was aware that he sounded pompous, but it didn't matter. 'I'd like everyone to leave the pool immediately.'

He glanced from person to person. One woman started to wade towards the edge.

'Urgh, no *way*,' said the boy with the rolling eyes. His smaller friend, very young, called out, 'He smells!' A lad with a tattoo and lean musculature called out, 'Sod off.' There was a flurry of movement to Martin's left and an overweight child ran to the edge, folded himself into a lump and dropped in the water, sending up a plume of spray.

Martin stepped back to avoid being drenched. 'I'm sorry to spoil your fun,' he said. 'I was young once and—'

'Doctor *Smell*-ingham,' said the boy with rolling eyes, as if he'd just discovered something.

'Smellingham Ellingham,' said his friend.

'That's hilariously funny,' replied Martin patiently, 'but this is actually quite serious. I'm trying to tell you there's something dangerous in the water.'

People's voices, which had begun once again to echo around the pool, now dropped to nothing.

'Thank you,' said Martin. 'So I'd like you all to swim calmly to the side, and—'

He was interrupted by a shriek, and a narrow girl in a blue swim hat pointed at the water. 'There it is!'

'Where?' came the question.

'There!' said the girl in the blue swim hat.

'No,' said Martin condescendingly, 'I didn't mean that . . .'

It was too late; no one heard him. There was pande-monium: everyone swam or waded or plunged to the sides and climbed out. The ladders were crowded with two or three people each. Swimmers stood at the edge of the pool, staring into the water.

Bob Thomas bounced in on the balls of his feet to see what the commotion was.

'I'll be off then,' Martin said to himself.

When he got back to the surgery, it was worse. 'Mrs Winter's in your upstairs loo,' said Elaine in her most insolent West-Country voice, as if it were all Martin's doing. 'Her couldn't wait.'

'Diarrhoea?' Martin asked unnecessarily.

'Fourteen, so far,' said Elaine gloomily, glancing at the figures seated around the edges of the waiting room.

Thank God he *had* made a fool of himself at the pool, thought Martin as he quickly went through to his surgery. This kind of situation called for immediate and decisive action.

Andrew, his first patient, was a lad of eighteen with black-framed glasses and an eruption of acne on either cheekbone and along his jaw line. 'You need plenty of fluids,' said Martin.

'Nnnn, OK.'

'And the prescription,' said Martin, writing quickly, 'is for rehydration salts?'

'Nnnn.'

'And when you're feeling better, you can come back and we'll talk about your acne.'

The lad stared. 'What acne?'

Martin tore off the prescription. 'When did you last use the leisure centre?'

'What leisure centre?'

'The pool.'

'What pool?'

'You don't use the swimming pool?'

Andrew shook his head slowly. 'Don't know what you're talking about. We mostly hang around up at the graveyard.'

Martin said impatiently, 'But you've been in contact with someone who uses the pool.'

'No,' said the boy, frowning.

Martin stood up. He said nothing. He was immersed in the puzzle, and he had put down what he thought was the right piece. It had looked dead right, but one corner, it seemed now, didn't fit. It would be the work of a moment to discard it and find a piece that did.

He accompanied Andrew out of the surgery and stood in the waiting room. He reminded himself to talk in a calm manner. 'Could I just ask everyone please . . .?' All four people looked up. He noticed Elaine cock her head on one side and frown. 'Have any of you *not* been to the leisure centre recently, or – *not* been in contact with any swimmers there?'

Three out of the four people put up their hands.

Anyone else would have felt that sense of blame, the pain

caused to the leisure centre by wrongly accusing them of being the source of the parasite, but Martin's only concern was to work along the axis made by the symptom-diagnosis-prognosis-prescription paradigm.

If he'd felt the effects of being wrong, he might not have gone on to make a worse, a bigger mistake; he might have been cautious. But he wasn't. He was a doctor, to the tips of his fingers. A leisure centre, or the economy of a small seaside village, didn't figure.

If it wasn't the leisure centre, thought Martin, it could only be the water supply, which was a worse scenario in terms of public health. From every tap in Portwenn the water came laced with cryptosporidium parvum; he was certain it must. He tried to remember a paper that delivered research on what percentage of a population drank tap water without first boiling it for tea and coffee. All the children with their orange squash. All the pensioners with their glasses of water to take to bed. He would need to be quick and decisive.

The next morning Martin was back in the radio shack, which was attached to the Bay Hotel. The radio presenter, Caroline somebody, he remembered, looked smug. Plainly she was proud to be in control of the means by which he could talk so quickly to the population of Portwenn.

'And we have a surprise visitor to the studio today: our very own Doc Martin,' she said.

'Hello,' said Martin, not bothering to correct her on the wrong use of his name.

'I gather he's got some health information for us, and he'll be taking calls later in the show.' She looked at him steadily from behind her table. 'Couldn't stay away, eh, Doc?' she said cheerfully.

Martin said bluntly, 'As some of you will know, there's a tummy bug making the rounds of the village.'

'Oooh, yes,' said Caroline, 'one or two of my friends have gone down with it.'

'I thought I'd tracked down the source to the swimming pool at the leisure centre, but that turns out not to be the culprit. So for the time being I'd like to advise people to boil the local tap water before they drink it, or use it for cooking, or make the children's orange squash, or—'

Caroline interrupted, 'So we have a mystery.'

'I don't think so,' said Martin. 'It's pretty clear the culprit is the water supply. So I'd advise people—'

'Hold on, Doc, we have to squeeze in a commercial break, and we'll come right back to you.' She said it in a friendly tone, but, when the jingle cut in, she tore off her headset and hectic patches of red showed on her cheeks and neck. 'What the hell are you doing?'

Martin was clueless as to his offence. 'What?'

'You can't say that about the water.' Caroline's jaw clamped shut.

'Why not?'

'If you bothered to know anything about the place you lived in, you'd know we had a scare not three years back that almost did the village in.'

'Right, but I have a duty to—'

'If the media gets hold of this, Portwenn is finished. No tourists. Full stop.'

Martin was furious. 'I'm doing my job,' he said, 'and you—'

'Tell it to the families without any jobs, the ones who lost their jobs, the ones who are still on the dole after the last balls-up.' There was a tap on the glass and she waved hurriedly and slipped on her headphones again. 'Welcome back,' she said sweetly, 'and first of all we wanted to reassure you that we didn't mean to suggest there was anything wrong with Portwenn's water supply, but –'

Martin leaned forward to his microphone. 'Yes I did. There is a possibility that—'

'That's right,' interrupted Caroline, 'the water is just a possibility.'

'No, what I said was—'

'And we go now to a caller on line one. Good morning, you're on air with Radio Portwenn, talking to Caroline.'

Martin heard the caller's quick, deadpan voice in his earphones. 'Hi. Ed Johnson, *Cornish Echo*. Can Doctor Ellingham tell us just how serious this infected water is? If I've drunk the water, is it best to go to hospital? Does he think there will be any fatalities?'

As he walked back down through the village, Martin worked out what would happen next: there would immediately be a substantial drop in cases because people would boil their water. He would have the water tested to confirm his hypothesis. There would be an investigation into how the parasite got into the water. The level of chlorination would prove to be insufficient . . .

Perhaps because he was so much taller and so couldn't see what happened at ground level, Martin collided with a much smaller man coming out of a shop – although later, when he thought about it, he realised there wasn't a shop along that stretch of street, and perhaps the man had deliberately walked under his feet. Martin's gaze hardly lowered; he took in a flat working man's cap, a baggy tweed jacket, and Martin was already saying 'Sorry . . .'

The other man's words came distinctly, and without pre-amble. 'Pissing – in – our – water.' But he didn't turn and look at Martin, or break his stride. He continued ambling down the street, a slight limp favouring his right leg, and the shoulder on the other side lifted a touch higher to compensate.

Martin didn't reply; he was wondering if he'd heard correctly, or if he'd imagined it. There was nothing he could do; he carried on, anxious to return to the surgery.

A car hooted and Martin turned to look; he caught sight of a lifted middle finger from the driver's window. He felt an unreasonable urge to run and bash the car with his doctor's bag. Did anyone seriously expect him not to warn the village, if their water supply was dangerous? What would the damage have been if he hadn't gone on the radio, and warned them so quickly? They were like dumb beasts.

It was Aunt Joan who summed it up most succinctly. She

stood, while Martin was carefully chopping sushi in his kitchen, and her white hair was a mad scramble around her head, like sheep's wool. She planted her feet and said, 'Marty, you do know the villagers are dusting off their pitchforks?'

Martin looked down; the food seemed a long way off, but it was neatly cut. His surgeon's skills were still useful. 'You've lived here a long time,' he said. 'Exactly how many generations ago did the in-breeding start?' And he pointed the knife and added, 'Do you want any of this?'

Joan shook her head. 'Not stopping,' she said. 'But listen, Marty. A few years back, there was a scare about aluminium in the water.'

'I know that. I had the unfortunate—'

'It turned out to be a false alarm. But it was too late. The national papers played it up. Summer came, and the tourists didn't.'

'I heard all that,' replied Martin, with confidence. 'But we're talking about public health. I can't help it if that means they sell a few less Cornettos down on the front.'

Joan wondered what it was like to occupy such a big tall body as her nephew's, all tightly bound up in a suit and tie. Maybe it separated him from common human decency. Her voice sharpened. 'The Nadlers lost their home. Old Mr Pearson hanged himself.'

'I still have to warn people,' said Martin pompously. 'If I didn't warn them, the pitchfork brigade would crucify me for that, instead.'

'Probably, but—'

'And when the water's tested and I'm proven to be right, can you see them coming up here to eat humble pie? I don't think so.'

Joan looked at him queerly. 'Tell me you had the water tested before you went on the radio.'

'It couldn't be anything else, given the pattern of incidents.' Martin was gruff, dismissive.

'Marty, it could be anything.'

'It couldn't actually.'

'It could be a viral thing. Portuguese flu gives you tummy trouble.'

'It's *not* Portuguese flu.'

'Could be dodgy shellfish, or . . . oh Marty.'

'It's the water,' said Martin, with certainty.

Later that evening, he ate his solitary dinner. He customarily went to some trouble to set the table properly – with knife and fork either side of a place mat, with a napkin rolled up in the silver napkin ring, which was the only family heirloom to have settled with him – and he would eat carefully and silently, alone. Occasionally he would have the radio on, particularly in bad weather.

If someone were to look in at the window and see him, it might bring to them a sense of pity, but there was no self-pity in Martin; his tendency to deal only in the very baldest truth, his sustained bouts of bad temper, and his single-minded attention to work, meant that he only wished to eat alone.

After dinner, he carried his plate to the sink and rinsed

it clean. He took a glass, held it under the cold tap and filled it. He lifted the glass to his lips and stopped, and looked into the water: a clear liquid. Life-giving, but also a frequent culprit in large-scale public health issues. Hence the chlorine that should be mixed with it, to kill the always-promiscuous bacteria. He sniffed, and there was no doubt, it was chlorinated. Could it be safe to drink? He poured the glassful into the kettle and switched it on.

It was late for the bell to ring and Martin walked to the door briskly, thinking it might be an emergency. It was a disappointment to see Bert Large standing there, round as a drum, another comical hat on his head, carrying a large cardboard box.

'Hear you don't like our water,' said Bert.

'Bert, it's been a long day. Take two aspirin and insult me in the morning.'

Bert said petulantly, 'Daphne du Maurier said our water was worth a pound a pint.'

'I'm sure she did, Bert, but—'

'Never touch the stuff, myself. Sludge. Got all sorts in it.' He shoved the box at Martin and then picked up a second one. 'Mind if I come in?'

'What?'

'Eats through the pipes. Imagine what it does to your innards.'

'The truth is, I might have been premature in questioning the water supply. It might be that it's safe, but I'll be making final, conclusive investigations in the morning. It's probably safe to drink.'

'You out of your mind, Doc?' Bert looked startled. 'Play it safe.' He split open one of the boxes and lifted out a bottle of mineral water. 'That's what I do.' He held up the bottle like a perfume salesman. 'Fine French spring water. Thought you'd need some in here, definitely, given the crisis.'

'Bert, I appreciate this is an opportunity for you, but—'

'Chateau Sainte Marie.'

'Look, maybe I shouldn't have been quite so quick to say what I did on the radio. It is my opinion, but it's not yet proven . . .'

'But you were right. And people do listen to you. And I'm stepping up, Doc, I'm here to help the population, you know. Bottled water, for a while, is going to be much safer and it's going to make everyone better, and if I, in my humble way, can provide—'

'We won't know anything until the water's tested,' said Martin impatiently.

'You don't need to test this stuff, though. It's from an ancient spring deep beneath the green hills of France. Or rather, the green mountains.' He planted the water bottle into Martin's hands, and kicked one of the boxes. 'So here you are. Give me a ring when you want some more.' He clapped Martin's shoulder reassuringly. 'Free delivery.'

*

The water bottle planted by Bert Large into Martin's hands followed Martin up to bed, and it was placed, unopened, on the bedside table.

During the night, Martin fretted at the accusations made by his Aunt Joan. She was often right; and unlike most people she said what she thought; she was unafraid of appearing rude. For instance, she had told him that he looked out of place in Portwenn; his habit of wearing dark blue suits, blindingly white shirts, striped ties and sensible lace-up shoes were perfectly acceptable in Harley Street, where all the doctors looked like that, but here in Portwenn it set him apart, made him look oversize, and alien. 'Can't you dress more normally, Marty?' she'd ask every now and again.

'This is normal,' Martin would say. 'It's everyone else who—'

'And you walk' – Aunt Joan would stiffen her limbs and imitate him – 'like someone has tied your arms to your sides, and stuffed a poker up your bottom.'

'Charming,' Martin had said.

She might have been right, but Martin could no more dress in a fisherman's jersey and a pair of jeans than he could bite the bullet that everyone fired at him.

Perhaps he had been too hasty in blaming the village's water supply? Perhaps he should have waited?

He didn't notice, as he fought his way through a number of restless night hours, how every now and again he sipped from the bottle of water put into his hands by the plumber, Bert Large.

The next day, at ten past ten in the morning, Martin picked out his usual dark blue suit and a pale blue shirt, and drove to the gates of the North Cornwall Water Company's offices in Wadebridge. In the figure of General Manager Tom Giddens he found an immediate irritant, and it took all his efforts to persuade the other man to undertake a test for cryptosporidium. Afterwards he drove straight back to Portwenn and immediately invited to the surgery the journalist from the *Echo*.

'Thanks for coming at such short notice,' said Martin. The journalist, he thought, looked too pale. Bloodless.

'Call me Ed. No, I should thank you. At last, a proper piece of news, not just lost puppies and new-born lambs and bake sales for the village hall. Sales will go through the roof.'

'I want to set the record straight,' said Martin, 'about the water.'

'Dish,' said the journalist.

'This has accelerated out of control. I don't know yet, for certain, that there's anything wrong with the tap water.'

'What's with the U-turn?' asked the journalist. 'You announced on the radio that the water was contaminated.'

'I didn't have all the facts. Tests are being done; that takes time . . .'

The journalist sounded gloomy. 'So now you're saying, what – the tap water is fine?'

'It's wonderful water down here.'

'So how come you're drinking bottled water, then?' The

140

journalist pointed to the half-full bottle of mineral water on the table between them.

Martin was frustrated; and it didn't suit him to say things that he didn't wholly believe; he was no good at it. 'I like it,' he said, 'and I drink it sometimes.' He stood up and went to the sink and drew a glass of water from the tap. He lifted the glass and said, 'Our Cornish water is worth a pound a pint.'

'What?'

'Daphne du Maurier.'

At the same time as he mentioned the famous novelist's name, Martin felt an enormous pain suddenly sharpen in his belly. 'The water is perfectly safe,' he began, his voice tightening.

'You all right?' asked the journalist.

'Yes,' said Martin hoarsely. 'Don't know. What all the fuss is about.'

'You're not . . . hey . . . are you?' The journalist had the scent of a story, and a half-smile appeared on his face.

'Certainly not . . .' But Martin had to clench, and run, because without question it was essential that he reach a toilet *right now* . . .

The journalist pointed and said, 'I'll quote you on that.' He stood up and stared, and put the cap on his pen.

The following day, the house had the plaintive, apologetic air of a place where illness resides. In the silence could be heard the tumble of water in the toilet bowl, and the sound of the cistern re-filling. Martin wore a dressing gown, and slid his finger along the top of the envelope delivered by hand from the North Cornwall Water Company. There was something wrong with the water; he himself had fallen prey to it – he hadn't moved to the bottled water quickly enough. All he'd be looking for, on this document, was the density of the coliforms in the count. His gaze flicked to the middle of the page, to the filled-in boxes, the results, and the figures on the right . . .

They were all zeros. No faecal coliforms detected. No coliforms of any sort. No contamination. The tap water was not the source.

The puzzle was thrown into the air, and the voice of his Aunt Joan came back to him – 'Oh Marty, tell me you had the water tested before . . .'

He looked for the missing piece to the argument. If it wasn't the water, what *could* it be? A foodstuff of some sort? It was too widespread . . . His anger grew – the sickness had even got to him; physician, heal thyself, he thought.

He poured some hydration salts into a glass of bottled water and stood there, as he drank, looking over to the other side of the valley, where the village was crowded so busily from the top of the hill down to the shore. The whole of the Willow family was ill, now – not just the son. He gazed at the white-painted converted chapel, the school building. Jean, the school secretary, would not be turning up to school today; she was off sick. The class rooms would have around ten per cent of their number absent.

Sometimes, as a surgeon, he had felt gifted with mighty

powers. He could transform, he could stay death's hand; he gave back life and limb. The brightest of lights shone into the mystery of the human body, and, brightly lit, his hands moved among the internal organs inside the machine, and made good. Now he felt dull, powerless, and ill. It seemed to Martin that he himself had cast a shadow over the village and, with each pronouncement he'd made, the shadow had become darker and reached further.

He realised, then, that without really seeing it until now, he happened to be looking at something very odd: just down the hill Bert Large, the plumber, stood at the back of his van, with the back doors folded open; and a huddle of people – Martin recognised the mother, Mrs Willow, and Jean, the school secretary – gathered around him. Each received and carried away a shrink-wrapped pack of Chateau Sainte Marie water.

With a gentle click, Martin set down the glass he was holding – and then he moved quickly. He was outside the door in a few seconds, the call on his lips, 'Bert!'

The plumber was just pulling the driver's door shut.

Even as Martin ran towards it, the van made the turn and drove off.

He hurried back into the house and went upstairs to get dressed. In ten minutes he was in the silver Lexus, the tiny streets of Portwenn practically grazing the vehicle's sides.

At the top of the hill, the village gave way to open country. He only vaguely knew the way to the Large family farm; he'd been there before but the lanes, the corners, the tiny junc -

tions and hidden sign posts proliferated and confused him.

With a 'brrr' of the tyres Martin crossed the cattle grid at the farm's entrance and jolted over the potholes into the yard. There was no sign of Bert, but the van was parked in front of a large slatted-wood barn. Martin walked in, and it took his eyes a while to adjust to the gloom. Underfoot a swept concrete floor spread cleanly to the walls. On every side, thin strips of light shone between the slats. In one corner was a stack of large cardboard boxes, some flattened and empty, others full and stacked like Lego, one of them open mouthed to reveal a supply of empty plastic bottles. A strange installation stood around waist height, on solid legs, in appearance like a miniature bale-wrapping machine. A roll of plastic stood on its spindle. Martin guessed: shrink wrapping.

Standing with his back to Martin was Bert Large. His round shape meant his trousers looked like a brown paper bag. The usual comical hat was perched on his head. In his right hand he held a hosepipe, which filled the plastic bottle in his hand. The sound of the water, plus the calling of sheep somewhere nearby, meant that Martin's footsteps weren't heard, and he came near enough to be able to speak quietly. 'So this is Chateau Sainte Marie.'

Bert was startled, but there wasn't a trace of guilt on his face. Instead the opposite: he was mildly affronted. 'If you don't mind. Private property.'

'Selling the local water dressed up as imported mountain spring water – not clever, at all.'

A stony meanness settled on Bert's expression. 'None of your business, now, is it? I told you before, shove it.'

'This operation is closing down, Bert, as of right now.'

'Look, maybe the water isn't French but it's spring water, just as good. Better in fact.'

'You're making people ill.'

'Oh, I see. First, it's the leisure centre you're shutting down, then the village's tap water's to blame and, guess what, our tourist industry is down the tubes, and now you're closing our little operation and all. Who's next then, for the chop?'

Martin said coldly, 'I've had the mains water tested – it's clean.'

'This is from my spring.' Bert thumbed his own chest and wagged his hose. 'It doesn't get any cleaner than that. Washed by the Cornish hillside.'

'Where is your spring?' asked Martin.

'Up North Field.'

'And are there sheep in that field?'

Bert shrugged.

'Lambing?' insisted Martin, watching the belligerent meanness disappear from Bert's expression. He went on, 'Sheep during lambing, a common cause of cryptosporidium.'

Like a switch had been thrown, a comical sense of Bert's humanity now illuminated his expression and replaced the previous greed. He looked hurt. 'I've given everyone the runs?'

'Collect all the bottles you've already sold, every bottle, and stop.'

Bert hesitated, while numerous thoughts – of money in his hand, of his fellow villagers ill, of what he'd done – chased through his mind. A minute later he uncoupled the hose, and kicked the half-empty cardboard box. Martin might as well not have been there because Bert looked inwards. 'It was for Al,' he said, talking to himself. 'I always knew he'd want to fly the nest.' He switched off the wrapping machine. 'That same morning he was born – no, even before he was born – I had this vision. Him and me. Plumbers together.' Bert's plaintive eyes met Martin's. 'We were going to be special, see. Maybe even invent a new toilet, or something like that. I don't want him to go. But it's coming, that time, I know. And I'll have to provide for him, I will.' Bert eased his hat to a different position. 'Ungrateful little tyke.'

'Close it down, Bert. For good.'

'Did I give everyone the runs?'

'Yes.'

'Consider it closed down, then. For good.' He meandered a few steps in the hollow silence of the barn. 'What can I tell Al, though? What shall I tell my boy? It's all very well for you, Doc, but you don't have a son or a daughter biting your ankles all the flippin' time. What shall I do with him? Shall I let him go off with the computers? What d'you think, Doc?'

'I've already told you what I think.'

Now seemed to be as good a time as any; together Martin and Bert went to find Al and tell him the news that, yes, he could go off and study computers. The Large and Son office was like a Portakabin, a cheerless place, with Al brooding behind the desk. Martin thought how different the son was from the father: taller, slender and lean compared to the father's weight, blue eyes to Bert's brown, and with a different voice. Things were obviously bad between them. The instant Martin and Bert appeared in the office, Al's voice came at them. 'What do *you* want?'

Bert rolled right around like a cannon ball on the deck of a ship that suddenly tilts the other way, and left the way he'd come in. 'Drop dead, dunderhead,' he threw over his shoulder.

Al stood up behind the desk. 'Is that the best you can do? "Dunderhead"?'

Bert said to Martin as he left, 'See how he is? I can't speak to him.'

'Bert,' called Martin.

Bert came back and obviously – you could see the struggle, the uncertainty in his face – he made a decision to face up to his son and be a good father. 'Al,' he began. 'Son. Son . . .' It was difficult.

Martin helped him. 'Your father has something he wants to say.'

'Son, I . . .' Bert gestured with his hand like a baritone singing in an opera. Then he seized on something easier to say. 'Are you warm enough? I could bring the spare heater.'

Martin looked down pityingly; he was impatient to move Bert along. 'Oh, for God's sake. Al, your father sincerely regrets his controlling attitude and it's fine with him if you go to college and study computers. All right? Thank you. Goodbye.'

It was Martin's turn to hope that he'd now be allowed to leave the scene. It really was none of his business after all.

But Al wasn't fobbed off with that. He'd come close to this result before, and it hadn't happened. Nothing would be good enough except a direct, straightforward word. '*He* didn't say that,' he said and pointed to Bert. 'Did he? Not him. If he means it, *he* should say it. To *me*.'

'Son . . .' Bert gathered up his disappointment, took a breath, and tried to have done with it. 'Doc Martin here, well, talked some sense into me, and . . . if you want to do that computer thing, then it's all right with me.'

Al stared hard. These were the words he'd waited for, and during all that waiting he'd chewed on his sense of duty to his father, and felt the chains around his ankles. Now it seemed they had been unlocked and had fallen away. 'Dad.' He moved out from behind the desk. 'Wow.' Al wanted to hug his father, maybe for the first time ever give him a hug, but the shape of the man – a human boulder, compared to his own sapling-like slenderness – made it difficult.

The human boulder, Bert, looked like he wanted to hug Al back, his own son, but perhaps it would be too comical. In the end they made do with a manly clasp of the shoulder, a handshake, and the embrace was left as merely a thought in the minds of both son and father, and perhaps it had a more tender existence, that embrace, as a thought they had shared.

They walked Martin back to his car.

'Dad, it's quite expensive, the college,' said Al.

'Don't you worry about that. Your old dad will sort that out for you.'

Martin heard Al's next question, despite the fact that Al lowered his voice. 'Not the . . . selling the water from the hosepipe thing again?'

'No, no.' Bert sounded affronted. 'No, son, I told you, stopped all that long ago.'

'How will we afford it then?'

'We'll sort it.' Bert rolled along, towards Martin's car. Beside him walked his taller, thinner son. 'Don't you worry.' He couldn't help it, but he tried, then, for a bit of an angle on the situation. 'Another option would be night classes. Y'know. I hear they have them at Wadebridge.'

'What, and do the plumbing in the day?'

'Just an idea, keep a few coppers coming in, while you study.'

Al felt a plummeting disappointment almost as severe as the elation he'd felt earlier. 'I suppose,' he said.

They reached the car. 'So thanks for that, Doc,' said Bert. 'And that other thing, consider it done.'

Louisa Glasson wrote a long letter to a friend who was out of work, and broke, and thinking of switching to become a teacher. She watched her own hand moving over the paper, and she wrote carefully, in the knowledge that when things were spoken or written, the hearts and minds of people were changed, and one had to take responsibility for that.

'What surprised me,' she wrote, 'was that in the very first teaching job I got, I found I could have fun. From day one there were bits and pieces of laughter, throughout the day. Children are always spirited, they are mostly hoping to have a good time, they are ready for anything, and keen to try new things.' She took a moment to think about her head teacher, and bent her head again to write, 'Children of any age are bored by some of the more lazy teachers, but I know you won't be one of those. You'll be great – look how kind you are, just to look at you is to know that you are kind, and you will exude that special quality that kids love: that you have in your heart a strong hope that every child in your care will succeed. There are boring bits to the job, of course. Christ, every teacher has to do a bit of the usual "Where's your homework? But you said that last time. Right, I'm going to speak to the head/your parent – and, by the way, take that fleece off, give me that conker, are you chewing? Is that nail-polish you're wearing?" But if you're any good that kind of stuff doesn't really intrude much. And think carefully about the love of your subject(s), because that will determine what year group you want to teach . . .'

She put down her pen, and flexed her wrist. Tiredness swept over her. After a day of teaching, and now writing this letter, she felt like she'd been talking, expressing herself, for hour after hour, and now the needle was on empty. Yes, the subject . . . music was *not* her subject, and never would be, and yet today she'd been faced with picking up the pieces of the after-school music club.

In the event, although she'd walked into the class unprepared and feeling that solid knot of dread, she'd walked out at the end with her feet hardly touching the ground.

It was her fault it had gone wrong to begin with. She'd thought it was something she could do for Roger Fenn: if she advertised for an after-school music club, and there were enough takers, then she could offer him the job of teaching it. She'd felt anguish at his bitterness that he'd been ousted from the school – and she had his job, after all. She'd wanted to help him back on his feet.

Enough parents had signed the form; the budget had been prepared. But when she'd naively presented Roger Fenn with the gift of an after-school music class ready and waiting for him the following evening, he'd turned her down. His voice was stronger, but he'd spoken kindly: he was engaged in a legal action in order to get his pension re-instated. He didn't want to do it. So it had been down to her. She'd unplugged her ghetto blaster from home and brought it in, along with a handful of CDs. What could she do – have the class write a song, write lyrics . . . ? She had to try something.

'Oh-kay,' she'd said to the eleven pupils who'd turned up in the Assembly Room. 'Attention everyone please, and that includes you Lucy Holmes. Welcome to the music club.' She looked through the CD collection. 'What we'll start with, is to listen to some music, and find out what we like . . . and then . . .'

'Where's Mr Fenn?' a boy's voice called out. 'He was supposed to be coming back, wasn't he?'

'He's got cancer,' chimed in another voice.

'Is he dead?' That was Lucy Holmes, sounding incredulous.

Louisa turned and made the announcement that she should have made at the beginning. 'We were hoping that Mr Fenn would be here for music club and that he'd give some music lessons, but unfortunately he was unable to come.'

'Are you any good at music, Miss?' It was typical of Jamie Springer to ask a question everyone knew the answer to and no one dared say.

'No, I'm not,' she admitted in her best optimistic voice, 'but this is by way of an introduction to the music club, some of its aims and so on, so I'm here just to start us off. You don't have to be good at music to listen to it, and decide if you . . .' It seemed unlikely, but she was winning – because the room was filled with smiles. It was a music class, after all; the room *should* be filled with smiles.

A nano-second later she realised the smiles were not directed at her but behind her; Roger Fenn stood quietly in the doorway to the Assembly Room, like he was waiting for a bus.

She swung back to face the children. 'Ah, that got you going, didn't it? You believed you'd been landed with me, didn't you? Ladies and Gentlemen, I give you the legendary teacher whose ghost still roams the corridors of this school, Roger Fenn.' She led the clapping until her palms burned. Maybe she shouldn't have mentioned the ghost part, she thought.

Roger Fenn strolled forwards and, when the applause had died away, he was straight into it – an old pro at work. 'Right then, my friends. Let's make some music. Next week I want each of you to bring in an instrument from home, but this week we'll make do with the instrument that we are all blessed with, from the moment of birth. The human voice. Everyone in a circle, please.'

The children began to talk and to take up position, squabbling to stand next to their friends. Roger Fenn spoke quietly to Louisa underneath the noise. 'You want to shoot off?'

'What happened to the legal action, the pension?' whispered Louisa.

Roger murmured, 'Can you imagine me with a walking stick and a sensible haircut?'

'What do you mean?'

'No, I mean it, can you? Walking stick, haircut?'

'Well, I suppose not.'

'Neither could I.' The class had started to fall quiet, although there was a stray boy left outside the group. 'John Dodsworth,' called Roger, 'is that your idea of a circle?'

That evening, the memory of the old church building was aroused by the singing from within its halls floating eerily across the village. Those who passed by caught the sound – and the fact that the church had clung to the side of this cliff for hundreds of years, and still could issue a song, sponsored in all these listeners a sense of hope, and of the beauty of things; the instant they heard their children's voices all matters were imbued with kindness; goodness became certain.

4

For the third time, Martin went on the radio. He was becoming familiar with the swivel seat, the desk that stretched between him and Caroline, and the sheet of glass behind which the technical person moved silently.

Caroline wore a cheerful voice. 'So, Doc, the crisis is over, there are no new cases of stomach upset, and our tap water has been officially contaminated, I mean vindicated. Vindicated! I am sorry. The tap water *is* clean; it *is* perfectly healthy. So you must be feeling a little red-faced.'

Martin's ears burned. He leaned into the microphone. 'Hardly. I . . .'

Caroline interrupted, 'Well, you were wrong.'

'With hindsight, yes, I was wrong, but I defend my—'

She interrupted again, 'People might say foolish, even.'

'Look . . .'

But then Martin suddenly saw himself as if he were looking down from a great height, and he was wriggling on a hook, and there was no way he was going to be let off, so he should stop.

He said, simply, 'You're right.'

'They'll say you almost put this village out of business for nothing.'

'That's right.'

'And have you at least identified the source of the infection?'

Martin had thought about how he would answer this question. A memory sprang to mind: of Bert Large standing with his back to him in the barn, hosing water into a plastic bottle. 'No,' he said.

'Well, I'm sure people will come to their own conclusions as to how well this has been handled.'

Martin felt an ordinary kind of calm, which was unusual.

'I'm sure we're all grateful it's over,' he said.

'OK, well thanks for coming in, Doc, and telling us about it.' She offered him a fake smile.

'Thanks Caroline,' said Martin, without needing to smile back.

That evening, alone in the darkened surgery, Martin sat down at Elaine's desk. He looked around at the personal bits and pieces that were arranged on her desk. There was an old iron ashtray, although she didn't smoke; instead it was filled with hair clips and ties. A striped mug held pens and pencils. Propped against it was a photograph of her father and his new wife, the woman who kept a dog in her handbag, in a cardboard frame, with 'SAMPLE' printed across it in transparent letters.

Martin fired up her computer and waited for the blink of

the cursor to tell him he could carry on. Like a burglar rifling through drawers, he went upstream through her files, every now and again typing, hitting the return, his right hand darting to the mouse to shift the cursor more quickly here and there. He spent an hour doing this, before closing down. Afterwards he knelt awkwardly and squeezed beside the desk to switch off the power at the mains. He then tugged all the leads out of the box, unscrewed six miniature cross-threads at the back and removed the housing. A few minutes later and he was done; he replaced the cover and plugged in the leads, and switched the power back on.

For a while he wandered through the darkened surgery, remembering how it had looked when he'd first arrived. At least the equipment was up to date now; it looked like a reasonably competent doctor worked here. There were still a number of cosmetic improvements he'd like to make. He noticed how his own mind – everyone's mind – rubbed away at what was wrong with any given situation. It was a process of continually moving the goal posts forward.

He went through to his living quarters, and poured himself a glass of tap water. He drank it slowly, not particularly enjoying the thought of all the processes that it had gone through. He remembered that unhelpful man up at the offices of the North Cornwall Water Company. Next he called up the image of Bert Large standing in his old barn with the end of his hose poked in the plastic water bottle. What had he called it? Chateau something. What an effort – the labels, the wrapping machine, the bottles themselves

. . . It was lucky for Bert that no infant or old person had died. Water from a muddy spring in a sheep field up the road, sold from the back of a van. Only Bert Large could think of doing such a thing.

Upstairs he loosened the knot of his tie. The dark blue suit jacket went back on its hanger, the trousers saved for the press. With his pyjamas buttoned, he sat on the edge of his bed and thought about the National Health Service, about the use-by dates on the drugs stored in the fridge downstairs. As he lay in bed he thought about Roger Fenn's prognosis, the eradication of tuberculosis, keyhole vascular surgery. He didn't think about Louisa, at all – except for one image: when the sun had shone on her face, at the wedding, causing her to shade her eyes with her hand. The eye in which he'd seen that acute glaucoma.

The next morning Elaine came in, dropped her bag and arranged her jacket over the back of the chair. She sat and leaned down to push the computer's 'on' button.

The first time she prodded the keyboard, she stopped chewing, looked thoughtfully at the screen and prodded the keyboard again. She frowned, put down the packet of crisps and used both hands to type. Her frown deepened and her jaw dropped. Her hand flew to the mouse and she pushed the cursor here, there. Without looking away from the screen she called out, 'Doc!'

Martin came through, wiping his hands on a towel. 'What is it?'

'Computer's all to buggery,' said Elaine.

'Oh.'

'Weird,' said Elaine.

'We'd better call Al.'

'Al? Plumber Al? You call a plumber to mend a computer?'

'He knows about computers as well,' said Martin shortly. 'Give him a call. Ask him to come as soon as he can. We can't do without it.'

An hour later, Al walked into the surgery. He wore his plumber's overalls, but instead of his normal tool bag he carried a square black briefcase. Elaine slipped from behind the desk and he took her seat.

In the doorway Martin stood watching.

After ten swift key strokes, Al pronounced, 'This is totally messed up.'

'I probably did something,' said Martin. 'I had to take a look this morning and I got a bit lost.'

Al frowned. 'Settings completely wrong. Network configurations are a shambles. It's like someone's run wild in here.'

'It was OK last night,' said Elaine.

Martin asked, 'Can you fix it?'

'Probably.' Al's fingers – all of them – flew around the keyboard like chattering starlings. His right hand darted out to move the mouse, and click, before it flew back again to the keyboard.

'Al Large,' said Elaine, standing with her weight on one leg and her arms folded, watching him. 'Who would have thought it?' Her eyes were large and inviting.

Al glanced sideways and caught her seductive look. 'What d'you want?' he asked.

'Oooh, quick lad,' said Elaine admiringly. 'Can you set this up so I can get free music off the net?'

'That's illegal, that is,' said Al.

'Yeah, but for me—'

'No can do I'm afraid.'

Elaine said in a sharp, commanding tone, 'Al.'

His new answer flew back at her, 'OK, yes. Will do.'

Elaine smiled. 'Good decision.'

From the doorway Martin asked, 'Can you see what's wrong?'

Al looked up. 'I can get it sorted, but something bad has happened in the box there.'

'Well,' said Martin. 'We can't do without computers, nowadays. Do you think we could arrange for you to come here and do a regular monthly check?' Martin saw his question sink in, and Al's effort to conceal his smile.

'Work something out, I suppose,' said Al.

'If I have to put up with this great lump every month,' said Elaine, pointing at Al, 'I want a pay rise and my own shelf in the fridge.'

'No chance,' said Martin.

Al asked her, 'What d'you mean, lump?'

Portwenn on a summer evening became self-conscious, like any good-looking creature. During the day its inhabitants worked, and its visitors didn't work; the inhabitants found their own way of thriving, or attempting to thrive, as they walked or sat in the sun, or stayed in the shade. At around six in the evening, when the village's latitude had taken that extra step further from the sun, the amount of infra-red expanded its share of the spectrum, which made the sunlight golden, more glad to the eye and, on the whole, people began to see each other in a new light. Susan Brading, helping in the garden, drew a weary wrist across her brow, and noticed that her husband, in this light, was youthfully handsome. Caroline, Radio Portwenn's disc jockey from nine until eleven in the morning, noticed the sparkle that ran through the white wine poured into her glass as she sat on the pub terrace. Portwenn's police officer, PC Mylow, sat back in his chair, arms dangling at his sides, and stared at the ceiling, before he jerked upright and told himself, 'No, do something about it.' Louisa Glasson, her towelled head grazing the ceiling of her tiny cottage, walked through a dust-speckled patch of sunlight let in by a bedroom window. She tugged open her wardrobe and batted the clothes from one end to the other, searching. Roger Fenn, up on top of the cliff, touched a fingertip on the keyboard to play one solitary note, before he sat with his hands in his lap, in silence. Sometimes the beauty of the sunset smothered him in a feeling of wonder.

Later, in The Crab and Lobster, at 8pm, Louisa and Martin weaved around the tables and looked for good seats . . .

Martin's presence washed over Louisa, and the day's ordinary troubles floated away; she anticipated their conversation would be immediately to-the-point; it wouldn't be polite, and she began, without a care in the world, to say thoughtlessly what came immediately to mind, confident that Martin, on the other end of the conversation, would take it and lead them somewhere interesting. 'Heard you on the radio,' she said.

'Which time?' asked Martin, dolefully.

'Does it matter?' Louisa wanted to jab him with a stick, make him laugh.

'Some were more painful than others,' he replied.

'Oh, really?'

He read the irony in her tone. 'No. All were terrible.' After every one of her smiles, thought Martin, he immediately looked for another one. He found himself seeing elements, contours of her face that he hadn't noticed before. It startled him, as though she were wearing a mask.

She cocked her head. 'What's the story, then, with the water?' She felt a sudden depth open in her stomach and it was like she had to hop from one stepping stone to another towards him, always with the likelihood that she'd fall in.

Martin leaned back. 'The whole story is . . . is over. Thank God.' As it happened, he could see Bert himself, and Al, among a group of drinkers not far off.

It didn't occur to Martin that he himself had been, in a way, corrupt: he'd kept quiet about Bert filling the water bottles with his hose and selling it as French spring water. There had been no swerve in his moral sense, because

Martin knew nothing of the panic that comes with wrong-doing. To have kept Bert's secret had been as automatic for Martin as taking his next breath: Bert would mend his ways and Al would go to college. The sickness had been mended, the puzzle solved. The village would be spared the ugliness of a prosecution. It was nothing more or less than sensible. He settled at a table. 'This do?'

'Oh come on,' she said. 'You can tell me. I know you were holding back.'

'How d'you know?'

'The way you allowed Caroline to lay into you. Of course you were hiding something.'

'I made a mistake and I admitted it,' said Martin.

'God,' said Louisa admiringly. 'Carry on like this and it might even be safe for me to admit I was on your interview panel.'

'I wouldn't break cover just yet if I were you. I've got one or two big cock-ups in the pipeline.'

'What are you drinking?' asked Louisa, just as he was about to ask the same question.

'Orange juice,' he replied.

Louisa went to the bar, while Martin slid into his seat. He realised what a small village he lived in, with Bert there, waving at him from the corner table, surrounded by his son and a tribe of males who leaned over their food and forked it in, and tipped their glasses down their throats. No doubt they were happily recounting the week's exploits and teasing each other. His disapproval of alcohol caused a frown to cross his expression. And that food, sticking to the sides of all their arteries. The fact that Louisa would return in a moment chased off his disapproving thoughts.

Perhaps Bert and his group were laughing at him. At the dark blue suit he wore? But who cared – Louisa would return soon.

A shadow crossed the edge of his vision and he looked – instead of Louisa, the slightly mulish, handsome figure of PC Mark Mylow stood there, not in uniform but in slacks and shirt, his hair neatly parted at the side, the usual expression on his face, one of troubled optimism and naivety. 'Doc!' he said, in a surprised tone.

'Mark.' Martin remembered the policeman's words in the car, 'People coming at you . . .' Yes, that's how it was, now. PC Mark Mylow coming at him, just when he shouldn't.

Mark pointed and said in a friendly tone, 'Listen, I should come and see you some time.' He made it sound like he would be doing Martin a favour.

'OK.' Martin could no doubt find him a slot among next week's appointments.

'Cos I'm still, you know . . .' His mouth turned down. 'The old depression thing.'

Martin remembered the Land Rover, Mark driving, the resigned, but interested tone as Mark had said, '*I'm* depressed.' He felt the looming, terrible irritation he was about to feel at the time about to be wasted on a conver-sation he didn't want to have. 'That's fine,' said Martin, 'but not . . .' He stopped in astonishment, because, with a whispered, 'Emergency, nee-naw, nee-naw,' PC Mark Mylow had slid into the seat opposite Martin – the seat where Louisa should be sitting.

'Thanks a lot,' said Mark, louder, and prepared to warm to his theme. 'I said "same old depression", yes, except maybe something's up, maybe it's a touch better now, because, I think I know at least what's *causing* the depression.' Mark wore a serious, open-minded expression. 'See, it's the girlfriend thing.' He paused, and then added, as though explaining the category to Martin, 'Not having one, that is.'

At the same time as he said these words, Martin looked over the policeman's shoulder and saw Louisa returning to their table carrying a glass of wine and his orange juice. The promise of an ordinary, perhaps even humorous conversation with Louisa seemed like impossible riches.

'I used to think,' went on PC Mylow, employing all the intellectual rigour at his disposal, 'that I was a basically *un*happy person. But now I think I'm basically a *happy* person – who just doesn't have a girlfriend.'

Louisa stood behind Mark, close enough for him to sense her presence. He turned and looked up at her, and, with right on his side, because obviously Martin had been sitting here all alone and he'd been first to come up to him, he politely asked, 'Hi Louisa, actually, you couldn't give us a little minute, could you?' He pointed at Martin and himself. 'Bit delicate.'

Louisa glanced at Martin, who returned a mute stare, a

frown of irritation. 'No, of course, that's all right,' she said hurriedly. The look shared between her and Martin seemed to last an age. She delivered Martin's orange juice, took a step backwards, turned, and carried her glass of wine back to where some people she knew stood at the bar.

Mark swung round in his seat and once more locked onto Martin. It was important that he got this off his chest. 'I do have girlfriends, of course,' he said. 'Regularly. Well, not *regularly*, but, it's not like it's always once in a blue moon, either. But I had one once . . .' His brow wrinkled with concentration, and then smoothed out again with the pleasure of making such an important confession, while, far out of reach, Louisa sipped from her wine, smiled, and talked to the people she knew. The affectionate policeman carried on, 'Well, she was the last one I had to be honest. But. She said something – I wouldn't have thought it would have been a problem, in fact I'd have thought it should have been a good thing, but she said that . . . in bed, I was too gentle?'

Mrs Potter's garden was set back a mile or so from the village of Portwenn, yet it overlooked the sea, albeit at a slight distance, and she took pleasure from the pattern of small fields that laced the hillside because the hedgerows were full of birds, which she could see through binoculars from her front window. This year she'd taken to visiting a cuckoo chick, which had outgrown its host's nest in the most outrageous fashion. Some of these birds she tempted closer by planting a forest of bird feeders on both her front and back lawns, and although the squirrels took much of the food, sometimes she was rewarded by seeing the strangest things: once, a kingfisher tried its hardest to cling to a wire cage and get at the food inside. The only birds she chased away were the magpies.

This morning Louisa Glasson and her colleague Mr Rundle lined up all sixteen pupils in Year Six on the pathway leading into Mrs Potter's porch, while Mrs Potter herself waited with hands folded inside the hallway. She liked to give a formal air to the proceedings.

'Peter,' said Louisa to the small figure who lingered in the road, as if he was thinking he could steal the mini-bus and drive it home.

Peter Cronk's solemn face turned to her, in a disinterested fashion. Louisa already knew there was extraordinary wisdom and intelligence in Peter, but these very qualities made it impossible for him to behave normally. He could not be cajoled, like the others, into thinking that the world was happy, well-ordered and constructive in its design. Peter understood that the world was vicious, and uniquely unfair, because it placed in the breast of every man and woman a passionate desire for fairness that was in itself the cruellest thing. 'What?' he asked.

'You might learn something.'

'Like what?'

'Mrs Potter is an expert on British wildlife. We are lucky to have her in the village.'

'I don't care about that stupid old biddy. I'll wait outside.'

'Peter.'

'I know what I want to know about birds. I read about birds when I was eight.'

It suddenly occurred to Louisa that she was looking at a miniature version of Doctor Martin Ellingham. The same reservoir of anger. The same impatience and intelligence. Straight to the point. The same social awkwardness and the ability to make enemies.

'Peter, you know already that if you refuse to co-operate I'll have to give you a consequence. Otherwise it's not fair on the others.'

'Common garden species,' intoned Peter in a dull voice, 'blackbird, black cap, blue tit, brambling, bullfinch. Do you want me to go on? Or do you want breeding habits, feeding habits?'

The tail end of Year Six was disappearing into Mrs Potter's cottage. The last one or two looked over their shoulders to check whether Peter was coming or not.

'It's not good enough to be clever,' said Louisa. 'Actually, it's not clever enough just to be clever. Sometimes you should know about politeness.'

'Why?'

'And sometimes you have to put some work in. Whether or not you come inside, you're still going to have to do the project, Peter, same as everyone else.'

'Why? If I don't care about birds?'

Louisa had had enough. If he was going to behave like a

three-year-old, then she shouldn't be indulging him. She followed the others inside.

Peter felt the loss caused by her absence. Without warning it was worse: he was swallowed up by a great human soup of loneliness. But then, if he'd followed her inside, he'd have been carried away by a torrent of anger and frustration. There didn't seem to be anywhere around here for him to occupy.

And so the day started well for some of Portwenn's residents, less well for others. While Mrs Potter chirruped to Year Six in her cottage, the fishermen lingered for another hour, waiting for the tide to crown the beach and lift their boats. The shops were open already; the builders on Mrs Brading's scaffolding had been at work since eight, and stopped for breakfast.

In the surgery Martin put his head around the door to talk to Elaine. 'Only one appointment this afternoon?' He used his brisk voice, which always shredded Elaine's nerves.

She twanged the hair-band on her wrist. 'Yes. That's a home visit, up on Bodmin. You'll need the afternoon for travel time.'

'What?'

'I told you. The Park Ranger? He's been asking for a visit for weeks.' She braced herself for Martin's bad temper, his voice even more clipped and short, like his haircut, and no doubt his footfalls would start to thud louder on the floor. Sure enough – like clockwork she thought – all these things happened.

'And I told you,' said Martin, 'if he's able-bodied he should come in.'

'Doctor Sim used to—'

Martin was already heading into his consulting room. 'Ring him back and tell him I'm busy, plus I dislike driving, and if he's not dying, could he come in please.' The door shut with a medium bang.

As it happened, Martin's next patient was PC Mark Mylow. Or at least, he was meant to be a patient. However, when the usual pleasantries had been dealt with in Martin's usual peremptory fashion and Martin asked, impatiently, 'What can I do for you?' the policeman's genial smile appeared and he said, 'Me? I'm fine, fine.'

Martin waited. There would be some reason, surely, that he'd booked an appointment, sat in the waiting room, and now appeared in the consulting room.

'I'm perky,' said Mark. 'I won't bother you with why I'm perky. Hold on, yes I will. It's because I've got a date, that's why.' His smile was as wide as a barn door.

'Good,' said Martin. 'Is that why, you've . . . er . . .'

'Yeah.' Mark brightened, but then his expression clouded over. 'No.' Then it lifted again. 'I just wanted to, you know, I thought you'd be pleased. I'm always telling you my *woes*, so now I can come to you and tell you . . .' He came to a halt.

'Tell me what, exactly?' Martin was bewildered.

'It's only a small thing. No, no, no. At least, when I say that, I mean . . . Hold on. Only a small thing, what am I saying . . . ?' Mark took a deep breath. 'As you know, I've not

been successful with people of the opposite sex. And uh . . .
lately . . . Are you on email at all? You must be on email. I've
just been wondering if, maybe, the problem is . . . Do you
get those emails about – or is it just me? I've been wondering
if maybe the problem is a size thing.' With his hand flapping
around, and his altering position in his chair, and his gaze
reaching all four corners of the room, there was no doubt
about Mark's embarrassment, and the courage he'd needed
to come here. 'Apparently,' he went on, 'no matter what a
woman tells you, it *does* matter.'

Martin was incredulous. Portwenn's amiable policeman
was in front of him, claiming . . . that he wasn't well enough
endowed? Martin asked, 'Do you feel you have a problem
with—?'

'I don't exactly *know*,' interrupted Mark. 'I mean, in the
showers is one thing, but you can't tell . . .' He held the palm
of his hand level, as you might to measure the height of a
small child. 'So I was hoping you could tell me, you know,
what's normal.' His hand lifted, and then dropped.

'There's a range of normality,' said Martin.

'I mean, I'm not talking . . . it's not like I've measured,
but . . .'

'I could speak to an urologist,' said Martin.

'Do you think – six,' blurted the policeman, 'six inches
would be normal?'

Martin nodded. 'Six? I'm sure six would be normal.' He
hoped this conversation was over, now. 'So that's good, isn't
it, that's settled now.'

Mark's expression clouded over. 'So five-ish . . . would be a bit small.'

'Not necessarily, not at all.'

'And a little bit less than five wouldn't be good,' said Mark gloomily.

'I should really make enquiries. I don't know—'

'Right,' said Mark.

'Let's make some enquiries, before we . . . shall we?'

'If we'd been talking seven or eight, we wouldn't have to make enquiries, would we?' Mark was overcome with the injustice of it, and fell silent, his hands in his lap. His stare aimed blankly, unseeing, at the objects on Martin's desk. 'Remember I told you,' he said eventually, 'about that woman who told me I was too "gentle"? That wasn't what she meant, was it? I understand now.' He fumbled in his pocket and brought out a white plastic pill bottle. 'I got these from the internet. Arm and a leg mind you.' He handed them over.

Martin took the bottle and turned it in his hands. The trade name 'Big Boy' was written in a large, bulbous print but what he was looking for was written in tiny letters. 'You should have told me about this earlier,' said Martin, and he gave himself a moment to read. 'I could have got you the same thing, for what it's worth. Which isn't much, by the way.'

'That's easy for you to say; you haven't got my problem. If you had a date with the woman of your dreams . . .'

A name popped into Martin's head, Louisa. Her face was suddenly drawn, like a kite, across his imagination. He blinked it away.

'That's great news,' said Martin. 'Who is she?'

'Louisa,' said Mark.

For a moment Martin was confused. The name chimed with the name already in his head. So it felt like an age before Martin answered, and he spoke in a tone of voice that made it sound like he disapproved, 'Louisa? Louisa is the woman of your dreams?'

Mark smiled. 'I've always . . . you know, from afar. Me and the whole village, I'm sure. I was always too frightened to say anything. Then out of the blue she invited me to the jamboree tonight. You know, the dance?'

A recent memory came back to Martin. Yesterday evening: Louisa's smile. Her words, 'I've been mugged by Bert . . .' He had replied, somehow. She'd said, 'I have two tickets to the Portwenn Players' dance. An auspicious occasion. Want one?' He could see her lopsided smile. And she'd held out the slip of paper. He had stiffened with dislike at the offer. He didn't dance, and he couldn't really perform any kind of jollity; public expressions of happiness and gaiety were not for him. He'd abruptly said no. And instead, obviously, she'd asked . . . He was brought out of his memory by the realisation that PC Mylow was talking.

'She is so . . . have you noticed the way she moves?' said Mark emphatically. 'She walks with this kind of swing . . . like she's dancing already.'

Martin was distressed to hear Louisa described by Mark Mylow in this way.

'Actually,' said Mark, 'I can admit to you, Doc, that

sometimes I walk past the school for no other reason than to catch a glimpse of her.'

Spoken with the naivety of a child, these words might just as easily have been spoken by Martin himself, because he had done the same – although he'd never have spoken of it to a soul, and even in his own mind the fact was obscured by layers of other reasons, which acted as camouflage even to himself. He stood up. 'Well,' he began, 'that's great.'

Mark stood up also. 'Sorry, Doc, course, you're a busy man. Thanks for the listen, you know. Cheaper than a therapist, crikey. Wish me luck tonight, though, eh?'

When PC Mark Mylow had left the room, Martin sat there, rotating just an inch or two back and forth in his swivel chair, his chin resting on his chest. His hands, clasped loosely in his lap, moved of their own accord, the thumbs slowly rotating. From outside came the call of a greenfinch: its cheerful trill, followed by a harsh, rasping sound. If he stayed like this, life would just carry him along. It was best never to try and work anything out, never to try and disentangle confusing thoughts and images that appeared out of nowhere, but instead just allow life to happen. Not to allow oneself to be jerked this way or that, by inexplicable and distracting thoughts or subconscious desires . . . He became aware that Elaine was in the room, holding a bundle of papers, and she was saying something.

' . . . this might come as a bit of a shock to you, but when I talk you're supposed to smile, you know? And say, "Thanks Elaine, you're as efficient as you are thin."'

'What was that?'

'I was saying I can't reach the ranger. The phone is down, d'you see?' She was ready for a new argument; Martin would shout at her. He'd rant and rave that he wasn't going to make a visit all the way out there for a man who was perfectly fit and walking and talking. He'd . . .

'OK,' said Martin, calmly.

Elaine felt her mouth drop open and she had to shut it with a snap otherwise she'd be looking gormless. 'So . . .' she began, carefully, hardly daring to trust her luck, 'you'll be driving out there, quite a long way, and he can expect you?'

'OK.'

There was something else that Elaine was nervous about, so she might as well get it over with while the going was good. 'Um,' she said, 'here's Mr James's notes.' She lifted the bundle of crumpled papers. 'Only when we had the flooding that time . . . Plus they were under that plant pot for a while. I've separated some of the pages.' Then she said earnestly, 'But let me *tell* you about him.'

'It's all right.'

'Everything's all right?'

'I'm looking forward to a drive in the country.'

'I thought you hated driving.'

'It's a nice day.' Like an automaton Martin rose and picked up his medical bag.

'Okayyy . . .' said Elaine, warily.

Martin pulled a road map from the shelf and walked calmly out of the room.

Elaine followed. 'Doc, let me tell you about him, cos . . .'

But Martin had gone already. He climbed into the car and drove up the hill to the top of the cliff – and it was as if the car lifted off and cruised through the sky – Louisa and PC Mylow? It was fantastical. And yet – policeman and school teacher; that's how things went . . .

Peter Cronk, aged ten years, was about to walk into the head's study and face a disciplinary panel composed of Portwenn's local policeman, PC Mylow, and the head teacher, as well as both Louisa Glasson and her colleague Mr Rundle. His self-confidence and his sense of calm, both inside and outside, could only have been explained by the fact that he knew something none of the grown-ups knew: he was innocent of any wrongdoing; he hadn't touched Mrs Potter's stupid bird tables and he was only here, he was only *alive*, at the moment, in order to enjoy the long, long wait, that maybe would *never end*, until that auspicious moment when the grown-ups found out they were wrong. And Peter was clever enough to know that the longer it took them, and the more heavily they punished him for something he hadn't done, the greater would be his achievement when they did find out.

Before they called him in, the head teacher, who had convened the disciplinary panel immediately on hearing of Peter Cronk's crime, asked for Louisa's account of what had happened earlier that day, during Year Six's visit to Mrs Potter's cottage.

Up on the side of the hill, with the warmth of temperate sunshine on her face, Mrs Potter had stepped out of her back door, leading out the trail of Year Six children to see her bird tables. 'Now then,' she had said in her careful voice, 'who would like to come out and see if Mr Black-cap is having lunch at my table? But Mr Black-cap doesn't eat pizza, he doesn't eat macaroni cheese, so what does . . .' It was the same speech that she gave every year, but it came to a halt as Mrs Potter turned to view the usually welcome, always familiar sight of her garden. This time, her eyes had glazed over in shock, and her mouth hung open.

She didn't notice the ten-year-old boy, loitering at the bottom of the garden, who at that moment picked up a stone and flung it at a grey squirrel. The squirrel galloped easily up a pine tree, with the faint sound of the scratching of its claws.

Instead, Mrs Potter had eyes only for the desolate sight of the four bird tables lying on the ground, smashed to pieces. Formerly they had stood artfully spaced around the nearest reaches of the lawn. 'My tables?' she said.

Louisa and Mr Rundle had looked at each other. Louisa was ready to swear that surely Peter couldn't have done such a thing, but already this morning they'd seen him outside the window making rabbit's ears to mock Mrs Potter, who'd stood calmly inside, talking away, completely unaware. It could only have been Peter who'd done this.

'Peter!' called Louisa. 'Did you do this?'

Peter had said nothing.

'Oh Peter . . .' Louisa had shaken her head.

The school trip to Mrs Potter's garden had been immediately cut short, and Year Six had been taken back to the school.

Peter, for a boy aged only ten, took an unusually analytical attitude when he was called in to face the disciplinary panel. The grown-ups all sat in a semi-circle around him and watched. Louisa Glasson had a notepad on her lap and a biro ready in her hand. Peter wondered if anyone would eventually read what she was writing down, in some kind of report, and he enjoyed the idea of an unknown person admiring his speech on the page. 'You don't *want* me to say sorry,' he said.

'It would be a start,' said the head.

'No. You . . .' – he waved a hand gracefully at the members of the panel – 'would like me actually to *be* sorry. That's what you want. And I'm not sorry. How could I be?'

'Peter . . .'

'The bird tables belong to Mrs Potter,' he replied, 'and she cares about the bird tables; she is feeling very sorry about the bird tables. And probably she is angry too. Angry with me, I would suppose. But how can I feel sorry, or angry, when the bird tables mean nothing to me?' He stopped, then, because he could see that he was frightening his audience.

A knock at the door of the head's study brought in the school secretary, briefly, who announced PC Mylow.

'Hello, everyone,' said Mark. His friendly voice had a

calming effect on most situations. He glanced at Louisa and tried not to smile. This was work. He made for the empty seat that had been left for him and faced up to Peter, a lad who was already familiar to him for having once tried to run away, and for various other misdemeanours around the village. 'So, Peter,' he began calmly, 'it's been brought to my attention that Mrs Potter is not the only villager to have her bird tables vandalised.'

Peter shrugged.

'I could ask you to help with my enquiries into a spate of similar incidents.'

Peter stared insolently. 'You can, if you want. Ask me.'

Mr Rundle leaned forward sharply. 'What's the point in vandalising people's gardens? How does it benefit *you*?'

'It doesn't,' said Peter. 'And surely that tells you something, doesn't it? Something important about me, and about bird tables, and, specifically, my relationship with bird tables?'

Mark's voice soothed away the increasing anxiety in the room. 'Peter, I don't want to arrest you for criminal damage. I don't want even to start out down that road. But I was thinking – Bob in the lifeboat house has some woodworking tools. Maybe you and I could spend some time in there? Make a few bird tables?'

Among the adults, there was a stir of interest and approval. Mark glanced sideways and caught Louisa's eye. She gave him the warmest of smiles and he felt his own kindness double in strength. It was a wonderful thing.

After this brilliant intervention, they all waited for Peter's agreement – as far as they were concerned he was a lucky boy to live in a small village with PC Mylow as its police officer. They could see Peter thinking about it; he was measuring the scale of what might be his penalty, compared to the generosity of Mark's offer.

'I would rather be arrested and go to jail for twenty years,' said Peter quietly.

There was a further humiliation for Peter: his mother was asked to come and take him home. For Peter, of course, who was certain of his innocence, this was another, further step they were taking along the path of injustice, and it would add to his reward.

Peter's mother, Mrs Cronk, was a fretful, overworked woman. She frequently touched or held one part of her head or another – as if it were in danger of falling off. She would clasp her forehead, or she would cover her mouth, or she held her head in both hands while slumped at the kitchen table, or she would try and pull back the sides of her face as if it had to fit through a narrow gap. Many of her troubles came as a result of Peter's behaviour. 'I'm so sorry,' she said; it was automatic for her to apologise because she'd had to, so frequently, before. 'How did it happen, what's he done?' When she'd heard the story she said again, 'I'm so sorry, I'll pay for Mrs Potter's bird tables. It can come out of his pocket money.'

Louisa said, 'And I have to tell you there are several other people in the village who have had the same treatment.'

'Oh no. I'll kill him.'

Mark was proud to be standing next to Louisa. He wanted to glue himself to this spot. He added, 'I don't have kids, but it seems to me kids are like the rest of us – if he knows he is loved, he could do great things.' He felt Louisa's approval, but didn't dare look at her. Instead he kept his benign gaze aimed at Mrs Cronk, who grew visibly calmer at this unexpected message from a uniformed policeman.

At the end of the corridor Peter appeared; a small figure next to that of the head teacher. Mrs Cronk hurried on her way to meet him, leaving PC Mark Mylow alone with Louisa.

Each second that passed seemed, for him, to be full of life-changing potential, whereas for Louisa the same moments passed by as ordinarily as the ones before he'd stood next to her, and the ones that would follow after he'd gone.

She looked at him and said, 'You know what? You're more . . .'

'More what?'

'I don't know. You're more . . . you're a really gentle person.'

Martin's Lexus wasn't built for Cornwall's rough tracks. The tyres sank in the ruts on both sides, which were deep enough to lower the car's belly onto the strip of grass that ran down the middle: the vehicle grounded from time to time. The hedgerows on either side reached out with long, scratching brambles.

Because he was moving at not much more than a walking pace, he noticed the hand-painted sign buried in the undergrowth – 'Ranger's Office this way'.

He should never have agreed to come out here, thought Martin, to visit a patient who was perfectly capable of driving into Portwenn. During the time he'd taken to come out here, and by the time he'd got back – an hour and a half for the round trip – he could have seen an additional eight patients. He felt himself heat up with irritation.

The track broadened into a clearing and the struggling Lexus was grateful for level ground. There was no way it would make it out here in winter. Ahead of him stood a plainly-built wooden structure; a rural cabin. All the way around was a set of eight-foot-high posts, carrying chicken wire. There was an obvious gateway through the fence, and Martin gathered his bag, climbed from the car and made his way to it.

'Doc Martin?' came a voice.

Martin turned to see a confident man approaching, aged somewhere around forty, dressed in what was obviously a ranger's uniform: a khaki green shirt and trousers, both with large, useful pockets. A circular badge was sewn onto the breast pocket of the shirt. Martin, without thinking, registered the man's above average good health: his gait was strong and unrestricted by any kind of pain, his eyes were clear, his skin colour was good, his breathing was easy, there was a strong physical energy in his movement and his manner was untroubled. 'Doctor Ellingham,' Martin corrected him.

'Oh yes,' said the other man, unashamedly. 'I heard you like to be called by your proper name and title. I thought surgeons prided themselves on being called Mr?'

'I'm no longer a surgeon,' said Martin with his usual shortness. 'I take it you're Mr James?'

'Call me Stewart.' Martin's unlikely patient spoke with an easy charm. 'Why is that, by the way – no longer a surgeon?'

'It was a personal choice,' said Martin. He followed Stewart through the locked gate, and into the house. It had the unmistakeable eccentricity of a house built from scratch by a half-good joiner. Martin's footsteps sounded thunderous on the wooden floor. In every corner there stood pieces of home-made furniture.

'Thank you for coming out,' said Stewart, as he switched on the espresso machine. 'I make incredible coffee – d'you want one?'

Martin was more concerned to repeat the message that he would deliver to anyone who called out a doctor unnecessarily. 'For future reference, unless you're in some way incapacitated, you must come into the surgery.'

'Oh, I can't leave here during the day,' said Stewart in conversational tone.

'Well, let's hope you don't need a doctor,' said Martin testily.

'It's true then,' said Stewart. He sounded happy. 'That you can be a touch bad tempered.'

Martin replied, 'It's true that I don't appreciate having my time wasted, if that's what you mean.'

'Of course. I understand. Portwenn must drive you mad.' Stewart clipped the coffee holder into the machine and switched it on. 'A bloke like you, famously sharp mind, used to barking and everyone jumping – Portwenn would be quite a shock. I'll bet half the locals came to your first surgery, just to see what you'd done to the place.'

Martin looked up sharply – that was exactly right.

'And then there's the aggressive unhelpfulness of – what's her name, the receptionist?'

'Elaine.'

'That's it, Elaine. And those girls that hang around the village in a group, and just giggle. What's all that about?'

Martin nodded ruefully. 'I know.' He took a seat in front of the window, and felt a pleasant breeze move past him. To breathe in such fresh air was delicious.

'I suppose that's one reason why I'm not in a hurry to come into the village; it can be . . . sometimes it can be . . .' and then he and Martin said exactly the same words at the same time, 'too much.'

They subsided into a momentary silence, both of them startled at the symmetry of their thoughts. Martin wondered if this might be the first person he'd met in Portwenn who was as sane and as straightforward as he was.

Stewart made another prediction. He pointed at Martin. 'Strong, black, no sugar, am I right?' He twisted the handle on the espresso machine and removed the mug from under the tap.

'Right.' Martin frowned.

Stewart said – as if he had only just thought of it – 'I'm really pleased to meet you.'

Martin took his coffee, and the smell already told him that it was as good as anything he'd get in Italy, France, or in Soho. It didn't happen often – meeting someone he could for a moment admire. He sipped the coffee and said, 'Perfect.' He suddenly imagined himself trading in the Lexus for a four-wheel drive Land Rover.

'I know how to make coffee,' said Stewart breezily. 'Of course you'd be lynched if you dared to say it, but they can't make coffee down here. Somehow you just get brown water.'

'Don't tell me about brown water. It was on tap when I moved in.'

'Portwenn should come with a manual,' said Stewart.

'Absolutely,' said Martin.

'And how about that neurotic policeman? What on earth's he up to? Nice guy, but you imagine him quietly sobbing himself to sleep of an evening.'

With the mention of Mark Mylow, Martin was reminded of the policeman's date with Louisa that evening and without thinking he veered away from the subject. 'Well,' he said, 'perhaps you'd better tell me what, um, seems to be the problem?' He was curious – this man was the healthiest specimen he'd seen in the whole of Portwenn.

'Nothing new, just the usual,' said Stewart, and handed Martin a pill bottle.

Martin read the label. 'Nitrazepam? Do you have insomnia or anxiety?'

'Yes,' said Stewart, without a trace of anxiety – he looked as fresh as if he'd just returned from holiday.

'I see.'

'I'm sure you know from my records that old Doc Sim used to prescribe me Nitrazepam.'

'I wasn't aware of that. Your notes were a bit . . . well, difficult to read. But in any case I have to be sure that it's the right medication for you. What are your symptoms?'

'Insomnia, anxiety,' said Stewart, sipping his coffee. In this sunny, beautiful spot, he looked like he didn't have a care in the world.

'Nitrazepam is a benzodiazepine. It can be highly addictive. It could be time to try something else. Or, how would you feel about trying to sleep without any medication at all?'

'That's not possible,' said Stewart. There was a strange kind of confidence in his voice – he wasn't defensive, he was just absolutely sure.

'Forgive me,' said Martin, his habitual frown once more comfortably inhabiting his expression, 'but we've just had a stimulating conversation; you don't appear at all tired, or anxious.'

After a while Stewart answered, 'I *am* tired.'

Martin waited.

'But I suppose I should come clean with you,' said Stewart. He looked hard at Martin, testing the situation, and making the decision to confess. 'OK, the Nitrazepam isn't for me. It's for a friend.'

'I see.'

'He's shy. He's—'

'What's his name?' Martin was prepared to be forgiving about this – but he would need to see and to assess the true patient, before writing a prescription.

'Ant. Anthony.'

'Well, you can tell Anthony I'd be very happy to see him. I don't bite.'

'Or you could just give me his Nitrazepam.'

Martin could sense the steeliness underlying this man's easy charm. His own stubbornness rose to meet it – not to mention his ordinary professionalism. 'I would have to see him,' he said.

'It's just he's very anxious.'

'He lives here, right?' Martin pointed at the floor.

'Obviously, but not officially. The Trust owns this place and—'

'But he's your partner.'

'I . . . look after him. He worries. And he's right to worry. There are greys everywhere.'

The strange sentence hung in the air. Martin hunted around for its possible meaning – because it had been said as though he should have understood. Greys? The only thing he could think of, was that Stewart meant old people – but why were they 'everywhere' and why would Anthony be anxious about them? He gave up. 'Greys?' he asked.

'Oh come on,' said Stewart, in an admonishing tone. 'They're everywhere. And they're so aggressive.'

Martin felt the cold, dead hand of mental illness suddenly take hold of the atmosphere in this lovely place. He remembered Elaine's last words as he'd left the surgery, 'Let me *tell* you about . . .' – but he'd left, and driven up here, unheeding.

'It's not brain surgery, is it, to understand why Anthony is so anxious?' said Stewart. 'Everyone knows the reds live in fear of the greys. *All* the time.' And with that, in one practised movement, Stewart swept up a shotgun, lifted it to his shoulder, and aimed it directly at Martin.

Martin became incredibly calm. There were the twin 'o's of a twelve-bore, like a pair of eyes set very close together, and he was staring straight into their expressionless, grey depths. He said, 'Stewart, can we . . .?'

Stewart took three steps closer and fired. The concussion of the sound hit Martin and made him think he'd been shot, but Stewart had fired through the window just behind him, and now walked forwards to lean out. 'See?' he called over his shoulder. 'The audacity. People think they're just a different colour. People think they're cuddly. They are actually the squirrel equivalent of Nazis.'

A clatter of birds had taken off, but a deep silence now filled the area that had previously been shocked by the sound of gunfire.

Martin stood up, his left knee shaking and his heart racing. 'So just to be clear,' he said, 'your friend Anthony – is a squirrel.'

'Used to be three million reds in this country,' said Stewart gloomily. 'Ant's not just a squirrel. He's a survivor. Least we can do is give him his tranquillisers.'

Martin suddenly felt tired; the weariness came from having the carpet pulled from under his feet, and the disappointment, and concern, that the one person in Portwenn with whom he might have had an affinity turned out to suffer from delusions, was probably schizophrenic and was certainly dangerous. 'I should be getting back,' he said.

'Of course,' said Stewart. 'I've kept you far too long.'

Martin was relieved it was going to be that easy. He picked up his bag, trying not to hurry.

Stewart followed him outside into the sunshine. The sounds of the countryside had begun to return. 'Shame you have to go. I was going to put some curry on. That's the other thing you can't get here.'

'Yes, well, we'll speak again,' said Martin. His anxiety infected his tone of voice.

'And you haven't met Anthony.'

'Another time.'

They approached the gate set into the chicken wire fence. Stewart stopped and lifted a hand to shade his eyes from the sun. 'But you'll leave a prescription for him?'

Martin said stiffly, 'I don't have my prescription pad with me.'

The two men stared at each other. After all the agreement between them earlier, it had turned on both sides to distrust. Martin made the last few paces to the gate, and Stewart went back inside.

When Martin reached the gate and slid back the bolt – it didn't pull free of the catch. It refused to slide back further. On the end of the bolt he saw a padlock had been attached.

He was locked in.

Martin looked back towards the house, half expecting to see Stewart carrying the shotgun, but there was nothing. The ramshackle wooden cabin stood beautifully in its spot.

He took out his mobile phone, but like in so many valleys in Cornwall, there was no signal.

There was nothing else for it; he had to go back in and ask Stewart to unlock the gate. He was cross, now, and the injustice carried over into irritation. He knocked loudly.

Stewart answered the door suspiciously quickly, and he was smiling broadly. 'You changed your mind!'

'Hardly,' said Martin. 'The gate, would you please . . .?' But with the door fully open, Martin could see the shotgun resting on its stock, the barrel idly held upright by Stewart.

'I'm glad,' said Stewart, 'because we were really hitting it off, weren't we? Tell you what, have something to eat, and then go.'

Martin tried to read Stewart's easy but fixed smile. It was dangerous to say anything.

'Good!' said Stewart. 'That's settled then.' He turned and went into the house and Martin followed.

In the kitchen, Stewart tied an apron around his waist and picked out vegetables from a rack. An enormous knife was in his hand and he waved it at Martin. 'I was thinking, surgery hours will be over by the time you get back, and I can't imagine you're going to the Portwenn Players' dance.'

Martin was astonished – how did a man living in this remote spot know about his surgery hours, or about the dance? 'I'm going,' he said quickly. 'Yes. I am.'

'God, why?'

'Sounded good,' said Martin.

'It's the annual meat market,' said Stewart. 'You'd hate it. No, as your new mate, I'm not letting you go to that.' The knife sliced expertly through green and red peppers; the tip noisily scraping out the pips. 'What made you say you'd go? It's fine if you want to get your tongue down somebody's throat.'

'Really?' Martin felt a wobble of strangeness at this ordinary dinner party conversation he was having, trapped in a madman's shack. And, presumably, he was about to have dinner with an imaginary squirrel.

'Didn't you know? You should look at your records. It's the night half of Portwenn's children are conceived. Excuse me, nature calls.' He wiped his hands on his apron. 'Talk among yourselves!' He began to leave the kitchen.

'Perhaps I could use your phone while you're . . .'

'It's down, I'm afraid. I had to call you from a phone box in Bodmin. Don't go away.'

When he was gone, Martin lifted the phone to his ear. There was no dial tone. He made a circuit of the kitchen, looking for ideas. His medical bag – he opened it quickly, and searched for . . . He could hear the flush of the loo, and the click of the lock drawn back, Stewart's footsteps. He pawed through the contents of his bag, looking . . .

Stewart came back into the room; Martin had only just dug out the bottle of pills and slipped it in his pocket, but his hand was on the bag and he didn't want to snatch it away; instead he opened the bag again, saying, 'Since I'm here, I may as well update our records on you, Stewart. Your details are practically unreadable. Can I take your full name and date of birth?' He drew out a notepad and pen.

'Stewart Edward James. Fourteen, ten, sixty-six.' Stewart went to a drawer and took out three knives and forks.

Martin watched as Stewart laid three places at the table. 'What's today's date, do you know?'

'You don't know the date?'

'It's slipped my mind.'

'It's the twenty-first,' said Stewart, warily.

'Of course. And your health? Any problems?'

Stewart went to the counter and came back to the table carrying a big plate of a yellow, mash-like substance. 'Not really.'

'Any illnesses or traumas?'

'I took a bullet in Belfast.' He put down the plate of food. 'I wonder if the big guy will show,' he said affectionately, and went to look out of the open window.

Martin felt a surge of anger. What on earth was he doing here, trapped in the wilderness, held hostage by – as it now turned out – a traumatised Northern Ireland veteran who had invented a red squirrel as his friend and life companion? By any chance, any chance at all, was the fact that Stewart was a shotgun-wielding fantasist written down in the stuck-together pages of the medical notes that Elaine had given him earlier in the day? 'Really?' he said, trying to keep an even tone. 'A bullet?'

'In the shoulder. Friendly fire, though. Tony bloody Bartlett. We stopped being friendly after that I can tell you.' Stewart came back to the table, and brought salt and pepper. 'Polenta's his favourite,' he went on, smiling at Martin. 'But feeding a six-foot-high squirrel on a ranger's salary is no walk in the park. This guy is pretty fussy.' He made another trip to the stove, and served food out onto plates. He came back and set them down on the laid table. He and Martin drew back their chairs and sat down.

'Oh, could I have some water, please?'

'Of course. Silly of me.' Stewart nimbly hopped to his feet and fetched two glasses of water. '*Bon appétit*,' he said, returning to the table.

'Thank you.' Martin had one hand thrust in his pocket, levering the top off the plastic bottle of pills and feeling them spill. He would need to move quickly.

Stewart took his seat, but his attention was on the window. 'I'm sorry he's not turning up,' he said. 'It's because you're here. When we're alone, he clings to me. I can't go out in the day at all, any more.'

Martin saw a possible gap in the situation. 'Then good heavens, perhaps I should go?'

'No, no, don't be silly.' Stewart put out a hand. 'You stay right where you are. You're the guest, after all.'

The meal dragged on. Martin answered questions about his childhood, about his training, about his life as a surgeon in London. When he described his own anxiety complex at the sight of blood, he felt himself uncomfortably in the same zone as Stewart, and the latter's concerned expression brought Martin – strangely – close to tears at the awful irony: here he was telling another complete stranger about something which, generally speaking, he kept tightly to himself; he hadn't even told his Aunt Joan about it. As he burbled on, he thought about Louisa, and the way she had idly put out her hand, that time down at the harbour, and a child had attached himself to it – how automatic was her kindness, and he wished to escape from here and go and stand stiffly, uselessly, at the Portwenn dance, whatever it was called, and watch her. It was dusk; she would be getting ready.

Martin's attention snapped back to the here-and-now: Stewart was standing up; he was going to leave the table in order to take the polenta back to the oven and keep it warm. While Stewart's back was turned Martin took two tablets from his pocket, dropped them into the glass of water on the other side of the table and stirred it with the handle of his knife. He tried to stir as hard as he could, while not letting the knife clink against the sides.

Even as the water swirled, Stewart sat down again.

At the bottom of the glass sat the two tablets – they hadn't dissolved. Martin tried not to look, but, when he did, an occasional bubble lifted from one or other of the tablets. If Stewart saw . . . Martin realised he might have made a fatal mistake.

'So you need a prescription pad, do you, for his pills?'

'Yes.'

An impatient edge crept into Stewart's voice. 'You can't just write a note? You can write a cheque on an eggshell. You should be able to write a prescription on a bit of paper.'

'I don't expect that's allowed,' said Martin. 'And even if it were, I don't think Mrs Tishell would oblige. You know how difficult she can be.'

Stewart's impatience was soothed. He said, in rueful agreement, 'True. Portwenn, eh?'

The moments ticked past. Martin couldn't think of anything to say. Half of him wanted Stewart to pick up the glass of water and drink; the other half dreaded that he would pick it up and notice the two tablets sitting in the bottom of the glass. Some of it must have dissolved by now, surely? The tablets looked smaller. 'But obviously the sooner I get back,' he said in a friendly tone, 'the sooner I can sort this out.'

'And you haven't got anything in your bag?'

'"Fraid not, no.'

The impatience returned to Stewart's voice. His jaw tightened. 'Old Doc Sim used to have something for Anthony in his bag,' he said and pushed back his chair and stood up. 'I'm going to look in your bag. I don't believe you.'

'Anthony, if you . . .'

'Stewart! My name's Stewart.'

'I'm sorry. Stewart. Why don't we have a drink? Talk about how to get this prescription to you. Soon as we can. And thanks for the dinner by the way.' Martin lifted his glass of water. 'Cheers.'

Stewart remained standing, but picked up his water. They clinked glasses.

Martin took a good long drink from his glass, while Stewart watched him. In his turn, Stewart lifted the glass to his lips – but then put down the drink and frowned. 'I'm not sure I like you,' he said meaningfully, and walked slowly to the kitchen counter, where the shotgun leaned. He stood it upright on its stock and looked back to Martin. 'I thought I liked you. But you're treating me like . . . You think Anthony's a figment of my imagination.' He effortlessly hoisted the gun and laid it over his forearm. 'Don't you?'

'I . . . Uh . . .'

Stewart's gaze switched from Martin to the doorway, and in a trice the gun was at his shoulder, the twin barrels level, pointed. Then a smile broke over Stewart's face, his body relaxed and he talked into thin air. 'Where've you been? We were worried.' He pulled back the third chair, straightened the knife and fork in front of it, and moved his glass of water across to the unused place setting. 'Sit down,' he said to an empty spot midway between the door and the dining table. 'It's all ready. Your favourite.' He went to the oven to retrieve the polenta, and positioned the dish between the knife and fork. 'This is Doc Martin,' he said cheerfully. 'I told you about him, remember?' He leaned closer. 'And I hope you don't mind, but I told him about you. Anthony, Doc Martin. Doc Martin, Anthony.'

It was obvious to Martin that he was going to have to say hello, but he balked at doing so, and he felt his customary irritation mix with his fear, and he opened his mouth to speak but nothing came out. He gave a sort of nod of the head . . . it was all he could manage.

Stewart clapped his hands and rubbed them together joyfully. 'Finally,' he said, 'the evening can begin!'

Lieutenant Colonel Gilbert Spencer flopped in the armchair, and dabbed the remote control to switch on the seven o'clock news. Outside, his wife carried her gin-and-tonic to the edge of the lawn; from here she could look down on the village of Portwenn as dusk fell and the lights brightened in the windows of the houses. Mrs Tishell, the pharmacist, turned her whole body – as she had to, with that neck brace on – in order to check for traffic in both directions before she crossed the alleyway. In various bedrooms scattered on this side of the hill, members of the Bevy of Beauties gathered in twos and threes to chuck back vodka shots and try on clothes and make-up; they were getting ready for the dance.

Peter Cronk, aged ten, paused for a moment, in his bedroom – he thought he heard a footstep on the stairs. He listened intently, but could hear nothing except the familiar sound of the television. He went to the door and opened it, and peeped down the stairs. The cat was laid out on its back on the bottom step as if it had fallen from a great height, but otherwise the stairwell was empty. He returned to his room and pegged open the top of his rucksack, and tried to pack his book-of-the-moment, titled *The Atom*. The rucksack made crinkling noises like it was a Christmas stocking, but he couldn't do up the zip. He took out the book and removed two giant bars of Dairy Milk before he tried again. This time, the book went in and he did up the zip.

For a while he stood at the window, and watched the houses below him on the slope. He could still see perfectly all right – so it wasn't dark enough yet. He'd put on his coat too early and he was overheating. He took off the coat and lay on the bed with his hands behind his head. He should think about what he'd forgotten. He started forward – of course, loo paper. He should take a roll with him.

At five past eight, when it was getting dark, the conductor of the Portwenn Jazz Band brought down his baton and they started to play 'A Tisket, a Tasket', while those who'd come early enough – mostly the older ones among the crowd, which would eventually fill the place – broke into a ragged applause. The coloured lights that hung here and there from the low ceiling gave the impression the revellers were on a vessel out at sea, since the smell in the air was of the ocean, and the men were either fishermen or looked like fishermen (even Bert Large) and the women were like the wives of fishermen, with that light in their eyes for their mates who had come back safely from their sojourns on the sea.

Louisa Glasson shone in this way; the eyes of the village watched her – all the eyes in here anyway – because she was a young woman with a fall of dark hair, with dark eyes, and happy. The music lifted her until she felt on the edge of dancing, especially when she saw others begin.

Excited laughter came from the bar where the first among the Bevy of Beauties was buying drinks.

In front of Louisa stood Mark, with his daft smile. She was fond of Portwenn's unlikely policeman. 'Mark!' she said and pointed at his glamorous white shirt. 'You look good.'

Mark's shirt buttons were undone to his navel. He had his first line ready; he'd rehearsed it beforehand, in front of the mirror at home, just so he could say something easily and quickly when he first saw her. He had even – embarrassing to remember – leaned in to kiss the mirror, just like he'd hoped to lean in and kiss Louisa's cheek, and he'd practised saying two or three times, 'Louisa, you're looking good . . . Louisa, you look good . . . Looking good . . .' And then he'd knocked back a whole fistful of the pills he'd bought off the internet, the 'Big Boy' tablets. They hadn't had any effect yet – he'd taken a ruler into the Gents and nothing doing – but hopefully after another week or two . . .

However, now that he actually stood in front of her, he didn't dare lean forward and kiss her cheek. But he remem - bered his words and he automatically said, 'Louisa, you look good.' As he deployed his opening line, he heard the same words come from her, 'Mark, you look good,' so his words clashed with hers. He pointed and exclaimed, 'You said that.' It sounded like he was congratulating her.

She looked bewildered. 'I did,' she said.

He felt unlucky, momentarily stupid. He stood there like a plank of wood, Louisa thought, and she smiled at him because she didn't mind that he was like a plank of wood. 'Let's dance?' she said.

'Ooh, not this one,' said Mark. 'But I do like to dance, you know, feel your body move.'

'Oh really?'

'I didn't mean *your* body . . .' he began, and pointed at it, tying himself up in a bigger knot, because that had seemed rude, so he went on, 'at least, not tonight. If that's what you – I mean, I'd have to wait a few weeks before . . .' He was thinking that he'd have to wait until the pills had had some effect, and made him less 'gentle'.

'Mark!' said Louisa, astonished at where this was going.

Mark didn't know how to explain what he'd just said, without telling her what he'd meant, which was impossible to admit. 'Not that I've got a disease or anything. It's hard to explain.'

She tapped him lightly and repeated, 'Mark? Hello!'

He could only happily tell the truth; he should stick to that. 'You know when you invited me, I thought God, you're brave. I mean, I've always wanted to invite . . . Well for years I've wanted to, but never had the courage.'

Louisa understood now that giving her spare ticket to Mark, which she'd done casually as one friend to another, had led him to mistake the gesture for a romantic one. Suddenly, she powerfully missed Martin, to whom she'd tried to give the ticket first of all. 'Mark,' she said, full of concern, 'I think I should say right from the start that—'

The band came crashing in with the first, long drawn out chord of the famous disco number from *Saturday Night Fever*, and Mark's face lit up. He interrupted, 'Hey! Let's dance!' He took Louisa's glass out of her hand and put it down on the table.

With a wry smile at her friends Louisa followed Mark onto the dance floor, but there he was already, right in front of her, striking a pose, with one hand on his hips, the other pointing in the air. Despite herself, she felt a lurch of excitement. He had struck a good pose; the music gathered them up and carried them into the centre of the dance floor and she could see with his very first move that this was Mark's thing, he could really dance, and it was electrifying. It made her feel she herself could dance much better. After only a few moves the other dancers gave them more room and those who stood watching around the edges began to clap. Louisa felt the intoxication of the music; it demanded stronger movements from her and she danced with more abandon yet at the same time with more precision, and she felt in the admiration of the crowd for Mark and for herself a new thrill of pleasure, which shot through her and made her grin madly, happy to make a fool of herself. Under Mark's admiring gaze, given he himself was such a good dancer, she felt powerfully elevated to somewhere . . . not animal, not human . . . somewhere musical, yes, it was as if, for a few short minutes, she *was* the music; it was a release from all her cares and worries.

A voice in her head told her, with certainty, 'Martin will never dance.'

Bert Large, still in his bobble hat, was one of those who watched the couple from the sidelines. 'Always knew young Mark had it in him,' he commented to the young lady next to him. 'People make assumptions and they shouldn't. For instance, not many people realise I, too, am a dancer of some ability.' He was looking all around the room as if he owned the place. 'Not that I am one to steal anyone's thunder. Wouldn't do that. No. Wouldn't be . . .' He turned to offer to the young girl the benefit of the benign, experienced smile that was currently plastered across his face, but it turned out she wasn't actually there. Instead there was only a yawningly empty space. ' . . . Wouldn't be fair,' he finished. The embarrassment was like a glass of cold water through his innards, but he was drunk enough not to mind. All part of life's rich pattern.

The song came to a finish and Mark and Louisa ended their display with a flourish, accompanied by cheerful applause from the onlookers.

'That was amazing,' said Louisa.

'Oh yeah . . . Ummm. Well I practise a bit, when it's quiet in the station.'

'Your secret's out now,' said Louisa.

Mark loomed closer. 'Talking of secrets.'

Yes, thought Louisa – as soon as he stopped dancing he was a bit like a plank of wood.

'Can I say,' went on Mark, 'you're looking really nice? Which I've always thought. But tonight . . .'

This was going to be uncomfortable. Louisa tried to speak over the top of the band, which had started up again. 'Mark, can we have a chat?'

'Cat?' he shouted. 'Well, I'd *prefer* a dog. I'm a dog person, really. But if you . . .'

She'd have to stand on tiptoe and speak right into his ear. Just as she went to do so, she caught sight of Doctor Martin Ellingham, standing in the doorway – stooped, to fit in. How small he made every doorway look, with his height. There was the strangest look on his face. She caught his gaze just as she was leaning right against Mark, and at the same time as she felt Martin's restless anxiety, she was eclipsed by disappointment herself: it was unlucky that he'd seen her just at that moment. In dismay she saw him turn around and leave.

Martin walked smartly outside and stood for a few moments, breathing in the salt-laden fresh air. He had found the person he'd been looking for – PC Mark Mylow – but his determination to commandeer the policeman's help in sectioning Stewart under clause 136 of the Mental Health Act had for some reason evaporated when he'd seen Louisa standing so close to him.

He breathed twice, three times. He couldn't go back in there. It could wait: he would find a community psychiatric nurse in the morning. He took a step or two, but then stopped: what he thought was a shadow turned out to be a couple locked in an embrace, kissing. He veered to the other side of the alleyway and it was the same again: another couple embracing. He saw a pair of white hands firmly planted on a girl's buttocks. And then he could make out other couples, further down, holding hands, or leaning into each other. He really couldn't walk down there. His feet wouldn't let him . . . Stiffly unhappy in his dark suit, harassed, still reeling from his recent escape from the trauma of his imprisonment at the hands of a squirrel-loving lunatic, he was besieged by evidence of everyone else's happiness and desire.

'Doc!'

The call interrupted Martin's thoughts and he turned to see the figure of Al, Bert's son, standing in the lit doorway of the village hall.

'Doc!' Al trotted down the hill towards Martin. 'What you said to Stewart?'

'What d'you mean, what have I said to him? What's he done to me, more like, I've only just . . .'

'You said something to him,' interrupted Al. 'Must have.'

Martin thought back to his final few minutes as Stewart's captive. What had he said? There had been that joke Stewart had made. 'How d'you make yourself attractive to a squirrel?' Stewart had looked between where Martin sat and the empty place where Anthony, the red squirrel, was deemed to be. Martin had played along. 'I don't know, how *do* you make yourself attractive to a squirrel?' The ranger had banged the table with his fist and answered, 'Climb a tree and behave like a nut.' He'd swept his hand sideways and knocked over the glass of water. Martin had really felt it was important to get out of there. He could sense a new, febrile mood take over Stewart. Martin had stood up and said, 'I really have to go,' and he'd been surprised to see Stewart think about it, and look over to where Anthony was supposed to be, before asking, 'What about Ant's tranquillisers?'

'I'll bring them tomorrow,' Martin had said.

And then Stewart had simply and easily said, 'OK, I'll see you out.' Martin had made for the door, but he hadn't been allowed to leave before one final indignity. The ranger had blocked his path to the exit and said in a confidential tone of voice, 'Anthony's very upset. You haven't spoken a word to him.' Martin had been obliged to look at the empty place at the table and deliver a polite greeting into thin air, 'Anthony,' he'd said, 'it's good to meet you. Good night.' And the ranger had told him the key to the gate was hanging off a piece of string attached to the padlock itself – Martin hadn't seen it. He'd fled, determined to find Mark Mylow and have Stewart sectioned.

Now he answered Al's question. 'If I did say anything to him, as I'm sure you know I couldn't divulge the content of a conversation between a patient and . . .'

'Yeah yeah, all that, but he's gone crazy down the back of Playstreet Lane. Completely Bodmin.' Al, who was as slender as his father was round, was already walking in that direction, and broke into a trot. Martin followed. The phrase 'completely Bodmin' was familiar to him from his childhood: it meant 'bonkers'. He had never been to Bodmin, a town not far away, but since childhood he'd always imagined it was populated by lunatics and zombies. What was Stewart doing? He was aware of other people spilling out of the village hall and following them. There would be enough people . . . He ran after the loping, shadowy figure of Al, running through the dark into Playstreet Lane, with an unknown amount of people following. They couldn't see much, but they could hear a series of groans and grunts – the sounds of a fight in progress. And a voice. Warily, they walked closer. They began to make out some of the words. 'They breed . . . feed and they breed . . . and they feed . . .'

Suddenly a halogen security light washed the whole of a back garden in brilliant white. There was the stark figure of the ranger, Stewart, his arms above his head, as he brought down a length of fence post – *crash* – onto a bird feeder. 'And they breed and they feed on *this* stuff,' cried Stewart and brought the stave down again. 'They love it.'

'Al,' said Martin, 'would you please run back to the hall and fetch PC Mylow?'

'Someone's already gone,' said Al.

A woman in a tight black dress and carrying her handbag hurried breathlessly up to them, wobbling in her party shoes. 'That's my back garden,' she began. 'That's my *bird table!*'

A small crowd had gathered to watch Stewart destroy the

bird table. 'That's the ranger,' a voice came to him out of the darkness. 'What d'you say to him?'

'I haven't said anything,' said Martin. 'I visited him, but . . .'

Mrs Beckett waved her handbag at Stewart. 'What you doing, Stewart?' she shouted, and then turned to Martin. 'You must have said something – he's very upset.'

A woman's voice came from the crowd. 'He's never done aught like this, before.'

'I simply refused him inappropriate medication,' said Martin.

'Yes, and now look at my fence, and my bird table.'

The same voice in the crowd echoed Martin's. 'Refused his medication!'

The owner of the garage at the top of the hill, Robert Thornton, swore, 'Bloody hell, that's no good.'

'It's not *his* medication, is it?' said Martin. 'He wanted it for his . . .'

'Bird tables,' Stewart shouted, from the spotlight. His face was white as fire. 'Bird tables.' *Crash!* 'Bird feeders.' *Crash!*

'What's he doing?' said a voice from the crowd.

'I'll tell you what he's doing,' said Martin. 'He's suffering from delusions. He thinks he's living with . . . with a squirrel. That's why I could not prescribe for him his medication – because it was for his "friend".'

'Anthony,' said Mrs Beckett, knowledgeably.

Martin was thrown by her mention of the name.

'Everyone knows,' said Mrs Beckett and rolled her shoulders. 'We've had Anthony for years, haven't we?'

'Yes, but Anthony . . . doesn't exist,' said Martin, irritated. If people wouldn't be told, wouldn't understand . . .

'Oh – Anthony the man-size gourmet red squirrel doesn't exist you say?' said Mrs Beckett, watching Stewart hurl her fence post across her garden.

'Whoever would say he didn't exist?' said Mrs Cooke, sarcastically.

'Long as you go along with him, Stewart's fine,' said Mrs Beckett. 'No need for all this lark, is there?' She swept her arm across her wrecked garden.

Bert was there, his face aglow from the halogen light. 'It's true, Doc,' he said.

Meanwhile Stewart had followed the fence post he'd chucked into the neighbouring garden, only to pick it up and start swinging it at a bird feeder hanging from the branch of a tree.

'How d'you think Anthony feels?' said Mrs Cooke. 'Knowing the greys come into the village to shove him out, and take his food?'

'He's actually a very clever squirrel, is Anthony,' said Bert, ruefully. 'And polite. Well-mannered you know.'

Mrs Cooke said, 'Doc Sim used to give Anthony what he needed.'

'You're right there, Bessie,' Bert said. 'He did, so.'

Martin walked closer to the garden where Stewart swung wildly at the bird feeder. 'Stewart,' he called. 'It's Doctor Ellingham here. Martin.'

Stewart turned to face the crowd, his face stricken and

angry in the pale wash of light. 'The predator doesn't think,' he said. 'Doesn't think what it's like to be the hunted one. Trust me, I know. He does his job with the satisfaction of being the stronger one.' He thumped his chest. 'The right one! Because in a fight, the stronger one is always the right one!'

The security light clicked off, and Stewart disappeared. There was only silence.

'Stewart?' called a different voice and Martin turned around. It was PC Mark Mylow, who'd just arrived, still dressed in his disco shirt.

'It's Mark here, Mark Mylow?' He sounded like he was calling on the phone for a friendly chat. 'How are you, my friend? Having a smashing time?'

Martin noticed that Louisa had arrived with him, and stood alongside him.

Mark Mylow tried again, 'Stewart?'

There was the sound of an engine starting – a green Land Rover in the warden's livery. It clunked into gear and roared off.

'Crikey.' Mark turned to Martin. 'Didn't you go out to see him today? What have you done to him?' He was light-hearted, but Martin was irritated.

Louisa folded her arms. 'Poor Stewart.'

'He was in Northern Ireland, you know,' said Mark.

'I knew that,' said Martin testily.

'We cut him plenty of slack, generally speaking,' said Mark.

Louisa stood precisely in between Mark and Martin, and she wished with all her might that she could step towards Martin and slip her arm through his. Instead her arms remained tightly folded across her chest. She felt cold. 'One important thing's come out of this,' she said.

'What's that?' asked Mark.

'We've blamed Peter Cronk for something he didn't do, and he didn't try and stop us. He let us hang ourselves with our own rope. I'll go and speak to him first thing in the morning.' She stood facing Martin, hoping for a sign from him, one inch of encouragement, but he stood stiffly upright, unapproachable. Instead it was Mark Mylow who came to stand next to her.

'I'll need your help in the morning,' Martin said. 'Something has to be done about this.'

'Course,' said Mark, before he took Louisa's elbow and steered her away, to join the other folk walking back up Playstreet Lane.

Later that night, some people were awake for hours, and most of them wore sorry faces. Deep in the woods, the ranger, Stewart, sat in the gloamy darkness in his wooden cabin, with only one candle guttering on a window sill. He sat, both hands on the table as if he were at a séance, and stared at the empty space where Anthony should be, the place still set with knife and fork, and with the bowl of stiffening polenta.

On the eastward slope of the village, Louisa Glasson, school teacher, lay curled up in bed, her face towards the window, from where she could hear the faint breathing in and out of the sea. Her eyes were wide open, and every now and again she would turn her pillow, or swap one pillow for another, in order to lay her cheek against a fresh, cool place. Her thoughts travelled back and forth between Martin, on the one hand, and her pupil, Peter, on the other. She had this image of Martin in Playstreet Lane, his figure unmistakeable even in silhouette against the halogen glare of the security light – and the thought occurred to her that he was like a cardboard cut-out, that he never would come fully to life. She was waiting for him without purpose, and time was passing by.

And then she'd swap her pillows around again, and turn to thoughts of Peter, of how he'd simply listened to their accusations, and let them run on, without denying them. Certain clues had been there, in what he'd said, like, 'And doesn't that tell you something about bird tables and about me, and about me and bird tables?' He'd allowed them to roll forwards with their punishments, because he knew it would come out in the end, and so it turned out that back then, in fact, he had been very busy earning himself this victory. Because they – she herself, and the school, and Mark Mylow – had been so very, very wrong, and now they looked stupid. She would go up to his house as early as possible . . . nine o' clock. And then her thoughts would switch back to Martin, whom, if she could fly, she could reach by stepping outside her window, winging across the bay, and in through his window . . .

Martin was not in bed yet. He was sitting at his kitchen table, attempting to un-stick the pages of the medical notes belonging to the ranger, Stewart. Some were irretrievably lost, the print or the handwriting lifted off. But there were some patches here and there that he could read, and Martin made up a new set of notes. In the quiet stillness of the night, it was as if the ghost of Doctor Sim entered the room and spoke to him, and Martin caught a glimpse of the actions of his predecessor.

Meanwhile, some two inlets further west along the coast, standing in the landward shelter of a rise of cliffs, a lonely shed stood hard up against the hedge. It was used to store feedstuffs and veterinary equipment for sheep, but currently it hosted Louisa's pupil, Peter Cronk, who had run away from home and had sheltered here, cold and lonely. He took out his books and a bar of Fruit and Nut. He broke off square after square of the chocolate and tried not to think of home, of his mother, or his bedroom with its warm duvet. This was the start of his adult life, away from home. In the morning he must make his way. He pushed the chocolate wrapper into a gap in the woodwork, and he wondered who would find it, and when. He stared into the scary darkness and he made plans: in the morning, he would stand outside the shed door, and he'd pull on his rucksack and he'd walk along the coastal path. He would ask for work from every farm he passed. He would find food, or buy food, and if he didn't find work he'd look for a hay barn in which to spend the night and he'd carry on until . . . well, until he found the place to stop. A place that wanted him.

Many others in the village of Portwenn slept soundly, the moonlight blue against their skin, their breath heating the air in the bedrooms. Dogs stirred in their baskets while cats stalked abroad, through the village, or along the hedgerows, in the barns. Some of the older residents lay awake and one or two rose from their beds and watched television, the light flickering in their darkened living rooms. The Bevy of Beauties stayed up all night watching films, and the fishermen, summoned by the tide, rose before dawn to take up their slicks and make for the harbour.

At 8.20am Peter's mother, Mrs Cronk, was surprised to hear the doorbell. She dropped her toast on the plate, rose from her breakfast table and went to open the door.

On her doorstep stood Louisa Glasson.

'Now what's he done?' she said and turned to call up the stairs, 'Peter?' She was breathing quickly, and patted her chest with a fluttering hand.

Louisa said quickly and emphatically, 'Nothing, Mrs Cronk. That's the whole point, he's done absolutely nothing.'

At the same time as Louisa and Mrs Cronk were walking up the stairs to Peter's room, Martin was climbing into Mark Mylow's police Land Rover. 'Is it just us?' asked Martin. 'Shouldn't we have more bodies?'

'What for?' asked Mark cheerfully, his expression as frank and open as ever. 'Stewart never hurt anyone.'

'You saw him last night,' said Martin gruffly.

'That was bad,' said Mark. 'And he's eccentric, yes, but not violent.'

'Try telling that to the bird tables. And he has a gun up at his place.'

'He's a Park Ranger though, isn't he? He's supposed to have a gun. This is the country, Doc.'

Martin couldn't see any reason why an armed, deluded madman should be tolerated in the country any more than in the town.

'Did he scare you?' asked Mark.

'I fear for his well-being and for public safety.'

'He scared you!' Mark was proud to be so observant. 'Did he do that thing where he takes some shots just past your shoulder at some greys? It's pretty scary when he does that.'

'He locked me in his compound,' said Martin.

'Locked you in?'

'There was a key,' admitted Martin, 'but I didn't know where it was and I felt like I was forced to . . .' He couldn't quite finish.

Mark glanced across at his passenger. 'What?'

'Have dinner with him. With him and with Anthony, the red squirrel.' Martin didn't like the way Mark was taking this so lightly. 'He clearly is in need of psychiatric care.'

'He stops by in Portwenn from time to time. We don't usually have a problem with him.'

Martin said, 'I suspect his next stop is a bed in a psychiatric ward.'

'What about a creative solution?' suggested Mark.

'What creative solution is there?' asked Martin.

'How about whatever Doc Sim did for him? We can't do that?'

'His condition has clearly worsened,' said Martin.

'Or maybe it's his doctor that's changed,' said Mark in a weird voice.

'Here's the thing,' said Martin impatiently. 'Everyone comes to you for an opinion, but when you give that opinion, nobody wants to hear it. Stewart thinks he's living with a squirrel. He needs help.'

Mark counted himself as well and truly ticked off, and for a while he drove in silence. However it only lasted for a minute or two. Mark's natural optimism and his straight-forward nature meant that Portwenn's policeman quickly forgot any argument. 'On a more cheerful note,' he began, 'I had a good night last night. Had a bit of a breakthrough.' He glanced at the sternly frowning doctor next to him, and pressed on. 'She's really good, you know, is Louisa. Have you seen her – I mean have you had a really good look at her? She's got a body and she knows how to—'

'Mark,' interrupted Martin, 'I really don't think—'

'Course not,' said Mark. 'But she can really dance. And then suddenly, it was really, really odd, but I realised I didn't fancy her anymore. All these years, but the truth is, she's just a really good mate. We had a laugh, don't get me wrong, but that's it. I just hope she's not too gutted, though, when I tell her. God, which I'll have to do, soon. Oh dear. Problems, problems.' He spared one hand from the driving wheel to fish in his pocket. 'Added benefit is,' he said, 'it gives me time to sort out the other trouble.' He took the plastic bottle of pills from his pocket and thumbed the lid, popped one as he drove. 'Who's the gentle one now, eh?' he said.

'Mark, they're placebos,' said Martin scathingly.

'Well, placebos work, though, don't they?'

'You mean the placebo effect?'

'Call it what you like,' said Mark, 'as long as it's an effect.' He snapped the lid shut, still with one hand steering the Land Rover. He went to put the pills in his pocket, but the container spilled from his hand and dropped between the seats.

Martin fished it out and turned it in his hand. The 'Big Boy' label was preposterous. It was a complete and utter fraud. How could Mark have any dealings with such a company? 'Mark, you don't understand, it doesn't mean you will actually grow . . . that's not what a placebo . . .' He gave up. 'Ah, never mind.'

The Land Rover turned onto the track that led to Stewart's cabin and the four-wheel-drive made short work of the rough ground. They drew to a halt outside the fence, and climbed out. The double slam of the vehicle's doors sounded alien to the deep, rural silence. Martin and Mark wandered up to the fence.

Stewart's face appeared out of an open window on the first floor; he was cheerfully smiling. 'Just coming down.' He disappeared from sight.

'Right,' said Mark in a low voice, 'give me a shout if you need a hand.'

Martin was astonished. 'I do need a hand. That's the whole point.'

'Well, technically I can't bring him in on a 136 unless I "find him in a public place". That's the darn Mental Health Act for you. Crazy.'

'Oh. I see.' Martin felt the customary irritation at just how stupid people could be. 'Telling me that *before* we got here – that would have been the Common Sense Act.'

Mark never seemed to be affected by anyone's anger, whatever the circumstances. 'I'll be right here if there's a problem.' He smiled. 'You'll be fine.'

Stewart was coming across the ground between them.

'Hi there, Stewart,' said Mark. 'All right? Doc Martin here wants a word with you if that's OK?'

Stewart teased out the key on its bit of string, unlocked the gate in the fence and held it open. 'Come on in,' he said in a friendly tone.

It felt ominous to step back through this gate. The last time Martin had done so he'd been trapped for hours and had ended up being forced to talk to an imaginary squirrel. None the less, alone he went through the gate, and alone, upright, with his stiff, city-dweller's walk, he followed Stewart into the wooden cabin where only yesterday he'd been imprisoned and shot at. How ironic that the only person he had felt an affinity with down here had turned out to be sectionable.

In the kitchen Stewart said ruefully, 'I've gone over the top again, haven't I?'

Martin watched as all the strength seemed to drain out of the other man's physique. He said, 'Mark and I would like to take you into Portwenn. See if we can't get someone to come along and give you the help you need.'

Stewart nodded, resigned suddenly to being taken care of. Staring at the ground, he spoke as if only to himself. 'It was so clear to me,' he said, 'aged nineteen. I was a soldier boy, you know. I saw some heavy stuff. I *did* some heavy stuff.' He sighed and lifted his gaze to meet Martin's. 'But I was fine. Left the army. Studied. I was successful, even. Then one day, out of the blue, I woke up screaming in the night. Now I guess I'm a bit, well, fragile. Smallest thing sets me off. A sound. A smell. And I go to pieces. A *smell* can put me right there, you know? You can't imagine.'

'I can, actually.' Martin felt anew – more strongly – that affinity between himself and the Park Ranger. Perhaps he, too, should invent an imaginary squirrel. It obviously worked.

'There's something about being out here in the wilds,' said Stewart, and waved his hand at the open window. 'If you're going to be fragile, it's the place to do it.'

Martin followed his gaze and looked out – he saw PC Mark Mylow perched on the front bumper of the Land Rover, reading a novel. It couldn't have been a more peaceful scene.

Stewart went on, 'Anthony's been a real support, of course. And I expect that he'll go when I'm stronger. But right now I'm glad he's around.' He looked carefully at Martin and said in a hopeful voice, 'I've made a start out the back on some replacements for the things I smashed up. Perhaps we can sort this out for ourselves?'

'I'm sorry,' said Martin.

It was the answer Stewart had been expecting. He pointed at the coffee machine and quoted the Dylan song, 'One more cup of coffee, 'fore we go?'

Martin felt such an aura of sanity and acceptance in this kitchen, compared to the madness of the previous day. He said, 'Why not?'

While the machine began to hiss, Stewart filled the little cup with ground coffee.

'I was reading your patient notes last night,' said Martin. 'Or at least I was trying to. I just wanted to ask – the pills that Doctor Sim used to prescribe for you – did you actually take them?'

Stewart nodded. 'Yes, I did.'

'And did they help?'

'They kept me . . . well, just the right side of things. Yes.' Stewart kept up with his coffee machine ritual.

Martin watched him as he worked. And the next thing Martin did happened despite his own professional intentions and beliefs – perhaps it was because he'd found himself and Stewart in the same lonely place, with the same kind of uncontrollable reaction, suffered because of some well of experience they'd shared. He reached for his medical bag and opened it, and rummaged within. At the same time he reached into his jacket pocket, and with his other hand fished out his pen from his inside pocket. 'I've been thinking about your case. After last night it's clear that you require medication.'

'Nitrazepam?' asked Stewart hopefully.

'No. These are new on the market.' He unclipped the lid on a fresh container and decanted into it a handful of pills. 'Take one every twenty-four hours, but be careful that you don't exceed the dosage.' He offered a single pill to Stewart, who took it tentatively.

'That strong are they?' asked Stewart.

'Yes.' Martin pressed home the lid on the unmarked container and wrote on the label, and then put the container on the kitchen table. 'That will do you for a day or two, until I can get you a further supply. D'you need a glass of water?'

Stewart shook his head. 'No, I'm OK.' He swallowed the pill down. 'Christ, they are magicians, aren't they, these chemists?'

Martin wanted at some point in the future to bring Stewart into a different mental space. 'Also, if I set you up with a therapist,' he asked, 'would you go?'

'Sure,' said Stewart reasonably. 'Yes, I would.'

'And I want you to get this phone working,' said Martin, and he tapped the dud implement. 'I'm going to pop in tomorrow and see how you're doing.' He stood up and clipped his bag shut. He was remembering how the last time he was here, only yesterday, he'd tried to fool Stewart into drinking a glass of water spiked with a sleeping draught. It seemed that every time he came here, he was trying to fool Stewart, and Stewart was trying to fool him.

Peter, at the age of ten full years, had never seen a hitch-hiker on the side of the road, nor had he ever been in a car that had picked up a hitch-hiker – and certainly he'd never actually hitch-hiked anywhere, himself. Yet he knew – from stories told by his mother and father – that it used to be commonplace. He knew the protocol from films he had seen, and so he'd taken the precaution of making – and packing in his rucksack – the A3-sized piece of white cardboard with his first destination, Bristol, heavily inked onto it in large capitals.

He knew to stand a good fifty yards ahead of a lay-by or on a slip-road with a hard shoulder, so that cars could stop safely. In his case, it meant a few yards ahead of a farm gateway that offered plenty of space for pulling up. He unfolded the A3 card and waited. The cold from the previous night was still in his bones, along with the pain in his hip and shoulder from lying on the hard floor of the shed. He still felt the strangeness of wearing the same clothes as yesterday, which were the same clothes that he'd worn during the night.

Within ten minutes a silver Vauxhall stopped and took him as far as the main road to Bodmin. There he waited at the point where a lay-by began to take a bite out of the verge, and for a while he was too shy to unfold the sign and hold it up. There were two lanes of traffic, now – one in each direction. Many more drivers would see him. Perhaps he'd gone far enough, and he should go home? He suddenly pictured his mother finding an empty bed, and how much that would frighten her . . .

No, he stuck to his decision: Bristol. Let them worry; let them search high and low . . . It served them right. He unfolded the sign and held it up with both hands. A car drove past without even altering speed. So did a second. A third gave a cheerful 'Peep peep!' A fourth, he could see, had every seat filled with children.

Somehow Peter didn't feel like a child any more. Childhood was behind him.

When the next car ignored him, he decided he would lean out into the road to try and make people stop. It was a Land Rover. Too late he realised it wasn't a roof rack on top of the vehicle, but a set of blue lights – a police vehicle. He snapped the card shut along the fold and with an uncontrollable, clumsy leap he turned his back, and then a voice in his head told him, 'Tie your shoelaces,' so he dropped on one knee and pretended.

The sound of the Land Rover's engine dropped in pitch as it slowed right down and swerved into the lay-by and came to a halt, diving forwards on its springs from the speed of the deceleration. He saw both its doors open and he recognised both the men who climbed out: PC Mark Mylow and Doc Martin. He dropped the sign and started to run.

He made for the gate into the field and scrambled over

it, his rucksack banging clumsily on his back. As he started across the field he heard the clatter of the gate as someone followed him. He kept going, heading for a gap in the hedge that he could see on the opposite side. Beyond the next field lay a wooded copse where he might be able to hide, if he could get far enough ahead. He didn't even spare a moment to glance back over his shoulder; he ran until his lungs felt they might burst and he ignored the pain as his ankle twisted on the hummocky ground. He could hear the breath of his pursuer and his footfall, and the sound became louder. He could not run any faster and the harsh sound of breathing, and the thump-thump of the person running, were close behind him, close enough for it to be no surprise that he felt a hand weigh on his shoulder, and grab the strap of his rucksack, and pull. He tried to lose the rucksack even as he ran, and so he stumbled and fell. The weight of PC Mylow fell with him. He put out his hands to save himself, and he felt the sharp pain as his arm folded too far over his wrist. They both landed in a heap, and he could hear the kindly voice of PC Mylow. He knew he was going home.

Later that day, both Mark Mylow and Martin sat in a corridor outside Louisa Glasson's class room while she spoke to Peter. She apologised to him and said she quite under-stood what a clever thing he'd done: by not taking the trouble to deny their accusations, he had allowed the adults to find out for themselves the injustice they'd committed in accusing him of destroying the bird tables, and in effect that was excellent teaching practice, and she herself, Louisa Glasson – here she pressed her hand to her breast – felt that as a result she'd learned from her mistake, and she believed the other adults had too. But, she added, she wanted Peter to realise that it didn't mean they didn't care about him; rather the opposite, they had been too quick to try and mend him when he didn't need mending, and all of them – the head teacher, herself, his mother – realised what an unusual and interesting brain he had, ticking away inside his head, and they hoped he would stick around for a bit longer before he left home, and take advantage of all the affection and respect that this small Cornish village had to offer, for the very short time that was left before he could leave home properly prepared for the outside world.

Peter nodded blankly and left the class room to find Doctor Ellingham and PC Mark Mylow sitting outside; and PC Mark Mylow rose to his feet and went into the class room to talk to Louisa, while Peter sat beside Martin.

'Nobody wants me here,' said Peter. 'They all gang up on me.'

'Let's see how that wrist is doing. Can you make a fist for me?' Martin felt the volume of heat. 'Everybody feels left out now and then, Peter,' he added.

'What do you know?' said Peter.

'I know your wrist is going to be fine.'

'Course it is, I could have told you that. It's a grade one mild sprain: ligament stretched maybe but not broken.'

Martin drew back in surprise. 'Yes. Quite right.'

'I want to learn about chemical pathways,' said Peter bluntly. 'Have you got any books I can have?'

'Yes I've got some books,' said Martin. 'But it might be useful for you to know that your manner of speaking makes it a touch more difficult for me happily to lend them to you.'

'People think I'm being rude,' said Peter, 'but I'm just saying what's in my head. You know?'

Martin nodded. 'Funny thing is,' he said, 'I really do know. Not just saying it. I really do know exactly what you mean. And people take offence, don't they?'

'Yes.'

'What do we do about that?' asked Martin. 'Can we change the way we behave?'

'I'd guess not, probably.'

'You're right; we're probably stuck with it.'

Inside the class room, PC Mark Mylow told Louisa that he had to seize this moment to tell her something important – that perhaps he had been leading her astray, toying with her affections, which he did realise amounted, in effect, to a criminal offence. He was sorry to cause her any heart-ache, but he couldn't possibly take advantage of the romantic affection that had recently sprung up on her part, because, as far as he was concerned, unfortunately, they could only be friends. He hoped he hadn't hurt her feelings too badly and that she'd be able to forgive him. He was proud of his speech, and he felt the wonderful cleansing power of truthfulness, as the reality of the situation was made clear to her, however much pain it might cause. He was relieved to see that she took it so well, and she even gave him a tentative, wry smile as she accepted the news, which boded well for her recovery.

PC Mylow was shocked later on, though, as he dropped off the doctor at his surgery. They had been talking about Stewart, and how Martin had decided to prescribe medication for him, after all. 'That was a good call, if you don't mind me saying so,' said Mark. 'I reckon this place is having an effect on you. Everyone will think the better of you for doing that. Why wouldn't a man like him need some tranquillisers? He was in Northern Ireland, you know.'

'Then you might be interested to know,' said Martin, 'that I didn't give him any tranquillisers.'

'I thought you said you gave him what Doctor Sim gave him.'

'I did, yes. But it seems Doctor Sim was cannier than I'd thought. From what I could piece together from his notes, I would say that the only pills Doctor Sim prescribed for Stewart were vitamin pills.'

'Ah – the old placebo effect?'

'Yes, in this case, exactly that. The placebo effect.' He carried on, 'Of course, I don't carry vitamin pills with me, but luckily for Stewart I was able to give him yours.'

'I haven't got any vitamin pills.'

'Yes you have.' Martin reached into his pocket and fetched out the pill container with the trade name 'Big Boy' splashed across the side. He shook it; and it didn't make a sound. He read the contents, 'Ascorbic acid, D-alpha tocopheryl, pyridoxine, thyamine . . . your enhancement pills are multi-vitamins.'

'You are joking.'

'I am not.' He tossed the empty container at Mark, who caught it.

Mark was indignant. 'You can't just give away my pills. That's not ethical. They cost me a fortune.'

'You'll get over it, Big Boy,' said Martin. He climbed out of the vehicle. 'Thanks for the lift.' He slammed the door shut and walked steadily, stiffly, into the surgery, carrying his medical bag, with his other hand just curled shut so the tips of the fingers trapped the cuff of his dark blue suit, and clean white shirt.

5

There followed a period of time when Louisa's absence from Martin's life was made even more insistent by the peculiar, ironic presence of other people, who approached him, and made use of him, in ways that seemed designed only to confirm, to the outside observer, that Martin remained wilfully alone, and that Louisa was not required by him even as a friend.

During these weeks, the sight of the surgery building on the other side of the bay prompted Louisa to think that it was a fortress occupied by an ogre, whom for some reason she found herself thinking about, more than she'd like to.

The first of these people who commented painfully on Martin's solitary nature was one from among the Bevy of Beauties, who appeared in the surgery – in fact Melanie was heard, wailing and crying, before she was seen, blue eye-shadow streaked with tears, holding out an arm as if it was an awful thing someone had asked her to carry. Her brother Joe seemed to be tentatively helping her to carry the damaged arm. Her figure was clumsy in her too-tight clothing, and her long hair was like a damp mop that someone had thrown in her face, and her brother was gloomy and rolled his eyes, and wore sparkling white trainers. When they came into the surgery Elaine regarded them with disdain – they brought in such dishevelment and *noise*.

Martin heard the screaming and put his head into the waiting room. 'What's happened?'

The brother and the sister answered at the same time. Joe, the brother, shouted defensively, 'It's not my *fault*,' while Melanie wailed, 'My arm! He killed my arm!'

'Let's have a look.' Martin approached the limb, which came out of her shoulder socket at a strange angle.

'You are not *touching* it,' shouted Melanie. 'Do not touch it!'

'What happened?' asked Martin.

'He karate-chopped me,' cried Melanie.

'I warned you though, didn't I?' Joe turned to Martin. 'She thinks she owns the remote control. Well she don't!' He turned back to his sister and shouted, 'You don't!'

'What's your name?' asked Martin peremptorily.

'Brain dead,' said Joe, 'that's her name.'

'Melanie.'

'Come in here, Melanie.' Then Martin instructed her brother, Joe, 'You stay here.' He led the wailing teenager into his consulting room. Elaine watched her go in, cruelly disinterested, popping another Rolo.

In the consulting room Martin felt gently along the arm, to find any evidence that there might be a fracture. Melanie stamped her foot and screamed, and the next moment she drew back the same foot, and she booted Martin hard in the shin. 'I told you not to touch it.'

It took a moment for Martin to swallow the pain and carry on. 'You've dislocated your shoulder,' he said, 'but I had to check for fractures before I . . .'

'Get off me!' Melanie carried her arm off around the room.

Martin followed. 'Melanie.'

She couldn't hear him; she was in such pain. Her white wedge sandal twisted under her and, with the sudden loss of balance, she jerked the arm. 'Ahhh.' Tears came to her eyes. She sank slowly into a chair.

Martin caught up with her. 'Melanie,' he said sharply. He brought up his foot and planted it firmly in her armpit, and grasped her wrist and her elbow.

'Agghh, what are you *doing*?'

Even as she screamed, Martin heaved on her arm, pulled with all his weight.

Melanie was ready to die, or faint, but instead, like a tide rushing outwards, the pain went away, almost to nothing. Her tousled, fearful expression cleared, to be replaced with one of wonder. 'Oh my God.' It was like the words emerged into calm, still air, after the storm.

'OK?'

'Oh my God. How did you do that?' She was awestruck.

'Dislocated shoulder,' said Martin. 'Might be a little bit sore for a while. You can make yourself a sling to rest it for a day or two, if you like. Any problems, come and see me.'

'Oh my God.' She looked at Martin, her eyes filled with reverence and thankfulness.

The next day, outside the school, in the very spot from where sometimes a glimpse of Louisa could be caught, the sight of Louisa was denied to him, and instead, as if on purpose, Melanie was there. Martin was striding at a solid pace when she appeared with her arm in a sling, holding an oblong tin with a picture of a ski chalet on the lid. 'Hiya,' she said and slumped her weight on one leg, and stroked the hair from in front of her eyes. 'How are you?'

'Why?' asked Martin suspiciously.

She said in a surprisingly grown-up way, 'You really saved me.'

'Well that's my job,' said Martin abruptly. He was uncom - fortable; the best thing was to continue on his way, but he heard her footsteps follow him.

'Made you a cake,' she said. 'To say thank you.'

Martin grimaced and stopped to find the cake tin right there. 'Cake? Melanie, I don't think . . .'

Melanie frowned and interrupted, 'I bet you, right, that no one remembers to say thank you.' She looked serious. 'Do they?'

'Actually, no, they don't.' Martin felt the onset of tears, which was *laughable*, and the moment had passed before he had time to think about why it had happened. But it made him appreciate the thoughtfulness of this child in front of him.

'Go on then. Take it. I used me mum's best cooking chocolate.'

'OK. I will.' He took the tin from her. 'Thank you, Melanie.' He didn't know what to say next. For a while he struggled to remember what to do with a cake. What to say, to a girl. The cake – oh yes – he should eat it. But not now. He could have done without this confusion. 'It looks very nice,' he said.

'You're very nice,' said Melanie. There was no trace of banter or flirtatiousness in her tone. She said it simply as a statement of fact. She gave a brief smile and lifted her free hand. 'See you around.' She turned and walked off.

Would he have done such a thing when he had been her age? Never. He had been too busy posting himself off to the island he'd made for himself, separate from other people of all ages, an island of cleverness, where achievements and exam grades arrived as if they were messages calling with increasing urgency from the world of work. And what about now? Could he behave in such a simple and gracious way? Might he walk into the school and say something affectionate to Louisa? You would as well have asked him to walk on the moon.

The next day, Melanie, in an even more painfully obvious way, again showed him how it was done. The surgery letter-box clattered at the wrong time and he arrived in time to see a bright green envelope fall to the floor. He went and picked it up and opened the door at the same time, to see Melanie walking back down the path towards the road.

She turned and gave a skip. 'Can't stop. Meeting my dad at the Leisure Centre. He goes mental if you're late.'

'Well, thank you.' Martin opened the green envelope and drew out a heavily embossed thank you card, illustrated with a furry angel. The inside was covered with Melanie's rounded handwriting, with all the dots drawn as miniature circles.

'How was the cake?' called Melanie and suddenly he realised she'd come back; she was standing in front of him.

'Fine, thank you.' He couldn't remember where he'd put the cake, in fact. Certainly, he hadn't eaten any of it. 'No need for a card as well.'

'Yes there is. You're lovely. People don't realise. They think you're Bodmin. But you're not. You're fab.'

Martin felt his ears burn. 'Melanie, any doctor would have done the same thing.'

'Yeah, but you're special. You were like the big boss in London, weren't you?'

'I was a surgeon in London, yes, but—'

She dabbed a finger at him. 'See? You don't go boasting either.'

'Melanie, listen—'

'Hey, did you notice our names begin with the same letter?'

'What?'

'Martin. Melanie.' She smiled.

There came the toot of a horn from the car waiting on the road. 'Gotta go,' she said. 'Dad gets furious.' A shout came from the car as the passenger window wound down and the same brother, Joe, called up to her, 'Oi, Brain Dead. What you doing? Come on.' Melanie's smile stayed steadily on Martin. She gave her standard small wave. 'Bye.' She turned and gave another little skip and ran to the car.

'Melanie . . .?' But she'd gone. Martin looked down at the card. She'd signed it with kisses and love hearts. 'Oh God,' said Martin.

The irony was that a middle-aged man who was imprisoned in a tower of loneliness, when someone young and innocent enough just walked in, with blind confidence, as if there were no walls, no ramparts, had to reject her, shut her out as a matter of urgency, for her sake as well as his own.

Martin was a professional; he did the professional thing – he reported his concerns to PC Mylow. He found Portwenn's policeman repairing a flat tyre on his Land Rover. 'Could we talk?' asked Martin.

'Sure. I've got good news, by the way. Discovered St John's wort. Definitely makes you happy. Early days, but I'm pretty sure the old spirits are on the up.' The policeman was genial and open as ever.

Martin ignored him. 'I need a bit of advice.'

'What's up, then?'

Parcelled up in his dark blue suit and tie, well past forty years old and standing at six foot three inches with size twelve feet, it did feel monstrous to say, 'There's a young girl . . . who seems to have become besotted with me.'

Mark's good humour closed like a curtain. 'Oh. Right.'

'Yes, it's a problem.'

The younger man said, 'Yes, well, it's a problem I wouldn't mind having.' St John's wort wasn't helping now.

'In this case, you'd—'

Mark interrupted, 'I mean, why d'you mention it? You know I haven't been exactly lucky in that department.'

'It isn't a competition.'

'It bloody is. You come running to tell me, don't you? I invite you for a drink, you don't really come – I got that malt whisky you like, and the bottle's still nearly full—'

'I don't drink alcohol,' interrupted Martin.

Mark Mylow carried on regardless. 'But now there's a young girl on the scene, and here you are. I'm not really interested to be honest.'

'Mark, she's fifteen. It's important that we take a professional . . .'

'*Fifteen*? I can't condone that.' Mark shook his head. 'No. Not right.'

'I'm not asking you to condone . . . Mark, she's a patient and I . . .'

'A *patient*? That's worse, that is.' He blew out some breath between his teeth.

'I know it's worse!' Martin was exasperated. Why weren't people capable of being moved to where they were supposed to be? 'Look, the idea is that I want to be completely clear that I have no interest, romantic or otherwise, in a fifteen-year-old girl who's chasing after me with . . .'

He was talking too loud; he had to stop and answer the

inquisitive look of a passer-by. 'Oh go away,' Martin said to the stranger.

He turned to Mark. 'I relocated her shoulder. Now I'm her hero.'

'That's right. Rub it in.'

'Mark . . .'

'I've been a hero too, you know.'

'I'm sure you have, but—'

'Is it Melanie Gibson?'

'Yes.' Martin was surprised at Mark's guess.

'And you've told her it's not on, presumably?'

'I made the mistake of telling her she was a nice person.'

'I'll remember that line. I might use that line, myself. "You're a nice person. Bend over."'

'Mark, that was before I realised she was . . . She'd made me a cake. I was being polite.'

'A cake?' Mark said, with sudden alarm. 'You do know, right, in Portwenn, if you take a girl's cake, it means you're engaged.'

For a moment Martin believed it, before he saw how far up his forehead were Mark's eyebrows. 'Yes, very funny.'

'Don't let her down, will you? Her dad's a martial arts nut up at the Leisure Centre. Tae kwan do.' Mark pulled a fighting stance. 'You know? Black belt. Advanced level.'

'Thank you, Mark.' Martin was already on his way. He'd done his duty: he'd informed the relevant authorities. He heard Mark's voice call after him, '"The way of the foot and the fist" – tae kwan do.'

Martin didn't waste any time. The next morning, when Elaine came into the consulting room with the day's paperwork, he asked her to cancel two appointments, which would give him the time to go and visit Melanie Gibson's parents before they even had a chance to take matters into their own hands. 'And find me their address,' he added.

'No need,' said Elaine in a low voice. 'Her dad's here already. Wants to see you.' Her eyes were round as an owl's. She shifted her gum from one side of her jaw to the other.

Together they went and peered through the inch-wide gap in the door that led to the waiting room. There was a man sitting there, with arms that stretched the cuffs of his T-shirt, and a chest as broad as Saunton Sands, and a determined expression on his face. He had a similar colouring to Melanie.

Martin murmured to the innocent-looking Elaine, 'You've told him I'm here?'

She nodded vigorously, and then seeing Martin's tetchy expression she added, 'What? You *are* here.'

She spoke so loudly Martin had to pull open the door and walk through, to drown her comment. The man's T-shirt must have shrunk in the wash. Martin could suddenly feel his broken nose twinge, for some reason.

'You Ellingham?' The T-shirt rose to its feet.

'Um, yes, come in.'

Elaine made quick little strides and left them together in the consulting room. The door shut with a soft click.

'Take a seat,' said Martin.

'No thanks.' The man's gaze was as steady as his frown. 'My daughter make you a cake?'

'Yes, she did, but—'

'You tell her she was a nice person?'

'Yes, I did, but there was no—'

The father looked irritated. 'I know she's been back here. She's been in your bedroom, probably? Agghhhh!'

'Mr Gibson, if I could take a moment to explain.'

'Has she been in your bed?'

'No she certainly hasn't.'

'That'll be the next thing though, won't it?'

'Mr Gibson—'

'I'm sorry she's done all that.'

'I beg your pardon?'

Melanie's father shook his head impatiently. 'I'm sorry. You know what young girls are like. I've seen her grow away from me in recent months. Classic early pubescent stage. Been expecting a bit of transference. You know, onto another authority figure. And here we are.'

'I see.'

'You just happened to be in the wrong place at the wrong time. You fix her shoulder – good on you – and you tell her she's a nice person, which she is, and the next thing you know she thinks you're God's gift and she gives you a goddamn cake. Silly girl.'

'Ah. Well. Yes.'

'I hope you haven't been overly inconvenienced.' Mr Gibson's movements were sharp, but concise, as if his body took the shortest possible route to the next position. He had an expression that remained solidly opaque.

Martin had the sense of an extraordinary willpower at work. 'Not at all.' His own movements were slow and vague in comparison.

'It'll wear off in due course, but I've spoken to her, and I'll keep an eye, for a week or two.'

'Thank you.'

'Nice to meet you.'

'And you too, Mr Gibson.'

'It sounds odd, but if there's any chance, I'd like to have the cake tin back? I'm baking tonight and it's the only tin we've got that will take a ten-and-a-half inch sponge.'

And so it seemed that the tower of loneliness that enclosed Dr Martin Ellingham without his being aware of it, or even giving credence to such a notion, was more dramatically exposed by the fact that *someone* was trying to reach him, and trying so nobly and with such innocence, with a genuine fondness for him in her heart – a young girl whose shoulder he'd put back into its socket. Melanie's misguided attraction towards him forcefully pointed out the absence of anyone else close to him – specifically the absence of Louisa, who might have, from time to time, wished to be close to him, when she wasn't thinking she'd like to be as far away from him as possible. For company, Martin had his suit and tie; for his sleeping companions he had the unmoving, unspeaking bits and pieces of furniture that stood in his room, waiting for darkness to disappear and daylight to intervene. The wardrobe, in particular, could be regarded as a receptacle that contained the many events, big or small, one by one, which had accrued to make him like he was – unapproachable, destructive of intimacy, distant – because the wardrobe was locked tightly shut and there was no key.

Melanie Gibson was young and surrounded by friends, and she could have reminded Martin, if he'd given it a moment's thought, that when he'd been as young as that, he'd walked alone, and at school had largely sat and stood alone. At the same time he could, if he'd chosen to do so, which he never did, look into the future and see that his heroically un-regarded loneliness would last until he reached the age of his Aunt Joan, because at the same time as Melanie had tried to steer herself closer to him, an old flame of his Aunt Joan's turned up and tried to reignite that past love affair. Martin, as if some didactic God on purpose wished to rub his nose in the nature of his own character, and make him actually *see* what was happening to him, was granted a ringside seat so he could watch and learn that in his old age, if things went on as they were, he wouldn't even be able to look back on any failed romantic adventures.

It started with the arrival in Portwenn harbour of an ocean-going Hanse yacht. A weather-beaten sailor could be seen on the deck, making anchor and locking up. He was unsteady climbing down into the tender, and as he started the motor and pulled away from the yacht he stumbled against the inflatable's side.

At the same time Martin had just come outside, followed by the dog, who slunk around his legs and continually glanced at him, as if Martin were the centre of its world and must always be kept that way, with continual adjustments to its stride, its pace and position. The dog was like an awful punishment inflicted on him by the county of Cornwall, for being an outsider.

As he strode down to the village Martin heard the rattle of the tender's outboard motor and he glanced out to the fine yacht at anchor in the harbour, with its orange satellite craft making a beeline for the shore. And even he recognised there was something odd about it: just when you thought the engine note should be dropping in order to navigate to the shore, the sound remained the same and, as the figure at the controls slumped forward, the pitch of the engine rose a notch and the boat accelerated.

Martin started to run – even from this distance he recognised unconsciousness in the form of the sailor's bent, motionless body. The noise of the engine intensified further and the breath sawed back and forth in Martin's chest as he ran down the slope. As he turned the corner and hit the sand on the beach he was in time to see the tender drive itself hard into the shallows and its propeller choke in the sand, where - upon it dived to a halt and threw the limp figure over the side and into the water. The heavy figure of Bert Large, plumber, was already splashing through the water, negotiating the rocks, to reach him. Martin thought for one moment about his suit, his shoes and socks, before following Bert.

The shock of the cold water had woken the incomer from his unconsciousness. 'It's all right,' said Bert, grabbing the stranger's arm and helping him up. 'I've got him. Everything's under control. When I was in the Scouts . . .' Bert slipped himself, then, and hauled on the stranger's arm. Bert kept his footing, but the stranger fell back into the surf and on the way down struck his head on a rock. '. . . I got my life-saving badge,' finished Bert.

By now Martin had reached the man, and somehow Louisa had appeared as well and was in the water alongside him. Together he and Louisa lifted the stranger and carried him to the shore.

Bert stood uselessly in the background. 'Mind your backs now,' he said, and spread his arms to the empty air.

He was quite light in their hands, and deeply tanned; it was obvious he had been sailing for a long time. They laid him down on dry sand. Martin looked down at the roguish, lined face, the eyes closed. 'Can you hear me?' asked Martin. 'I'm Doctor Ellingham. Can you tell me your name?'

The man stirred and his eyes flickered and stayed open. A confused expression grew on his face. 'Marty.'

'OK, Marty,' said Martin. 'Let's see if you can sit upright, shall we?' Together with Louisa, Martin began to help him sit up.

'No,' said the man. 'Not me. You. You're little Marty, aren't you?'

Louisa looked at Martin, and saw the uncertainty spread to his face, too. He obviously didn't know who this man was, or how he'd been recognised on a remote Cornish beach, and given the name used in his childhood.

An hour later, Martin had changed his clothes and was sitting at his surgery desk, making notes. A knock sounded expectantly on the door, and Martin knew who would appear. 'Come in?'

It was John Slater, as they now understood he was called, dressed in the clothes Martin had lent him, but without shoes or socks. He was a handsome man for his years, short and wiry in stature, a mane of golden hair just short of hippyish, with a knowing look in his eye that spoke of involvement in deals, in the give and take of life. 'Thanks for these,' he said, indicating the oversized clothes.

'Right, well, now you're dry let's have a proper look at you.'

John Slater submitted peacefully to Martin's examination. There was something practised in the way he offered his bare arm for the blood pressure cuff: it signified he'd done all this many times before.

Martin checked John's pupils with the torch. 'Look at me. Good, thank you. How come you lost control of your launch?'

'Don't know,' said John. 'Throttle jammed, I suppose.'

'I'd like you to stay in the surgery for an hour for observation.'

'Appreciate your concern,' said John, 'but I've got things to do.'

'Uh-huh.' Martin remembered the figure slumped in the boat. 'Nevertheless. If you need to call your wife or family and let them know you're here?'

'No family. No wife – or at least, not one I've spoken to for twenty years.'

Martin looked down at John's bare feet. 'Your ankles are swollen.'

'It's being at sea. Hasn't stopped me dancing, though.'

Martin could sense the pieces of the puzzle slotting into place. He knew it was best sometimes to wait, until further pieces appeared. 'Any light-headedness or dizziness?'

'No.'

'Well, you're not concussed. Take the shirt off for me; I'll have a listen to your chest.'

'Thanks, but I'm fine.'

'Look, if you don't let me examine you properly, I can't—'

John interrupted, 'I'm fine.'

Yet Martin could tell from the way the other man buttoned his cuffs – in fact the whole way he behaved in the surgery – that he was used to this sort of place. He thought about it for a moment – taking into account the man's age. 'OK,' he said, 'whatever. If you'd like to give me your details, I'll report your *fine-ness* to your GP.'

'You don't remember me, do you? I'm a friend of Joan's? Used to live here many moons ago. I took you and Joan on a day trip to Padstow in my boat, once.'

Martin tried, but couldn't remember either the man or the boat trip. He shook his head.

'We had to come back early. You wet yourself and Joan didn't have any spare trousers.'

'Right, well, that must be an amusing memory for you.' Suddenly, Martin wanted to get rid of this Slater – whoever he was. 'Can I have the name and address of your GP?'

'I haven't got a GP. I live in Hong Kong. How are they?'

'Who?'

'Joan and Phil.'

'Phil? Phil's dead.'

'Dead?'

'Years ago.'

'And Joan?'

'Joan's as strong as an ox.'

'I bet,' said John meaningfully. He remembered for a while – Joan and Phil. 'What happened to Phil – how did he die?'

'I don't know.'

'How can you not know?'

'Well, as you've just reminded me, I was about ten years old at the time and busy wetting myself, so you'll have to forgive me. If you're a friend of Joan's, why don't you ask her yourself?'

John didn't answer for a while. He was thinking about Joan, and remembering the farm – the path leading to the door, the stone flags underfoot.

Martin mentioned it when he next saw his Aunt Joan: she was unloading vegetables and carrying them into the farm produce shop. He stopped and said, 'Chap in town claiming to be your friend. John Slater. Obnoxious. He didn't know Phil had died and so I assumed he couldn't be much of a friend.'

Joan looked at him from beneath her sheep's wool hair. 'John? Where?'

'His yacht's just outside the harbour. Presumably he's on his yacht.'

'John Slater lives in Hong Kong.'

'Well, he crashed his launch in Portwenn.'

Joan couldn't carry another box of vegetables. Not at the moment. Memories came rushing back. 'Good grief. Is he all right?'

'Think so, yes. Bert tried to knock him out, but didn't quite manage.'

Joan found that she was repeating herself. 'Is he all right?' It was a different question for her – it meant, was he alive, after all these years; did he actually exist? Was he happy? Married?

'Yes, I just said. He's fine. Why?'

Joan was flustered. She felt like her life had been turned around to face backwards, suddenly. She didn't like the feeling that she might lose control. 'For God's sake,' she said, 'stop asking me questions! I'm just not here.' She started to head round to the driver's side of the vehicle.

'He's already asked about . . .' Martin stopped because he realised that the figure coming towards them was John Slater himself. He looked like a retired rock star, one of the shorter ones, wearing Martin's outsize clothes. Instinct told Martin to keep this man away from his Aunt Joan, but it was too late.

John, arriving at a slow pace up the slope, had recognised Joan from the way she carried herself, just the imprint that the shape of her character made on the world. He said, 'Joan?'

Joan was flummoxed; she'd no sooner been reminded of his past existence than he was here, a new version of him, anyway – a shorter, more tanned version – but still the same. The surprise meant she couldn't speak; she had to wait until different thoughts chased each other through her mind: same old John; the depth and number of wrinkles on his face; the same expression of amused intrigue.

'I think Joan would like to be left alone,' said Martin.

'Bugger off, Little Marty,' said John, without even sparing one second from looking at Joan.

Martin loomed closer. 'I don't think you understand,' he began.

'It's all right, Martin,' said Joan. 'I'm fine.' She felt in an extraordinary position suddenly: she spent so much of her life going about the place practically invisible, which is what it felt like for older women who *had* previously been looked at; and yet now she was in the street getting into a fight with an ex.

Martin moved away a few paces. He didn't want to leave his aunt alone with the man, but at the same time it was obvious they needed to talk in private. He held his peace and waited.

John Slater squinted quizzically at Joan. 'You're looking good,' he said. That line always worked.

Joan had found her way back to normal life. She began to lift a crate of vegetables. 'What do you want, John?'

'Just passing through. Touring on my yacht.'

'You can't just . . . pop up. After . . .' She couldn't even count how many years ago it was.

'I was thinking of mooring here for a couple of days.'

It struck Joan that this was a bad idea. 'John,' she began.

He interrupted, 'We could meet for coffee or sex.'

She remembered that habit of his: knocking polite conversation out of the water suddenly. An old roué's trick.

John said, 'I love that school teacher look. Make the funny lady do it again.'

Joan was already climbing into her vehicle; and so was John climbing into the passenger seat. However, she felt that enough had been said. Certainly, more than enough had been actually *done* all those years ago. 'I think it would be best if you got back on your boat,' she said, but without rancour, 'and sailed off into the sunset.' She waited until John had got out, and then she drove away.

The incident was finished with, and Martin didn't really expect to see John Slater again although he suspected already that John had a medical history behind him. A normal person wouldn't have lied about losing consciousness while at the controls of a motor launch: it was a sign he was doing something he already knew he ought not to. Martin had prepared himself to accept he'd lose the clothes he'd lent, but as it turned out John not only returned them, but had also cleaned and pressed them beforehand.

'Had them washed and ironed,' said John, holding out the bag from the launderette. They were in the surgery's reception area; Elaine looked at John as if she'd just lifted up a stone and found him there.

'What have you been doing?' asked Martin in a peremptory tone.

'I told you,' said John, 'getting your clothes washed so I could . . .'

'No, I mean you look flushed. Out of breath.'

John waved at the cliff outside the window. 'Ah, I've forgotten what it's like in Cornwall. You have to *walk*. Sometimes even uphill.'

'Your breathing shouldn't be so laboured. It's only a small hill. Unless you ran? Come this way, let me have a look.' Martin walked back into his consulting room.

John followed, only so he could try and escape; but Martin wouldn't let him.

'You have a history of heart trouble,' stated Martin, with certainty. He plugged the stethoscope into his ears.

'In more ways than one,' said John. Suddenly he felt tired and old; he wanted to sink into a chair and be looked after. He resented the familiar sheen of sweat on his skin.

'Why didn't you tell me?'

'I haven't come here to get medical care.'

Martin listened to John's heart. 'Abnormal rhythm,' he said.

'Atrial fibrillation,' said John in a bored voice. 'Rheumatic fever when I first got to Hong Kong. Embolism. Angioplasty. Stent. You name it.'

'Are you on medication?'

'You joking? The boat rattles every time I go about.'

'You lost blood pressure when you were in the launch, didn't you? That was no accident.'

'I forget what the technical term is. Yes, when I stand up, sometimes my blood pressure drops suddenly.'

'Orthostatic hypotension.'

'That's the one.' John buttoned his shirt. 'I lose control. Doesn't last very long. Not, generally speaking, very serious, at least not on the open water.'

Martin unwrapped a fresh syringe. There was something satisfying in brand new, sterile, medical equipment. 'Not too clever on a motor launch though, at close quarters. You could have killed someone.' He found a plump vein on the inside of John's elbow, and as he drew back the plunger to take the blood, he turned away, so as not to see the chamber fill with red. He met John's eye.

'You all right?' asked John.

Martin didn't want to give way. This was his profession and it was required of him to retain authority. He carried on, 'I'll send this sample for a sedimentation rate check. I presume you know what I'm talking about?'

John nodded.

'And I'll get you into Truro for some tests, pronto.'

'No thanks.'

'You understand, I think, that you could be seriously unwell.'

'I've lived with a dodgy heart for half my life. Don't get your knickers in a twist, Little Marty.' John looked at the tall, large-scale person that 'Little Marty' had become, and immediately knew that he, John, had been small-minded. 'Sorry. Difficult not to be living back in those times, coming here.'

'Luckily for you, Little Marty grew up to be a vascular specialist.'

'But I haven't come all this way to sit in a hospital in Truro.'

'And I dare say you haven't come all this way to be buried in Portwenn cemetery,' said Martin. 'Just to be clear, I'm not suggesting tests because I *like* you.'

'Just to be clear,' said John, 'I'm not going to the hospital. Whether you like me or not.'

'Fine,' said Martin, sealing the specimen envelope. 'That's your look-out. The blood test will take a day or two. Goodbye.'

John looked at the doctor on the other side of the desk. Fancy that – Little Marty had grown up to be a tetchy GP, practising here in the village where he'd taken his summer holidays as a boy. 'Blood,' said John, quietly – watching Martin's reaction. 'Blood.'

'Like I said, the results will be back in a day or two,' said Martin stiffly. 'And I'd ask you not to—'

'Not to what?' John was on the way out of the consulting

room. 'Oh. You mean, not to mess around with your Aunt Joan?'

Martin stared, mute. It's what he had meant, but he could see that his interference was ridiculous.

'You're right,' said John. 'It is none of your business.' He left the consulting room with the feeling that the person he'd left behind – was Little Marty, after all.

Martin didn't feel that way – he was Grown-up Martin, and he was protective of his aunt: it was unfair that a seriously ill man had descended on her and tried to recruit her to tend to his years of failing health. John Salter needed to be picked up and moved further away from Joan, and *vice versa*.

He made the time for a specific trip to Haven Farm, to see his Aunt Joan, to try and get people to where they ought to be. He found her leaning into the frame of a shed door with a screwdriver, re-affixing a hinge. 'Just wanted to see if you were all right,' he said.

'I'm always all right,' said Joan. 'I've been all right all my life. Good old reliable Joan. All right, all right, all right.'

'This Slater chap.'

'John, you mean.'

'There's something wrong with him. I think he's looking for someone to sit beside his hospital bed.'

'Oh for goodness' sake. Maybe you think he's come to stake a claim on my millions? Martin, Slater Containers could *buy* Cornwall. He could have a whole row of people sitting beside his hospital bed. He can usually get anything he wants.'

Martin felt like he was the parent – warning her off unsuitable men. 'I just think it's . . . well, clearly he's hurt you once already.'

'Marty, Marty . . .' She was going to question his qualifications in giving any kind of relationship counselling, but she looked at him standing there, her tall, clever, solitary nephew, and she felt in her bones how cruel that would be – that she'd be kicking the door down to reveal a large empty space, where a close, intimate human relationship should have been, but never had. 'Your idea of relationships is straight out of the eighteenth century,' she said instead. 'Marty, it was *I* who hurt *him*. I sent him packing. So please don't make assumptions about whether people are decent or not, until you know the facts.' She gave a last twist of the screwdriver, and wagged the shed door back and forth to check it worked. She slung the screwdriver in the box, clipped it shut and headed indoors. She could feel her grown-up nephew following her. How much she'd *always* loved Marty. Ever since he was small he'd been following her about the place, here at Haven Farm. A haven. Yes.

Martin was digesting the idea that there were things he didn't know about his aunt's life. He'd always thought that when he wasn't there, her life stopped, or at least only ticked over in a minimal way, until he reappeared.

They went into the house. 'You were enamoured?' asked Martin.

Joan almost did laugh. 'We bonked, Martin. We were lovers.'

'But you married Phil.'

'Indeed I did. Evidently.'

'And – what – John couldn't accept it? That you chose to marry Phil?'

She rolled her eyes and said tetchily, 'Martin, I was *already* married to Phil.'

'Oh.'

'Yes. Oh.'

'I, uh – right. Sorry.'

'Sorry's no use to anyone. Go and do your job. Cure a few people.'

Joan fretted away at her memories of John Slater: she leafed through them as if they were a set of old postcards – messages from the past – that had suddenly fallen out of the attic. Several times she went through what had happened, picture after picture: the hotel room, the picnics at The Longstone where once he'd arranged in advance a table and two chairs, the motor car and their various parking places – each event held its meaning, and marked her progress through the affair and out the other side, back to her marriage, with John Slater gone.

After a while, she realised she must go and find him. No doubt tomorrow he would weigh anchor and leave, and she'd regret it, if she didn't *talk* to him.

She was certain where she'd find him: the same place he always went when he was moored offshore: the pub. Sure enough, she glimpsed him through the window before she went in, and it was a classic snapshot: he was leaning one elbow on the bar, weight on one leg, the one ankle just neatly cocked against the other, and with his hand wrapped comfortingly around a pint glass. He was talking, and there were several people listening, including two smiling women. He caught her eye and moved from his position. She went in just as he was coming out; and his hand was on her shoulder, asking her to come in for a drink. She asked if they could go for a walk instead of staying in the pub. She didn't want to join that group, to be overheard or watched.

They fell into the same matching stride they'd always had. It could have been twenty years ago. 'Martin came over, and I found myself defending you,' said Joan, 'and so I found myself speaking up for you. And then it seemed churlish not actually to speak *to* you.'

'I've been hearing about Phil,' he said. 'I'm sorry.'

'I hope there's a nicer way to go than motor neuron. And I hope there are people around who know how to nurse their loved ones better than I did.'

'Wish I'd known,' said John.

'You were just married. What would have been the point? Sorry I couldn't come, by the way.' She took a breath and asked, 'Is she with you? Slaving in the galley?'

'Amy? Amy and I . . .' he shook his head resentfully, 'we lasted five minutes. She wasn't you.'

'Oh don't be ridiculous.' Joan wasn't going to be doing with such smarmy nonsense. She always did have to slap down his chat-up lines, while at the same time she rather enjoyed them.

'It's true. Gave up with women after that.'

'Course you did. Then why didn't you come back?' Their footfall was like a gentle metronome. They'd always talked better when they walked.

'You sent me away; what could I do? I was a man in exile, alone and without a penny to my name . . .'

'Oh, sob, sob. How long did that last?'

'I admit the finances sorted themselves out.' He added, 'So listen, if it's not full-on sex, what about coffee?'

They were down by the harbour, where her car was parked. The secret life of the sea continued beneath the surface, black as oil in the darkness. 'John,' she began, 'I haven't got room in my life anymore. And we're both a hundred and five.' She could see his disappointment like a shadow in the moonlight.

John Slater soaked up his old girlfriend's face, the same face he'd loved so much, thirty odd years before.

It might have been a time for looking back; but when Martin fixed the top button of his pyjamas and propped himself up in bed, he thought about the way in which bilirubin is processed by the liver, the remarkably clear pictures of the kidney offered by ultrasound; he thought about strep throat, ovulation, hypertension and myocardial infarction – heart attack; he wondered about the effect of a fresh fish diet on atherosclerosis. He thought about incontinence, abdominal hernia, gastric ulcers, about discharge from the ear, breast lumps, osteoma, sinusitis, neurapraxia.

Somewhere in the room, among his possessions – but Martin wouldn't have a clue where it was or even if it was there – was a battered cardboard box that he had never opened, which had inside it several fat, satisfying envelopes full of old photographs from his childhood; and they would have matched up with some of the memories recently discussed by his Aunt Joan and John Slater: a row of ten legs and feet all standing together, big next to small, during a picnic in the dunes; Smartie, his aunt's collie at that time, resting his jaw trustingly on Martin's chest, eyes closed in the sun; Martin's father standing up to his waist in the sea, body board at the ready; the bike Martin had used whenever he'd stayed at his aunt's; his mother a tiny figure standing on a hilltop. There was one photograph that showed a much younger John Slater, in the background but unmistakeably him, leaning over to scoop up a beach towel, his swimming shorts clinging to his legs. Joan was half turned away from him, wearing a brilliant smile. All these pictures had remained unseen for many years.

A disturbing image came into Martin's mind, of all the hearts in Portwenn lying in all the beds in all the houses, beating away. He found himself for some reason worrying about keratoconjunctivitis, and the inadequate production of tears in eyes suffering from various conditions, and in such cases artificial tears being required to be applied at frequent intervals.

*

John Slater wasn't on his boat the next morning, as Joan had thought he would be. Instead he arrived at Haven Farm in a taxi; and even though she called over to him that he'd better ask the taxi to wait because it was a long walk back, instead the taxi reversed and left the yard and John Slater walked towards her, strangely, with one arm held behind his back. 'I thought flowers would be cheesy,' he said.

'Too bluddy right they would be,' said Joan.

'So I brought some,' he said, and out they popped from behind his back, and she remembered: same old John – the 'flowers' were just bits and pieces that he'd picked from the hedgerows: ferns, ivy, cow parsley, bracken. She loved him for that.

He asked her to spend the day with him, and claimed that if she refused he would come back once every thirty years to try again, so she might as well give in now and get it over with. She looked at the flowers, and funnily enough it was the length of gold ribbon that tied them together, neatly fastened with a bow, that did it for her: the beauty of the ribbon, attached to the casual amateurish nature of the collection of greenery, from a man who was so rich, after all – it nearly broke her heart. She went in and got cleaned up and changed, and they headed off together in her car, for a destination that John wouldn't reveal. She knew several miles before they got there where they were heading: many times they'd met here, at The Longstone, a curious outcrop of rock that stood at the head of a secluded cove, with beautiful views along the valley upstream and, the other way, out to sea. It was a bit of a walk and John made sure to arrive first, even though it meant a sheen of sweat arrived on the surface of his skin and he was out of breath. He reached into his pocket and his hand closed around the pills; he popped the lid and took a celebratory medication. He'd keep going. It was all here; it was ready.

When Joan looked up she smiled and said, 'You should have told me. I'd have brought the cheese and pickle sandwiches, and the thermos flask.'

'Ah,' said John.

They moved a pace or two further, to the other side of the rock, and there it was, exactly as it had been in her memory: a picnic table and two chairs. On the table was a Tupperware box, of the old type, the plastic clouded and opaque, and a cheap plastic flask, orange, again straight out of the seventies. She could not believe it – but he nodded, yes: cheese and pickle sandwiches and a flask of coffee.

By the end of that picnic – no, halfway through – Joan knew she'd made a decision: pack up Haven Farm and run away with John Slater. It filled her with a marvellous recklessness. The air was suddenly more full of oxygen; the future was a mysterious mist rather than a rut. Her physical self had been transplanted into a different world – the world of John Slater. It was a moment, she realised, of great femininity, and she hadn't felt like a female for ages.

The very first thing she had to do was to tell Martin. She looked at Martin's frown, at his unhappy face, so different from John Slater's optimism. 'I think I still love him,' she said simply. It was that same evening, and she'd hurried to Martin's surgery to ask for his permission – that's what it felt like, anyway. They were standing in Martin's kitchen, and Joan was having the same feeling she'd had all day: that everything was upside down, and she was in a rush, and this might be the last time she stood here, or did this, or talked to this person. 'I do,' she repeated, 'I *know* I still love him.'

'Right,' said Martin.

'I always did. Yet I sent him away, told him I didn't. Martin, I hope you never have to know what that is like. But now, it's *possible* to love him. There's nothing in the way. Before, there was Phil and you, and then there was *his* wife, or so I thought. But now I can't think of an earthly reason why we shouldn't . . . Apart from the fact that I'm a certified ancient monument. Is it mad for a woman of my age to . . . ? It *is* mad, isn't it?'

'I don't think it's a good idea,' said Martin.

'Of course you don't. You're Martin, aren't you? You don't think anything's a good idea.'

'I really don't think it's a good idea.'

'Why ever not?'

The truth was – Martin wasn't able to say; he was bound by patient confidentiality. He was bound *not* to mention that two hours previously, in the surgery, John Slater had come to find out the results of his blood test. Not to mention that John not only had rheumatic heart disease, which he already knew about, but that he'd also developed an infective endocarditis; he would need a hospital visit for intravenous antibiotics and probably surgical intervention, and without it he'd be dead from septicaemia within six weeks. And that even with that intervention, even with some more work on his leaky valves and on the heart's lining, he probably had only as long as a year to live.

Martin was bound not to mention these things. He was obliged to watch his aunt walk towards a catastrophic grief and be unable to do anything about it. 'I just think it's a bad idea,' he said.

'Look at your face!' said his Aunt Joan. 'What's the matter with you? You live in one of the most beautiful places in the world and you go around like someone stuffed a cactus up your botty.'

'It's just that he's not . . . He's not . . .'

'Martin, apart from your father, who never liked John and never will, you're my only family. I don't need your blessing. But I would like it.'

'What did you mean,' asked Martin, 'when you said there was Phil, and there was me?'

Joan suddenly saw herself as if from a long way off: an old woman whose life had just been upended in the most unexpected way by the re-appearance of a former lover, and who now found herself saying things she never thought she would, with feelings she'd never thought she'd feel . . . If it was a season for honesty, then perhaps it was time for Martin to know the truth. When she spoke, her tone of voice was urgent. 'Remember you asked me why your summer visits to me stopped, when you were a child?'

Martin gave the answer before she could. 'Dad.'

'Yes. Your father. He found out about John and me, and he wouldn't countenance sending you to stay with a woman guilty of such gross moral turpitude.' She could feel again the horrible twist of the punishment – the way it caught and held her, as if at the point of a knife. She carried on, 'It was cruel of him. He knew I loved you like a son. And still do.'

In Martin's mind, all the years he hadn't come down to Portwenn began to count themselves, and with each year the sense of injustice added to the sense of loss. Martin felt how that one decision of his father's had made his teenage years a kind of desert – a long trudge through suburbia. This woman standing in front of him was the key that could unlock . . . He stopped himself. He was overwhelmed with confusion and a sense of loss. He said, 'But you broke it off with John. So I *could* have come down, then.'

'He still wouldn't send you. I can't forgive him for that.'

'You sent John away, for me?'

'Don't get carried away. Not just for you. For Phil, too. For the sake of my small but precious family. My husband, and my son. My virtual son.'

Martin couldn't perform embraces, nor tears. Yet what he needed, at the moment, was both of those things.

'Say something, Marty. Come on. Be *happy* for me.'

Yet he couldn't. He was bound not to tell her something

she didn't know: that it would end in grief, in tears, and soon.

Joan held out her arms, and Martin obligingly stepped into them, and they felt themselves in the unfamiliar territory, for both of them, of an embrace. For Joan it was a sign of Martin's approval of what she was doing; for Martin, it was a rehearsal for when he'd have to console his aunt and watch while she suffered.

After she'd gone, he drank his usual glass of water, and found himself standing uselessly, without purpose, in various parts of his kitchen, while recent events played out in his head. He made a tour of the downstairs rooms to switch out the lights, and then took to the stairs; and each of the wooden treads sounded hollowly – dum, dum, dum.

He went into his bedroom and switched on the light, and the wardrobe with its mirror sprang to life: and it was like seeing a ghost; there was this sudden haunting, because the wardrobe had, whether it wanted to or not, become a prop in the reckoning of his own emotional life, or rather, lack of it, because a girl's *face* was brilliantly illuminated in the mirror: a young girl, smiling now, a pile of dark hair, impossibly real – because it *was* real, and the strangled expression of horror died in Martin's throat. There was no need to be frightened; the mirror held a reflection of his bed, and in his bed lay Melanie, the one with the cake-baking father, holding the covers up to her shoulders.

It took just two seconds: Martin determinedly ordered her

to get dressed and leave immediately, while he stood like a post facing in the other direction.

Melanie burst into tears and stumbled from the bed; she clumsily pulled on her underwear. 'I thought it would be like Romeo and Juliet,' she moaned, but the soldier-like stiffness of Doctor Martin Ellingham didn't alter. She hoiked up her jeans and tied her trainers and buckled her little blue sparkly belt. 'I'll be leaving now, then,' she announced, more calmly but her breathing still ragged. She headed for the window.

'Not through the window,' ordered Martin.

'Ohhh . . .' Melanie huffed and dragged herself off through the door. There was the clump of her footsteps down the stairs. When the front door slammed Martin breathed a sigh of relief. The bedclothes, thrown back, made their comment on this invasion of his empty life. When he was in his pyjamas and he climbed between the covers, a trace of Melanie's warmth was left behind, like a signal from a far-off land.

For one whole day Martin had to disallow all feelings of abandonment. His aunt, who was more than his aunt, more like an honorary mother, was leaving him behind. He was, as always, buried in his work. It was like a blanket, or a dense fog through which he moved, with the rest of his life thankfully invisible; he only saw – or maybe he only chose to see – the medical puzzles that emerged in front of him, in his consulting room and out in the village.

Louisa saw him, the next morning, staring at women's

breasts. She was on her usual Sunday-morning perch in The Crab and Lobster, reading the papers in the cool interior, and from the window she saw Martin, the only person in a suit and tie, incongruous among a throng of holiday-makers. There were two attractive forty-something women, one of them taking an ice-cream from her friend; and both of them arranged themselves to catch the sun. Martin ogled them – there was no other word for it, thought Louisa – as he passed by. And then he came back and stared harder at the woman's breasts. Louisa remembered when he had first stared at her, on that train . . .

The two women were perfectly relaxed about being stared at while Martin went past, but when he came back, and stared harder – that was rude. 'Excuse me?' said the one, with a seasoned tone of voice that spoke of many men being rebuffed.

'Do you mind?' said the second one.

Martin, ridiculous in his suit and tie, said, 'I want to examine your chest.'

'I don't think so,' said the second woman.

'Just above the right breast.'

'What?'

'Have you had that looked at?'

The second woman, the friend, stood up and pointed her ice-cream at Martin. 'What the hell are you going on about?'

'I wouldn't sunbathe,' said Martin.

'Bugger off.' She waved the ice-cream. 'Go on.'

Martin decided gloomily to do what he was told. 'Might

be a melanoma,' he muttered as he turned around and walked off.

He hadn't gone more than a few paces when he felt Louisa's presence alongside him. He glanced at her, and the sudden chocolate-box beauty of her face, her expression, the kindliness there, offended him. It felt dangerous, and was accompanied by fear.

'Martin!' she said. 'Martin.'

He felt her hand on his arm and he paused. 'What?'

'I saw what just happened – that was unfortunate. It reminded me of the train . . . I just wanted to say, maybe you should introduce yourself before you try and . . .' She stopped, because Martin was walking determinedly onwards, obviously offended. She added, 'Don't worry, I'll go back and explain.' She couldn't help smiling, especially since she remembered her own confusion, when he'd done the same to her: staring rudely at her eye.

'I don't need you to apologise for me,' said Martin, and kept going.

Louisa fell back and watched him go. She was used to the sensation, now, of being hurt by his clumsiness; but somehow, for a reason that she couldn't quite bring herself to think about, she didn't mind so much; she found she could wear the hurt easily, as if she had partitioned it off in a separate area where it was not quite real.

She returned to the outside of the pub and found the two women still enjoying the sun. It felt good for her to be able to explain they'd just enjoyed a typical encounter with

Portwenn's eccentric and unlikeable doctor. And somehow, she thought as she wandered back into the pub, the dysfunctional, charmless nature of Martin's social interactions afforded him, in her eyes, a rare integrity.

As it happened, Martin didn't lose his Aunt Joan, after all. Her tone of voice was different when she rang him to ask if he might come up to Haven Farm – and the invitation itself was proof something had gone wrong.

When she pulled open the door to answer his knock, and there she stood – grey sheep's wool hair a cloud around her face, the frank, open expression, the determined set of the mouth and the purposeful stride back into the house – he even knew what it was that had happened.

'I've been a stupid, stupid fool,' she called out.

They sat at the kitchen table and Joan described how John Slater had asked her down to The Crab and Lobster and told her that he was, in fact, married; he had quite a new wife, called Laura, and his dalliance with Joan had only been a bit of fun while his wife was off the boat, and he hadn't realised Joan would take it so seriously . . .

Joan moved bits of paper pointlessly around the kitchen table, adjusted the position of the vase of flowers, and carried on.

John Slater had revealed that Laura, his *wife*, was flying in unexpectedly, so he had to end things with Joan, now, but perhaps it was for the best. She described how angry she had become: she'd told John Slater (she couldn't call him by just his first name anymore) that he used to be a decent man but he had become a monster, hadn't he? She didn't know who to feel the most sorry for, John Slater himself or this Laura. She had left the pub in tears, she confessed to Martin – 'like a teenager,' she added, with new tears standing in her eyes at the memory. 'So there you have it,' she said. 'Maybe he was taking his revenge for my sending him away all those years ago. But tomorrow, he's sailing at first light. Off, on his boat. He'll probably have forgotten me after his first tack out of the harbour.' She placed the palm of her hand on the table between them. 'You knew there was something wrong, didn't you, Marty? But I wouldn't listen. I thought you were behaving like a big baby with your nose out of joint. I thought you'd have said anything to put me off him. I'm sorry about that. I underestimated you. Who'd have thought it, hmm? I'm so sorry.'

Martin couldn't remember feeling such anger on someone else's behalf. The Lexus spat out chips of stone and clouds of dry mud when he reversed out of Joan's yard and took off; he found himself driving through the country lanes as fast as a local, which he'd never done before.

Later that evening, it was easy enough to find John Slater in The Crab and Lobster. Martin walked into the pub fuming, but half an hour later he walked out with all anger having drained away, replaced by sorrow, a sense of the weight of suffering that pressed down on all human lives, big or small. He considered driving back up to Haven Farm, but it was already eleven o'clock at night and he made the decision to drive up at first light.

He slept heavily, and dreamed of being dressed in the wrong clothes at a golf tournament, of all things. He'd never played golf in his life.

The next morning he awoke at 5am and his eyes repeatedly opened even after he'd tried to sleep again.

There was one phrase his aunt had used, last night, which had stuck in Martin's head: she'd said, 'I hope you never have to suffer this heartache, Marty . . .' But he looked around at his life, at the borders of it, and found he was quite safe; no such heartache would have to be looked back on, at all.

He rose and dressed with his habitual care, and drove back up to Haven Farm. There was no one there. The chickens had been let out; the dog lay peacefully in the yard. She'd risen, and she'd gone somewhere; Martin thought he knew where.

It took another half an hour in the car, and a twenty-minute walk along the rim of the wooded valley that was so familiar to him from his childhood, but he found her – yes – at The Longstone. There wasn't a sail in sight. The sea was an even, solid blue, as if it soaked up and condensed the pale blue of the sky.

Joan wore a coat, against the freshness of a summer dawn. Her hands were thrust into the pockets and she stood as if braced against the tilt of the sea. 'I'd like to be on my own, Marty,' she said – there wasn't a trace of criticism or rancour in her tone.

'All those times we came here,' asked Marty, 'were they always to watch him sail?'

She nodded. 'Affairs taint everything. But they were good times, too, weren't they?'

'Yes. They were.'

Her gaze returned to the sea. It was still empty, faintly corrugated with a light swell on its distant surface. 'Well, you hated his guts, Marty. We'll both be pleased to see the back of him.'

Martin felt that he had received so many confidences that it was uneven, and he, too, should say a few things that were difficult to admit. 'What you said before, about my behaving like a big . . .' He couldn't bring himself to say the word 'baby'. He went on, 'My feeling displaced. Perhaps there was some truth in that. I would have said anything to put you off him, it's true. You didn't underestimate me.'

'You are forgiven,' said Joan easily. 'After all, you were right.'

'But,' said Martin, 'I underestimated John Slater.'

'What do you mean?'

Martin put aside any idea of patient confidentiality. Out here, with such a landscape at their backs, and in front of them the whole scope of the sea and the sky, he told his aunt about John Slater's heart, his test results, and how short a time he had left to live. He told her how, last night, he'd found John Slater in order to confront him, but instead he'd learned there *was* no wife – Slater had invented the story in order to drive Joan away, and keep her away, while he went about the business of a solitary death, and meanwhile saved her the grief, for the second time in her life, of nursing a beloved into the grave.

Joan, unblinking, watched Martin closely while he spoke of these events, about which she knew nothing, and hadn't guessed. She felt a renewal of her filial love for her nephew and recognised the weight of responsibility he'd carried on his shoulders as if she'd carried it herself. At the same time the love and belief she'd held for John Slater returned, redoubled, and she picked it up again – she was exhausted by feeling, and rooted to this unmoving spot.

Together they waited until a dainty white triangle appeared, a tiny shape against the blue: it was John Slater's sail, carrying him away.

6

Louisa Glasson, school teacher, counted twenty-eight children's heads. She waved her arms, and shooed them along the corridor towards the gym. 'Come on 5G. Sometime this year would be good.'

Lingering resentfully to one side was Peter Cronk. Louisa couldn't look at him without thinking of the broken bird tables, and how he'd allowed them all to think he'd done it. 'Come on, Peter. That means you.'

'Miss, I've got a note,' he said in a desultory voice.

'OK. You can sit in the library.'

'Thanks.' Peter shouldered his bag and wandered off.

There was something about that walk, thought Louisa. Years of experience told her that the slight roll, the move - ment of the shoulders, the half-glance backwards meant the note didn't actually exist, or he'd written it himself. 'Hold on,' she called out. 'Let's see the note.'

Peter made an immediate about turn and stomped back towards her. 'I don't know why we do PE,' he moaned. 'It's not education. It's just running about.'

'Well, Peter, why do we do anything?'

Peter slumped along, behind the others. 'Oh, right you are, Miss, it all makes sense now. Thanks, Miss.'

Louisa caught him up. 'That's all right, Peter.'

'Look, I hate sport and I'm not learning anything. It's a waste of the taxpayers' money.'

'Sometimes we just have to get the heart beating, the blood pumping,' said Louisa.

'That's not a reason. Saying you have to do something doesn't explain *why* you have to do it.'

'Enough, Peter. There's only a small amount of time I can give to useless listening.'

Peter moved along reluctantly, dragging his bag on the floor.

Outside the changing rooms, she did have to admit that Peter was the kind of boy who shouldn't have to do games. His body looked incapable of co-ordinated movement. His skin was as white as cheap margarine. There wasn't a muscle on him. He was all brain.

'Can we *not* play a team game?' he asked, sticking close to Louisa, embarrassed by his ghastly gym shorts. 'I hate team games.'

'That's why you should play them.'

'There you go again. Do you actually think that's logical?'

'Do you actually think I'm stupid enough to try and argue with you?'

'"Team games" just means everyone *teams* up against me. I don't fit in.'

'Yes you do. You will. I'll make sure of it. You are my

special project, young man. The rescue, and the fitting-in, of Peter Cronk.'

'Is that because you've given up on the rescue and fitting-in of Doc Martin?'

'I'll give up on you, if you don't mind your own business.'

'I can mind my own business very satisfactorily,' said Peter in a stentorian voice, 'in the library.'

Martin's haemophobia had somehow become common knowledge. He first realised when he was treating Neville, a surfer who was so laid back as to be horizontal, and Neville, in his drawl, asked, 'I don't need a blood test, then?'

'You have an ear infection, Neville. There's no need for a blood test.'

'Just wondered. You'd have to take the blood, wouldn't you? I mean, there's no nurse or anything to do it for you.'

'There's no nurse,' confirmed Martin.

Another time, he was treating a mole on Don Hennessy's neck. He pressed the freezer against the skin and Don asked, 'Will it bleed? I'm another one not keen on the old red stuff.'

Martin had grunted, and pressed down harder on the freezer.

'I'm just saying,' said Don, 'I'm not big on blood. Mind, I don't have a phobia about it like you do.'

Martin worked the freezer much harder.

'I can feel that,' cried out Don. 'I can feel that.'

'Really?' said Martin.

But then an incident arose that threatened to damage Martin's reputation permanently. It started with a call from Elaine. 'Bert's hurt himself in the Crab!'

Martin grabbed his bag and ran. It was only a few hundred yards downhill and he was there, pushing through the swing doors. There weren't many inside; it was still early, before the lunchtime crowd.

'Through here,' said the landlord, his arms spread wide.

Some figures – two, three people – were standing around on his way through to the kitchen. There was an atmosphere of intense concentration.

Among the stainless steel surfaces, sinks and shelving units in the pub's kitchen Bert was an incongruous figure, sitting on a stool someone had fetched from the bar. He was missing his woollen hat, which made him look vulnerable. People gathered around uneasily – Martin recognised some of them, including Bert's son, Al.

'Bert,' said Martin. At least his patient was conscious, upright and breathing, he thought.

Bert smiled benignly. He looked right as rain.

'We thought we were going to lose him,' said Al.

'Got me real good,' said Bert. 'The drill bit went right in. Saw the old life flash before the eyes.' He touched his left arm – and the sleeve was soaked in blood.

Suddenly, Martin got it. He felt the anger like a stone in his throat. 'I see,' he said. 'Oh, hilarious.'

'What?' asked Bert.

Martin swung round to face his audience. 'The doctor has

an issue, let's set him up. I do actually have real patients in the surgery.'

The eyes gazing at him were embarrassed, some of them; others looked shocked.

'Doc?' began Al.

'No.' Martin glared at Al, a young man whom he'd chosen to help. 'If you play practical jokes, then be prepared for the victim to be less than amused.'

'It's just that Dad's hurt,' said Al.

Bert had slid off the stool and stood there, clutching his arm.

'Oh, right.' Martin was ashamed to have been caught out – he'd let the conversations with Neville, and with Don, get to him. He'd made an embarrassing mistake. For one short moment he was grateful to be a doctor again, instead of being at the fag end of people's jokes. He could go back to work and forget what people knew about him. He stepped towards Bert, about to find the site of the injury. But then he saw that not only the arm but the whole of one side of Bert's shirt was covered in blood, below where he held the arm against his chest. The familiar panic froze his muscles and he couldn't move.

'You all right, Doc?' Bert's voice was a faint whisper.

'Let's get you . . . cleaned up.' Martin felt the shakes take hold. A sweat sprang from his forehead and from his collar. His breath was shallow. He pointed. 'We're going to run cold water over your arm, to wash away . . . if you could, wash away the . . .'

'The blood?' asked Al.

'You all right?' asked the landlord.

'I'll just get the . . .' Martin lifted the medical bag but missed the clasp and the bag fell from his grip. The contents scattered at his feet. He could feel the sweat spring from his palms as he kneeled to scoop them up. A bottle rolled away from him and he took a step to follow it, pick it up – and at the same time a powerful smell of vinegar reached him. He stood up, and for a while stared at Bert's blood-soaked shirt. His gaze moved to the stainless steel work surfaces; he was looking for proof. Sure enough, among the mustards and olive oils there stood three empty ketchup bottles. He stared at Bert and said in a low voice, 'Maybe you could do us all a batch of chips to go with the blood?'

Every face around him wore a grin.

Bert held out his ketchup-soaked arm. 'Ahhh, Doc,' he began affectionately. 'No need to take it hard, just a little joke on our old village doc. You're part of the community now. No harm done.'

Martin knelt to pick up the contents of his medical bag. 'I have patients waiting in my surgery,'

'They'll live for a moment longer, I spec,' said Bert. 'Meanwhile, we'd all like to buy you a drink for being a good sport and, more to the point, being a good ol' doc, you know . . .'

Martin straightened and without saying a word he was gone.

The smiles among those left behind broke into something

more: a sort of awe at what they'd done, and a touch or two of laughter, and a bit of fear. 'Should have seen his face!' said the landlord.

'I tell you,' said Bert, 'I didn't know if he was going to patch me up or faint in my arms.'

'You should be so lucky,' someone cried.

'You did always like 'em large-sized and comfortably off,' said the landlord.

But Al was serious. He remembered all that the doc had done for him, and he felt a bit frightened. 'He wasn't laughing,' he said. 'I don't think he will ever find that funny.'

The anger and humiliation stayed with Martin all the way out of the pub, along the narrow street and back to the surgery. This village was too small for him. He barely fitted down this alleyway. He could lift up these cottages and toss them into the sea. Through every doorway he had to duck his head. The village was populated by trolls and midgets and idiots. He walked blindly along and almost wilfully knocked aside a tourist who strayed into his path, and he cursed her, 'Will you . . . bloody well watch where you're going?'

When he arrived back he slammed the door to his consulting room, threw down his bag and slumped angrily in his seat. Outside the window, here at the back of the house, the cliff face reared up, hemming him in.

For a while he didn't hear the timid knock on the door. He didn't want to see another resident of this village ever again. When Elaine put her head around the door he couldn't bear the sight of her. When he learned there was a child injured up at the school he muttered under his breath, 'Boo hoo.'

Yet he had to pick up his bag, walk out through the waiting room. Without a word he left the building. As he walked down the slope he'd just climbed, the anger stayed with him. What did they think they'd been doing? He was a doctor, not a . . . well, not a . . . friend in the school yard or something.

He passed along the harbour and up the other side of the slope to the school. He already knew where the Sanatorium was, and went straight up without announcing himself. Some woman or other – he'd treated her once before for something – fluttered in front of him like a moth; and as she went ahead of him into the San he plainly heard her say to whomever was in there, in a low voice, 'Bad mood.'

'Too right I'm in a bad mood,' he said as he walked in. 'I understand a child has had a fall.' The sight of Louisa was like a knife between his ribs – she would hear of the practical joke. She would see his bad mood, right now, because he couldn't rein it in.

'It's Peter Cronk,' said Louisa, 'and he's fine, but I thought you should check him over in case he's cracked a rib or whatever. Just to be on the safe side.'

'He's fine, but best to be on the safe side?' Martin couldn't stop himself from biting her hand, as it were. 'Whereas a woman with a melanoma on her breast should be ignored?'

Louisa sprang back, angry at the injustice, 'That's not fair, and it's not what I said . . .'

Martin had moved on already; he leaned over Peter Cronk who lay on the bed, minus his school sweatshirt and with his shirt unbuttoned. 'Peter,' he said.

'I'm all right,' said Peter.

'Well, when you're the doctor, you can make that judgement, hmm?'

From behind him came Louisa's tight, angry voice. 'Right – I'll leave you to it, then.'

'Where does it hurt?' asked Martin.

Peter's face was solemn against the white of the pillow. 'It doesn't.'

'From how high did you fall, and how did you land?'

'I fell off the climbing bars, and I landed across one of the benches, on my front, here.' He patted his chest. 'Just bruising. Nothing broken.'

Martin pressed against Peter's sternum, and his ribs. The solemn face remained unmoved.

'Told you,' said Peter. 'I happen to know that with a cracked rib you get a crunching sound, or breathing difficulty, or—'

'Do you mind?' Martin wanted to concentrate without any more insane chatter from the boy.

'I've done some reading,' said Peter. He fully expected to win his way back into Martin's approval.

'Have you graduated from a medical degree with distinction?' asked Martin coldly.

'I was just—'

'Be quiet.' Martin's voice was actually loud.

Louisa, who'd lingered at the doorway, listened with dread. She ducked back into the room. 'Martin, can I have a word?'

Immediately Martin dropped his examination of the boy, picked up his bag and strode into the corridor outside the room. Louisa followed him and shut the door so Peter couldn't hear. 'What d'you think you're doing?' she whispered. 'He's ten years old . . .' She tried to read what was going on, but Martin's face was a mask, unmoving. It was frightening. For several seconds he was immobile. And yet she felt as if there was a torrent of thoughts and feelings passing between them. What had happened? What had she done wrong?

'Take him to the hospital,' Martin suddenly erupted, and strode off down the corridor.

'What?' Louisa followed – she was confused and hurt.

Without looking around Martin said, 'Obviously ten-year-olds and nursery school teachers know better than I do. That's fine.' And he added, airily, 'Get him checked over at the hospital.'

Louisa stopped, floored by that dismissive qualification – 'nursery school teachers'. She watched Martin's stiff, upright figure retreat down the corridor. His shoes seemed to make a thunderous noise compared to anyone else's. Any space he walked into he took over, and it was invaded by whatever mood he happened to be in. When he disappeared from sight, it was as if life itself – this place, the people in it, the colours and the shapes of things – dropped back to a more safe normality. She violently wished never to see him again.

She returned to the San and found Peter Cronk feeling more wounded than before. She sat on the edge of the bed and said carefully, 'I don't think that was anything to do with you; I think that was my fault.'

After a while Peter said thoughtfully, 'Mum says – don't show people you're clever, because if *they* aren't clever, they won't like it. But he *is* clever.'

She didn't have any answer for him – which often happened. Instead they got themselves ready for a drive to the hospital, as they'd been instructed. Peter was sore across his chest when he exerted himself, like on the stairs, but otherwise he was in good spirits. She accompanied him to her car, in the staff car park, and they both got in.

As usual, the business of the car – seat belts, steering, gear changes – together with the lack of eye contact, made a fertile area for conversation. 'If it's any consolation,' said Louisa, 'saying the right thing at the right time to the right person, let alone *doing* the right thing – no one finds that easy.'

'Do you love him?' came Peter's voice from the passenger seat, *her* passenger seat, right next to her. It felt shocking.

'No,' she said, and then, 'Who?' followed by a slump backwards into using the old stand-by, 'Mind your own business.'

Peter's smile was invisible to her, but she could feel it spread wide enough to reach her; it filled the car.

At the hospital they checked themselves in at the desk and then sat in adjoining plastic chairs to wait. After a while they were taken to Radiology where Peter was manoeuvred into the correct position for an X-ray. He felt curiously lonely when everyone else abandoned him for those few seconds it took the radiation to pass through his body. It felt incomprehensibly stagey, all the opening and closing of doors.

Afterwards they waited again, sitting on the same type of plastic chairs but in the corridor outside the Radiology Department. At a quarter to five the radiologist came out and headed in one direction, while a young female doctor, carrying the X-rays, came towards them, carrying a large brown envelope, with the flap loose at the top. She addressed Louisa. 'Mrs Cronk?'

Even as Louisa replied that she wasn't Mrs Cronk, but that she was Peter's class teacher, Louisa felt a curious wistfulness, actually, to *be* Peter's mother; it seemed like it would be an especial privilege.

The doctor smiled. 'Well you can tell his parents that no bones are broken. Just a bit of bruising, or what we call . . .' and now Peter's voice chimed with hers and they said the same thing at the same time, 'intercostal sprain.' The doctor looked at Peter and Louisa. 'You must have taught him well,' she said.

'If only,' said Louisa. 'Sometimes I think it's the other way around.'

'Well, take it easy. There'd be no harm in taking the rest of the week off school, OK?'

On the way home Louisa pulled over on the top of the cliff, seeing the ice-cream van was there, and she bought herself and Peter a cornet each and they sat on the top of the cliff looking out to sea. They talked about Dr Ellingham and how the whole village had found out he was afraid of the sight of blood, and they talked about Peter's mother who was afraid of her own shadow, and they asked themselves what they were most afraid of. Louisa said snakes, and Peter admitted he was afraid of heights, but then, as they worked their way through the ice-creams, they agreed that these initial answers didn't really count, because everyone was sort of afraid of snakes and heights – what was more important was for them to admit to what they were afraid of, in terms of other people. Peter said he was afraid of never really knowing anyone properly, not in the way in which he knew himself, and Louisa said she was afraid of dying alone and without having had children. Peter, in a very ordinary voice, said he would like to offer his services as Louisa's child, just as a stand-in until she had children of her own, and she gave his arm a squeeze and felt a wordless outpouring of love for the very odd and very clever Peter Cronk, aged ten, sitting next to her, while at the same time the terror descended, quickly, because this moment, now, might be the only time that life, or fate, would provide for her, to feel maternal love.

She drove Peter home; and his mother opened the door of her cottage. 'It's all right,' began Louisa; she'd heard of

Mrs Cronk's panic attacks but she was too late. For a moment, at the sight of Louisa, Mrs Cronk couldn't breathe. She clapped her hand against her chest and tried to suck in air.

'It's all right,' repeated Louisa.

'What's happened, what's wrong . . . ?' interrupted Mrs Cronk. She was fraught, breathless, moving her weight from one foot to another. She was pale and her hair was damp with sweat.

'Mrs Curnow got in touch with you, I believe?'

'Yes, but what's happened, I've just got in from work, what's happened?'

Peter walked in, adopting a jolly tone of voice. 'Mum, what's for tea? I'm starving.' He turned round to Louisa. 'Thanks for driving me home, Miss.' And then he added in a low voice, 'She always panics, sometimes.' A moment later he bounced back along the hallway, shrugging off his bag and dropping it, his mother waiting for him. 'Come on,' he called loudly, 'I fancy those potato wedges, maybe with the battered cod thingummies.' His mother followed him, blocking Louisa's view.

Louisa stepped backwards two or three steps, and pulled the door shut, suddenly excluded. As she walked back to the car, Peter's incoherent sentence echoed in her mind. 'She always panics, sometimes . . .' From a boy, about his mother, it seemed to Louisa that his contradictory response was filled with the deepest of human tenderness and forgiveness, and it spoke of Peter's effort to understand his mother and at the same time present her in the best possible light to the outside world, for his sake as well as hers. Louisa was touched with humility, thinking of the difficulties of those two lives, a worried mother and her clever son, so closely and permanently entwined in that tiny cottage.

When she got home Louisa showered and changed her clothes to reclaim herself, clean and whole, from the day's troubles. The emergency was over. She took her glass of white wine onto the tiny balcony.

She sat, alone, and felt the presence of the ocean not so far below her, as it weighed heavily in the bay, the tide drawing it back, now, inch by inch. She liked the thought of seawater, this heavy, life-and-death force, as old as the hills, named only recently the Atlantic ocean, touching the skirts of the place where she lived, and at the same time touching thousands of other places as well around its borders: in Canada and North America, in Spain and Portugal and France; and in all such places there were human hearts at work, trying to make the best of themselves.

It was around 6.15pm when she looked down onto the house below her, and saw the top of her neighbour's grey head of hair. She called down a 'hello' and received in return news of Martin's earlier debacle at The Crab and Lobster. It was a rumour that had been going around, but she hadn't quite believed it – a surgeon with an aversion to blood? She'd heard something about it earlier on the car radio, before Peter had turned down the volume. It sunk home: this was why he'd been in such a bad mood.

Her feeling of goodwill towards all people led her to decide to walk the short distance down past the harbour and up the slope the other side, to the surgery, where she thought she might knock on Martin's door and spread some of her new-found understanding and forgiveness in his direction – and at the same time tell him that Peter was all right.

With the sun dropping close to the horizon even as she walked along, and the coolness of the evening air making itself felt as she climbed into the shadow of the westward side of the valley, she felt all would be right with the world if only she could mend Doctor Martin Ellingham a little, now, and persuade him to join her, or let her join him, maybe, in keeping each other company for a while.

When he opened the door to her knock, she jumped in first with a big smile because there was good news. 'I took Peter to the hospital and he's fine. At home eating his tea with his mum.'

'Thank you.' Martin's answer was curt, but she now knew him well enough to believe she could get beyond that. She wanted it just to be simple, for him not to stand there like a doorman but to invite her in – or for her not to need an invitation, and simply walk in. He still had his suit and tie on. Did he never change out of work mode? 'I heard about the thing in The Crab and Lobster—' she began.

'My private concerns seem to provide this village with an endless source of amusement,' said Martin.

'I don't think the radio was the best—'

Martin interrupted, 'Don't you people have anything better to do than gossip?'

'"You people"? Is that me? Forgive me, Martin, but maybe a doctor being frightened of blood is worthy of discussion. Maybe not practical jokes and maybe they shouldn't have talked about it on a radio station, but—'

'I have a minor . . . blood issue. I don't need your sympathy.'

Louisa felt all the goodwill she'd harboured drain away. 'I was a lay-member of the panel that interviewed you, and I don't recall your minor blood issue being mentioned. That amounts to negligence at least.' As soon as she'd said this, she realised she'd lost all hope of achieving what she came here for: reconciliation and forgiveness. 'I'm sorry, I didn't mean that,' she said.

'For the record,' said Martin, 'I wrote in advance to the head of the PCT explaining in full—'

She interrupted, 'I said I didn't mean it.'

'What did you mean, then?'

Louisa sank underneath the sense of loss, and waste. An honest plea fell thoughtlessly from her lips. 'I don't know why *every* conversation we have is so . . . combative. Do you?' What she'd said, and how she'd said it, had left her vulnerable, open to hurt, and for a while Martin stared, and didn't answer.

And then Martin said, 'When I speak, it just makes things worse.'

She found this statement unbearably moving. At the same

time it made her angry, because it was the voice of a hurt child, and she didn't want a child, she wanted a grown man, and she should tell him so. 'That is so childish,' she said. 'I've spent all day with a ten-year-old; I don't want to spend the evening with one as well.'

'I think you just proved my point.' Martin felt miserable.

'Peter would have said that, too. You know something? Both of you deliberately stand outside the crowd, and then you wonder why you feel isolated.' She turned to go, but threw a parting comment over her shoulder. 'Apart from anything else, it's so selfish.'

She walked home quickly and went straight to bed without even cleaning her teeth or washing – she just wanted the covers over her, and to escape into sleep.

Two hours later Martin also went to bed, following his usual routine: water in a glass, carry it upstairs, undress and bathroom, pyjamas buttoned up, bed.

The village of Portwenn sank into an uneasy sleep. Here and there a light shone: the blue emblem above the police station, the school's emergency exit lights, various porch lights set above cottage doors, some of them automatically sensing movement and switching themselves on, and then off again. Landing lights spilled dimly down stairwells and showed faintly through glass front doors. A child's night light would cast an upstairs window with an eerie glow. Occasionally a pair of car headlights would sweep across the sleeping buildings. On Louisa's wrist, the dial of her watch cast a faint luminosity on her sleeping face.

In an upstairs room of the Cronk household, a light came on. Some minutes later, a downstairs light appeared, also. In these smallest of hours, the house began to stand out from its neighbours. It awoke.

Next, on Louisa's bedside table, the phone's screen silently lit up, and a half-second later it loudly announced its ring tone. Already Louisa was sitting up and breathing in. She fumbled to answer it. 'Hello?'

She heard the sound of heavy breathing. 'Oh sod off,' she said and put down the phone. She batted her pillow, turned to face the other way and cursed being woken. If she couldn't get back to sleep, now, she'd . . . She'd . . .

An image came to mind: of Mrs Cronk's hand clapped against her chest, and her being unable to breathe – out of panic. Louisa sat up sharply, swept up the phone and dialled 1471. It had been a Portwenn number. She pressed 3 for ring-back.

Across the bay, in Martin's house, a landing light usually remained on overnight, and the bedroom door was ajar so a section of it fell into the room and glinted in the wardrobe mirror. Martin, who slept like the effigy on top of a tomb, could hear Louisa's voice, 'Martin? Martin.'

He sat up with a jolt, alone in the room except for the dog, which was nosing at his face, despite the fact that it had never before come upstairs. 'Bugger off, dog,' began Martin, but even as these words instinctively escaped from him, he stopped talking because he could, after all, hear Louisa's voice – it was coming from the answering machine downstairs. In the darkness of the surgery, the red light blinked its warning and her electronic voice filled the room. 'Martin? Something's wrong at the Cronks' house. Can you hear me? OK, if you get this message meet me there; I'm going over now.'

Upstairs, Martin was already half-dressed.

Louisa fled to the Cronks' house up on the hill; it took her five minutes. She banged heedlessly on the glass front door. She hoped for a shadow to break up the pattern of light, but it remained obstinately unmoving. No response. She ducked on one knee, pushed open the letter flap and peered through. All she could see was a few square feet of hall carpet. She called into the house, 'Mrs Cronk? Are you there?'

Still there was no answer, nor any sign of movement. Louisa looked around for something with which to break the glass, but could only think to use her fist. She took off her jacket, wrapped it around her hand and walloped the glass, which splintered; she put a hand through to find the latch. One twist and she was in. She ran down the hall and into the kitchen, to see Mrs Cronk lying on the floor, her hands pressed to her chest, fighting for breath. 'Mrs Cronk,' she called, 'it's all right, I'm here. It's only panic. I'm going up to look at Peter, OK?' She trotted as fast as she could up the stairs, knowing that to make sure Peter was all right was also to make sure his mother was all right. She burst through all the doors up here: bathroom, a bedroom, and then Peter's bedroom. He was lying there, mumbling incoherently,

291

underneath a duvet that had had its cover removed. Piled on the floor, here and there, were two duvet covers. She sat on the bed and touched her hand against his forehead. 'Peter? Can you hear me?'

His eyes stared into the middle distance, even though his head turned towards the sound of her voice.

'Peter? It's Miss Glasson. Can you tell me what's wrong?' She already had her mobile phone in her hand but was shaking so much she could hardly press the right buttons. Just three. When they picked up she said, 'Ambulance.'

Martin, when he arrived, plunged through the broken-down door and called out 'Hello' at the same time as he saw Louisa appear down the stairs to meet him.

'Peter is very ill upstairs,' she said quickly. 'I've called an ambulance. Mrs Cronk is having a panic attack.'

Martin took the stairs two at a time. He called out, 'Find a paper bag for her to breathe into.'

He found Peter's bedroom. 'Peter, it's Doctor Ellingham. Peter?'

Peter's head flopped from one side to the other and he moaned.

Martin felt Peter's stomach and noted rigidity and tenderness. His examination told him one thing, while he looked around the room for more clues: the duvet covers piled on the floor. Evidence of vomiting. And there was something else: underneath Peter's left shoulder was a rolled-up towel, serving as a support cushion. He swore quietly, 'Christ . . .'

He got to his feet, left the room and rushed down the stairs, to find Louisa supporting Mrs Cronk in a sitting position. 'Is Peter having neck pain?' he asked without preamble. He noticed the uneaten supper still on the table.

Mrs Cronk stopped breathing into the paper bag and said, 'Should have rung you sooner.'

'Mrs Cronk, his neck – there's a towel under his neck.'

'He said it was stiff, that it hurt.'

'On the left side?'

She nodded.

Louisa looked stricken. 'What does that mean?' she asked.

'Where's that ambulance?'

'I just called. It's probably still in Truro.'

'Not good enough. Call Mark, tell him we need him and his Land Rover, fast. We can get him up to the top and take him by air ambulance.'

A minute later both Martin and Louisa were talking into their phones at the same time – Louisa to Mark, and Martin to air ambulance control. 'Ten-year-old male, suspected rupture of the spleen . . . been leaking since lunchtime. Tell the duty surgical team that speed is of the essence.' He looked up at Louisa, who was dealing with Mrs Cronk's increasing shock. 'Let's carry him downstairs, so we're ready.'

Martin lifted Peter in his arms; Louisa scooped up his duvet. Minutes later they heard Mark's shout from the doorway, just one word, 'Where?'

Outside the house neighbours were gathered; as Louisa followed Martin she could see pairs of legs, and slippers, caught in the circle of light thrown by the open front door. A call came from the darkness, 'Anything I can do to help?' It was a woman, a mother's cry.

'Can someone drive Mrs Cronk and follow us?' called back Louisa. The back of the Land Rover stood open and Mark, running ahead, hopped in and moved a stack of traffic cones out of the way. Martin, carrying Peter in his arms, hurried after him, his stride shortened because of the weight. Louisa was there just as Martin handed Peter over to Mark, and she pushed the duvet in underneath him. Mark held Peter, now, as Martin climbed in, and the duvet was arranged as a mattress on the floor of the Land Rover. Mark laid the boy down and Martin folded the duvet over him. When Mark jumped out, Louisa climbed in and sat next to Martin, with Peter wrapped up at their feet. The door swung shut.

The Land Rover's engine started; the headlights brought a brilliant light to the narrow street, reflected from the white cottages on either side. The blue lights began to spin and the vehicle took off cautiously and smoothly. At the bottom of the hill the headlights could be seen to make a right turn and point up the hill. The vehicle moved quietly, without a siren, but in the dead of night the revolving blue lights made patterns on the ceilings of people's rooms.

In the Top Field, where often the village held its firework displays and bonfire parties, the Land Rover and its anxious occupants waited for the air ambulance to arrive. Louisa crouched on the floor of the Land Rover and held Peter's head on her lap, and smoothed his brow. 'Where is it . . .?' Martin's growl made them sound like swear words. He was out of the Land Rover, again, and he walked to the car, which had pulled up behind them. Through the passenger window he saw Mrs Cronk, a paper bag pressed to her mouth. Her eyes were round with fright. Martin leaned down and said, 'I don't think you'll be happy to fly, will you?' She shook her head. Martin went on, 'I suggest you say goodbye to Peter now and set off for the hospital by road. It will take you longer than us.' He opened the door for her, and helped her out. The darkness enveloped them and a breeze tugged at their clothing. The driver of the car, a neighbour called Robin Thornton, leaned over and said, 'Doc, I'm not sure she should come with me, in the car. She's breathing funny.'

'Take her,' said Martin. There would be no argument. He went back to the Land Rover.

Mrs Cronk stood at the open rear of the vehicle, leaning over her son, fretfully stroking his forehead as if trying to wipe something away. 'Mum will see you soon,' she said between half-breaths. 'Very soon.'

Martin chipped in, 'She'll be just a few minutes behind us.'

Mrs Cronk looked up at Louisa. 'Promise me you'll stay with him?'

Louisa looked at Martin. She wasn't sure. She wanted to say yes, but would she be allowed to travel in the air ambulance? 'I . . .' she began.

Mrs Cronk lifted the paper bag to her mouth again. Standing next to her, Martin nodded imperceptibly.

'Yes, I will,' said Louisa. 'I'll stick with him, all the way.'

Mrs Cronk leaned over Peter and kissed his forehead. 'See, you've got your Miss Glasson with you, Petey, haven't you? You've got your favourite Miss G with you, all the way.'

Louisa smiled at her, and lifted Peter's hand, which she was holding in hers. Mrs Cronk turned and went back to Robin Thornton's car.

Martin climbed in the back and picked up Peter's wrist between his thumb and forefinger. After a while he said, 'Pulse is racing.' He checked his watch and cast an anxious gaze at the night sky. 'Where in God's name . . .?'

For an instant they confused a flashing blue light on the horizon with the helicopter, and expected it to lift higher in the sky, but it remained obstinately travelling along the horizon and they realised it was an ambulance. Mark, still in his pyjamas and a coat and boots, ran down to the entrance of the field to wait for it, and flag it down. Five minutes later the ambulance turned into the field, and pulled up next to the Land Rover.

When the ambulance driver jumped out, Martin called, 'Have you got a radio line to the helicopter?'

'Yes. You the GP?'

'Then can you find out where the bloody hell it is?'

'Still at Delabole. Mechanical fault. No engineer, no chopper.'

'What?'

'Funded by donations,' said the driver simply.

'Then we have to move very fast indeed,' said Martin.

'New one on us, that is.' The driver's voice rankled. 'Ron?' he called back to his co-driver. 'Over here in the back of this vehicle.' He turned to Martin. 'What have we got? Abdominal trauma?'

'No.'

'Oh. They told us male, ten years, abdominal trauma.'

They stood at the open mouth of the Land Rover. Louisa looked between the two men.

Martin said pointedly, 'He's not a male abdominal trauma. He's a boy, and he's called Peter, with a suspected ruptured spleen.'

'Right you are,' said the ambulance driver. 'Peter?'

Five minutes later Peter was strapped onto the stretcher and installed in the brightly lit interior of the ambulance. 'OK,' said the driver. 'We'll take him from here. We'll look after him, don't worry.'

'I'm coming with you,' said Martin. It was said with certainty, and it was meant as a rebuke.

'So am I,' said Louisa, and joined them in the crowded interior.

The two ambulance men swapped roles – one of them going to drive, the other to attend the patient. They crossed paths at the side of the ambulance. 'Pushy GP alert,' said the driver. 'And his girlfriend.'

The second paramedic rolled his eyes. 'If you see anyone waiting for a bus, give them a ride, too.'

The ambulance moved off the field – cautiously at first, but when the wheels hit tarmac it got up to speed; the lights and the siren went on. Inside the vehicle, a canula was inserted into Peter's arm and a drip attached, and his blood pressure was taken. It was low.

Peter's eyes flickered and his mouth opened. He was trying to say something.

Louisa leaned closer and squeezed his hand. 'What, Peter, what is it?'

'I was wrong,' mumbled Peter. 'Intercostal sprain . . .'

A sharp right-hand corner pulled Martin and Louisa backwards against the side of the ambulance. 'We'll see,' said Martin. 'Let's get you to the hospital. You might have been right all the way down the line.'

'No,' said Peter. 'You tell the truth. Most adults . . . but *you . . .*'

'OK,' said Martin. 'I think when you fell in the gym, you damaged an important organ. You have shoulder-tip pain on the left side. I suspect it might have been your spleen.'

Peter held his breath, tried to speak but then failed. Suddenly the words all rushed out at once. 'I can live without my spleen can't I?'

'You can,' said Martin. 'But you may be bleeding inside, and that's why we have to get you to hospital.'

'Mmm . . . Am I going to be OK?'

'If I have anything to do with it.' Martin spoke the words with such determination, that it sounded like anger, injustice. Louisa glanced at him. This was a man, she realised, whom it might be possible to love absolutely and without reservation.

Peter's voice came more faintly and, with the sound of the engine grinding up a hill, and the sirens, it was difficult to hear. Both Martin and Louisa leaned closer.

'What was that?' asked Louisa.

'Got to let them tease you,' said Peter.

Louisa glanced next to her and saw that Martin wore his customary frown.

He turned to her. 'What did he say?'

She replied, 'He said, "You've got to let them tease you."'

'Why would he say that?'

'I said the same thing to him earlier, after his accident, when I was trying to tell him how to join in, how to be part of . . . how to . . .' She came to halt. 'And he just repeated them.' The ambulance's braking threw them together, momentarily.

Peter spoke again, even though his eyes were closed, 'After a while they say, oh yes, he's one of us.'

They'd arrived at a junction and the note of the engine descended to a momentary silence, to a tick-over, until once again it climbed and the clutch bit; now they were on the main road, so the going was faster. The ambulance lurched, and the sirens resumed. The tyres thrummed on the white lines.

Martin took Peter's wrist between his thumb and forefinger. His voice sharpened. 'How long before we get there?'

The second paramedic, whose name was Rowe, answered, 'Thirty-five minutes.'

Louisa felt the transmission of anxiety from Martin and knew it was too long.

'Can we get more fluid into him?' asked Martin.

Rowe pumped air into the cuff around Peter's arm. 'We'll take his BP again first,' he said.

'He's bleeding internally,' said Martin.

'I always say the little ones drop like flies,' said Rowe, 'but bounce like balloons. Couple of days, and he'll be cutting the legs off spiders, right as rain.' He ducked forward to read the dials and all his workaday joviality, his professional bedside manner, disappeared. 'Blood pressure's too damn low,' he warned.

The vehicle swayed and sent them all grabbing for something to hang on to. Incomprehensible words and sounds came from Peter's mouth.

'He's exsanguinating,' said Martin. He was suddenly on his feet. 'Now do *exactly* as I say. Give me gloves. Give me another line.'

'For what?' asked Rowe. His manner had changed utterly.

'What have you got? Plasma?'

'No. Haemaccel.'

'That will do. How many?'

'Two.'

'Better than nothing.' Martin pumped air into the cuff and let it out. 'No BP. We need more fluids in him – now.'

Rowe struggled with the line, the tilt of the vehicle throwing him off balance. 'Can't find a vein.'

'Veins are collapsing because nothing's in them.' Martin took the needle off Rowe, the line like a snake in his hands. He simply and quickly thrust the needle into Peter's neck.

Louisa hadn't seen. She'd been stroking Peter's hand and suddenly was sure that it felt different. 'He's going cold,' she said.

'Louisa,' said Martin, not sparing her even a glance, 'put some gloves on.'

She obeyed immediately.

Martin asked Rowe, 'D'you have a Martin pump?'

Rowe braced himself against the side of the ambulance, reached into a shelf and handed it to Martin.

'Louisa, this is a bit like a salad-spinner.' Martin connected it to the drip and worked the handle to show her. 'It pushes fluids into him faster.'

Louisa spun the pump, and her eye followed the line – and she was shocked, then, to find it ended with the needle sticking grotesquely out of Peter's neck.

The ambulance's tyres bumped over the white lines on right-hand corners; on left-hand corners it brushed the hedgerows. Truro was still fifteen minutes away.

'This has finished,' said Louisa, having watched the bag of fluid empty into Peter's neck.

'Blood pressure?' asked Martin.

Rowe sounded grim. 'Not recordable.'

Martin could only afford a nano-second to weigh up the options. 'I need a blade,' he said.

'We have no anaesthetic,' warned Rowe as he handed it to him.

'Where he is, he won't feel anything,' said Martin. He stripped the blade from its sterile wrap. 'Do you carry Spencer Wells forceps?'

'Yes.'

'And disinfectant.' Martin yanked open Peter's pyjama top to expose his chest. He took the disinfectant and sluiced his hand with it, and Peter's chest – the left upper quadrant. He pointed the blade, there was nothing left for him to do except open it up. The hesitation lasted for one second longer and he heard Louisa pray under her breath, 'God help us . . .'

Martin looked at Louisa and her frantic gaze was glued to his. He said, 'I may vomit. Sorry.' And he made the cut.

Louisa looked away sharply.

Blood welled out – and a splash leapt across Peter's skin. Martin cut down further. 'I'm in,' he said. 'It *is* the spleen.' He could see the rupture, the discolouration and the rush of arterial blood. He picked up the Spencer Wells. 'I'm going to clamp the splenic artery,' he continued. 'That should buy us a little . . .' And then his tone of voice changed; it became impatient. 'It's broken,' he said.

'What is?' Rowe sounded desperate.

'The clamp. Got another?'

'No, I don't think so, no.'

'Martin . . .?' called Louisa, in a pleading voice. 'Please tell me that—'

'I will hold it 'til we get there,' said Martin curtly and looked up at the ceiling of the speeding ambulance. His gloved hand was thrust into the opening in Peter's chest. Blood was smeared across his front; a smudge of it was on his face.

Louisa was faint with panic.

'That's all we can do,' said Martin, still looking at the ceiling. 'Radio ahead. Tell them what we know and tell them to have a functioning Spencer Wells standing by at the other end. Give me some water.' He spoke each word as if it was the next in a queue, a list.

Rowe produced a container of sterile water. 'Where d'you want this?' he asked.

'In my mouth.'

The ambulance sped through the night; a solitary vehicle between the sleeping hedgerows, through sleeping villages. From a distance it appeared to move gracefully and sedately through the darkened landscape, its revolving blue lights like radar, but close up it drove ferociously fast, and the blue flashes from its roof and from its front grille were blinding.

When it reached Truro it ignored all traffic lights and encountered no delay in its flight to the A&E department of Truro Hospital. The doors were flung open and the Spencer Wells was snatched out of the doctor's hand when it was offered. Martin's right hand ached as he unclamped his

303

thumb and fingertips from the artery. Peter was lifted onto a gurney and a crowd of nurses and doctors, together with the two ambulance paramedics, wheeled him towards the hospital doors. They asked for precise details of what had happened and Louisa walked alongside, to tell them.

She remembered how he'd gone to the gym in his shorts, with his legs as white as margarine. And of course during obstacle tag the others had picked on him as an easy target, and Peter, with a reproachful glance at Louisa, had tried to climb the wall bars; and just as he'd gone to jump down Emily had caught hold of his ankle. The bench had been right beneath him and he'd fallen across it, and for a moment the whole room had turned completely still, as if to statues, before Louisa had rushed forward. Peter had opened his eyes and calmly asked, 'Now can I go to the library?' Instead they'd taken him to the San and Peter had diagnosed himself with intercostal sprain, and Louisa had taken advantage of having him to herself for a few minutes to lecture him. 'Peter, if you take part in things, eventually you'll *be* part of things. *Let* them tease you,' she'd said emphatically. 'See the funny side. Then people will think, oh, he's all right, he's one of us.' And Peter had worn such a mournful look.

'We've got him now, thanks.' Surrounded by his medical team, Peter was wheeled through the swing doors and into the hospital.

Martin and Louisa were left standing next to each other under the A&E canopy, cast in a slightly yellow, unflattering light. Both of them were exhausted.

'OK?' Louisa asked him.

'Yes.'

'Martin?'

He looked at her, so close beside him, and then he looked down to see that his right hand, the still-bloody hand that had squeezed shut the artery for all that time, was squeezing hers, too tight, and it was trembling uncontrollably. It was difficult to let go.

Later, Martin and Louisa occupied adjacent seats in the A&E waiting area, and the minutes passed by painfully slowly. From time to time they got up and stretched their legs. At other times they fell into bits and pieces of desultory conversation.

Louisa asked Martin, 'How can you have a thing about blood? You're a doctor.'

'A minor anxiety disorder,' said Martin, 'resulting from exposure to a . . . a high-stress environment.'

'What about in English?'

The usual hound-dog type wrinkles appeared in Martin's forehead, and he replied in a gloomy voice, 'I think I worked too hard. And for too long. I lived in the operating theatre; it was the one place where I felt in control. Then, one day, I was operating on a woman. I'd been to see her in the ward. Her whole family was there: husband, sister, son – sort of clinging to her. They wouldn't let her go. And a few minutes later, there she was, on the table, in front of me. And I couldn't do it. Blade in hand. Everything ready. I couldn't make the first stroke.' He drew his hand over his face.

'Haven't operated since. Which is a shame really because it's about the only thing I was ever any good at, and now . . . just the thought of it terrifies me, really.'

Louisa, because she kind of knew the answer already, had been looking at Martin just as much as she'd been listening; it was something to do with the harshness of the light inside the A&E waiting room but she marvelled at how the hair around his ears was so very neatly trimmed, at how perfectly clean shaven he was. What he had said – his confession – somehow combined with this new intimacy, this desire she felt to look at him more closely, and notice and count the physical imperfections, and it filled her with tenderness.

Later, she fell asleep, and Martin found himself having to maintain an uncomfortable position because her head rested on his shoulder. On the opposite bank of seats waited Mrs Cronk, forever alert. She whispered, 'Going to the loo. Shall I get us some coffees?'

Martin shook his head. He didn't want to talk; he was afraid it would wake Louisa.

Mrs Cronk didn't go. She whispered, 'You're sitting on my coat.'

Martin was confused – why did she need a coat to go to the loo? He remained motionless and silent; that was his priority, but he couldn't help feeling that everyone wanted something from him that was impossible to give, and when did he, Martin, ever get to ask anyone else for something, when did he . . .?

He was saved by the appearance of a nurse who walked

and stood neatly, like a ballet dancer, in front of him and Louisa. 'Mr and Mrs Cronk?'

Louisa's head lifted quickly from Martin's shoulder.

Mrs Cronk stood up. 'I'm Mrs Cronk,' she said. 'What's wrong?'

'The surgeon's coming down to talk to you, if you'd like to follow me?'

Louisa and Martin were left alone in the waiting area. A hollow silence pervaded the place after the others' footsteps had faded away. The vending machine made its hum and an occasional rattle, but there was no human traffic.

After a while Louisa said, 'I loved that boy.'

Martin's eyes were glazed over.

After a while a figure appeared and walked towards them. A middle-aged man of Asian descent, with a balding crown and an amiable face. 'Dr Ellingham?' he asked.

'Yes.'

At the same time Louisa asked, 'How is he?'

'Minus a spleen, but he'll live.'

Louisa burst into tears; she was helplessly caught up in the relief.

'Any complications?' asked Martin quickly.

'Tiny bit of pancreatic leak.'

'Any secondary spleen?' asked Martin.

'There was, actually, which we were careful to leave behind.' He smiled and said in a very simple tone of voice, 'Your actions in the ambulance saved him. My job was easy in comparison.' He offered Martin his hand; and Martin felt its warm clasp, before the surgeon shook Louisa's hand, and turned and went. They realised they hadn't even found out his name.

They rang for a taxi to take them home; the first pink fingers of dawn were painting the sky as they left Truro behind, and fields and hills once more filled the view from either side of the vehicle being calmly driven along. Louisa glanced at Martin and he felt her gaze but couldn't bring himself to look at her.

'How you feeling?' asked Louisa.

Martin nodded. 'OK.'

She said, 'You did a very special thing today.'

He replied, 'You do a very special thing, for Peter, every day.'

The taxi carried them homewards calmly and steadily. There was no emergency; no blue lights.

Louisa said, 'Maybe the truth is, people like Peter, they're never quite going to fit in, they're never quite going to be ordinary. And maybe that's not such a bad thing, and maybe that's why we love the Peters of this world, maybe that's why we, or I . . .' Her nerves whipped tight, and she couldn't finish what she wanted to say.

A glance was shared between them that was thrown with all the wildness of a love affair that was just about to end, rather than one that might begin; and then both were looking out of their respective side windows at the Cornish countryside, which served the useful purpose of taking anyone from any point in Cornwall and leading them quickly to the most romantic shoreline in all of Europe. And, as the taxi carried them along, the stripes of pink in the sky turned to a turquoise blush, as the sun threatened to rise.

In the back seat of the taxi, Louisa very carefully placed her hand on the seat, in the space between herself and Martin – and left it there. His own hand was adjacent; he only had to pick up hers . . .

Martin shifted in his seat. He was uncomfortable. That hand . . . He leaned forward and said to the driver, 'Actually, I'm too tall for this back seat – do you mind if I come in the front, with you, bit more legroo—'

He was silenced by the palm of her hand, which arrived gently to hold the side of his face and turn him to face her, and he could say nothing more because she loomed impossibly close, and he felt a shot of adrenalin, like an accident was about to happen, as her lips touched his; she was as soft and warm as the underneath of any creature, and he discovered that he knew how to kiss Louisa Glasson.

For Louisa it was as if she met with her own feelings; for the first time she saw them in a full light – she felt them as permanent, and deserved, and earned, true. The connection between them electrified her. She remembered – it was like a snapshot suddenly held up for her to see before it was taken away again – how she'd met his gaze for the first time, on that train . . .

She had held his face in her hands; they had kissed. Now she scolded him, 'What was that – "Mind if I go in the front"? Martin Ellingham, where *are* you?' She squeezed his hand. 'I've been wanting to do that for a long time.' She looked into his preoccupied, worried face. 'Martin, say something.' She poked him with a finger, knowing it was hopeless. 'It's your job to say something.' She watched him open his mouth but then, like a fish, he closed it again. 'What?' she asked.

'Nothing,' said Martin.

'No, go on, really I mean it, say it.' She smiled encouragingly.

'Presumably you have a thorough dental hygiene regime?'

She couldn't believe her ears. 'Pardon, are you serious?'

'No, because—'

'I mean obviously not in the last few hours because – but, thank you very much, yes, I have.'

'Of course. So that would suggest maybe rhinosinusitis or gastroesophageal reflux.'

'Hang on,' said Louisa, bewildered, 'are you saying I've got bad breath?'

Martin said soberly, 'I just think it might be worth ruling out any cancers of the aerodigestive tract.'

Louisa stared at his frank, hurt expression. He wasn't joking; he was deadly serious.

'Of course,' added Martin, 'a dietary explanation would be the happiest outcome.'

The edge of the landscape had just come into view, and made the seam between the green of the fields and the blue of the sea, with the first blush of the sky thickening now into the reality of daylight, as the sun rose.

The taxi was the only car on the narrow lane to Portwenn, and an observer from on high would have noticed how it slowed down, and came to a halt. The nearside rear passenger door opened and a middle-aged man dressed in a crumpled suit, the collar undone and without a tie, climbed out. There was a slight delay as it seemed like he didn't want to close the door, but eventually he pushed it shut. The taxi pulled away immediately and Dr Martin Ellingham began to walk the last mile or so into Portwenn.

Not long afterwards, the figure of a dark brown dog appeared, seemingly out of nowhere, and joined him, trotting along at his heels.

Coming soon from Ebury Press:

DOC MARTIN

MISTLETOE AND WHINE

Another novelisation of the hit TV series Doc Martin.

Meet the ultimate Scrooge . . .

The festive season in the small Cornish village of
Portwenn is going to be anything but easy for the
curmudgeonly Doc Martin. His idea of a perfect Christmas
Day is to remain steadfastly alone and catch up with back
issues of *The Lancet*.

However, Portwenn is fighting off the cold and frost with a
period of determined revelry before it heads into its deep
winter sleep, and his patients are even more exasperating
than usual. Not to mention his on-off relationship with
local school teacher, Louisa.

It will take all of Doc Martin's willpower to fend off the
attentions of the Christmas spirit . . .